BLACK SHEEP

BY THE SAME AUTHOR

Ortog (translated by Brian Stableford)
Blood Light (*The Books of Anguish 1*) (translated by Sheryl Curtis)
The Improbables (translated by Michael Shreve)

BLACK SHEEP
and
THE CHILDREN OF HISTORY

by
Kurt Steiner

translated by
Michael Shreve

A Black Coat Press Book

Visit our website at www.blackcoatpress.com

ISBN 978-1-64932-198-5. First Printing. June 2023. Published
by Black Coat Press, an imprint of Hollywood Comics.com,
LLC, P.O. Box 17270, Encino, CA 91416. All rights reserved.
Except for review purposes, no part of this book may be reproduced or transmitted in any form or by any means, electronic or mechanical, including photocopying, recording, or by
any information storage and retrieval system, without permis-
sion in writing from the publisher. The stories and characters
depicted in this novel are entirely fictional. Printed in the
United States of America.

TABLE OF CONTENTS

André RUELLAN

A biography, bibliography and filmography of André Ruellan, a.k.a. Kurt Steiner, is included in The Books of Anguish No.1.

Foreword

My first step: 1948, first year of Medicine. *Hebdo Latin*, a small broadsheet launched rue Gît-le Cœur. First story published: the students are so badly treated that they will soon be forced to feed on the corpses they're dissecting. A few poems that will remain mostly unpublished follow.

My second step: 1950, *Le Hérisson* [The Hedgehog], a newspaper printed on green paper, published one of my stories: "Beware of Widows," the theme of which I recycled in my first novel for *Angoisse* at Fleuve Noir. Some unpublished short stories follow, such as "Rendezvous under the Autobus" but others are published as "The Infernal Chair" in *Voir Magazine*.

My third step: a science fiction novel at publisher La Flamme d'Or, entitled *Alert Monsters!*, then a whodunnit at publisher Faucon Noir: *Blood on the Elbows* –its sole value being a cover by soon to be *Barbarella* creator Jean-Claude Forest.

The year 1954 is, as everyone knows, exactly nine hundred years after the schism that split the Eastern Church from the Western Church. Incidentally, it is also the date of birth of the *Angoisse* imprint at Fleuve Noir, with a translated novel by Donand Wandrei.[1] There were still people in publishing who had taste and loved such terrifying works.

I was finishing my fifth year of Medicine, with courses in Forensic Medicine along with its cortege of amusing autopsies. So I immediately started writing a novel for this new and providential imprint. I finished it at the beginning of the following year, and entitled it *The Sound of Silence*. Then I left it in the care of a small pharmacy in the rue Vercingétorix, the street where I knew the publisher lived.

---

[1] *The Web of Easter Island* (1948).

A fortnight later, I was given a telephone appointment at a café called La Rhumerie where I met "Benoit Becker" (as I found out later, there were two other writers that also used that house name). He told me that not only was my novel accepted, but he asked to write two more. With some aplomb, I answered affirmatively even though I did not believe myself capable of it. At the time, Fleuve Noir to own the nom-de-plume of its writers, so in accord with them, I found one that was neither French nor Anglo-Saxon (too many others in that vein), but German.

Was it too soon after the war? I had nothing against German culture: it was, after all, against it that Baldur von Schirach, leader of the *Hitlerjugend*, had cocked his revolver. So that's how I became Kurt Steiner, who admired Heinrich von Kleist.

After that, I often had the opportunity to visit the small office where, face to face, sat on either side of a desk, publisher Armand de Caro and Guy Krill, his partner. I had signed a contract which gave them the rights only to my nom-de-plume (there would be only one Steiner at Fleuve Noir) but which quickly led me to deliver one book after another to keep the monthly checks (written to my real name) coming.

Then Krill and his family died in a road accident so violent that his big American car was pulverized by a truck. It was a real loss for Fleuve Noir.

Two years later, Fleuve Noir moved to Boulevard Saint-Marcel. My new editor, François Richard, had an office that suited his stalwart, ruddy complexion and his mustache. He looked like an English officer back from India. I continued to write my scary stories, at the rate of six novels a year, more or less.

However, *Angoisse* was selling only six thousand copies, while its sister imprint, *Anticipation*, was selling more than twice that figure, and *Espionage* reached one hundred and twenty thousand copies. My tastes and my abilities thus prohibited me from earning a fortune, sometimes even obliging me to spend weeks doing fascinating research, like for my novel *The Other Side of the Mask*.

Then, de Caro offered me a place in *Anticipation*. I embarked immediately, leaving the stygian waters of *Angoisse* to navigate the rivers of Time, Space and Parallel Universes.

At that time, I was tempted to join a friend who had decided to spend his 1967 vacation in Saint-Tropez going about on a bicycle – an undertaking easier than going to Betelgeuse other than by imagination.

During the war, the Germans had confiscated my old bicycle on which I had traveled thousands of miles, so I bought a new one and quickly relearned to ride it. I made the trip in ten days, sleeping in hotels whose single star was waning, crossing admirable stretches of land without hurrying, and, after hiding my bicycle, knocked at my friend's house. His parents asked me where I had parked my car. There ensued many explanations and exclamations that I still remember today.

Thus being filled with a new spirit of adventure because of this whimsical escapade, I became a Revolutionary in the beautiful month of May the following year, writing *The Children of History* for Fleuve Noir, and other works under my own name, that other Publishers soon agreed to publish. These in turn opened the doors of the worlds of Cinema and Television, and a new life began.

André Ruellan

ANTICIPATION

F N

FICTION

Kurt STEINER

BREBIS GALEUSES

fleuve noir

BLACK SHEEP

CHAPTER I

Leaning on the guardrail, Rolf admired the world. He was at the top of the fifth tower, the one that looked over the city. From here he had a complete view of the horizon. He just had to turn his head, twist his neck as far as it could go and then back to first position. Like that he had a view of the world.

Rolf smiled. No, you couldn't see everything from a single spot. The world was too big. From the suburbs, which were already far off, his eye could drift toward the hazy horizon. Beyond, and very gradually, was nothingness. The ground merged with the sky, by rising up. If he kept looking higher, he'd have to close his eyes because he'd be gazing into the sun. He could always open them after passing it by, then he'd see another part of the sky and shortly another part of the horizon.

See, this world had the shape of a huge egg with the Sun inside. You could go around the Sun without ever leaving the ground... at least theoretically. Practically, it was really too long and too risky. Since the world was around 600,000 miles at its smallest diameter and double that in the widest part, it was preferable to use the aircraft that followed a secant line across the oval space. It greatly shortened the trip. As for the travel time, already brief because of the unparalleled speed of the aircraft, it was made even quicker by the shortcut. Not to mention, of course, all the dangers lurking around the unknown territories between the cities.

But, naturally, you had to follow the secants that didn't form a very wide angle with the ground, otherwise you'd need a spaceship. And then, you'd have to keep your distance from the Sun if you didn't want to be vaporized. That's happened to spaceships in distress whose pilots miscalculated the trajectory—at the limits of the gravitational layer from the ground, they got caught in the magnetic sphere of the Sun.

Rolf pondered all this. The grandeur of the world overwhelmed him, but he felt more than just awe. And anyway, this kind of sacred fear that big things emanate is always a little unsatisfying. Of course, there were official theories. But who was really satisfied with them?

He glanced around him. The terrace was almost deserted at this early hour when it was still chilly. Only one other person, maybe 20 yards away, who shot him a quick glance. A glance that he felt was both ironic and sympathetic at the same time. Without knowing why, he answered with a vague smile. Without knowing why? Of course he knew! Rolf needed to confide in someone. Too many things were tormenting him deep down inside.

Responding to the smile, the man came over. "Not very warm," he said when he was close enough not to raise his voice.

"Oh," Rolf replied, "within an hour you'll have to take off your coat. But in an hour..."

"Yes?" the other waited. "In an hour..."

"I'll be at the office," Rolf finished.

"And me in the lab," the man replied.

He looked at Rolf and tilted his head, an asymmetrical head with almost colorless eyes. A friendly smile played on his lips. "It's all so beautiful, isn't it?" he stretched out his rams to the horizon.

"Indeed it is," Rolf agreed. The conviction of his response made him forget the banality. He added, "But it's very complicated..."

"Ah!" the man nodded, "it certainly is complicated..."

Rolf said nothing. Was the other stroller interested in metaphysics, astronomy, all those sciences steeped in politics? Maybe he preferred not to talk about things like that exactly because of the politics involved. But as if to prove Rolf wrong the guy finished for him:

"It's complicated even in light of the official interpretations."

He leaned closer, looked back over his shoulder to made sure nobody was listening, then went on, "To tell you the truth, I don't know if those interpretations really explain everything."

He raised up his two open hands in front of him and cried out, "Attention! I'm not doubting anything, get it!"

He lowered his voice worriedly, "But maybe there are one or two details that might have been… how to say it… left out."

Rolf looked at him sympathetically, "One or two details? You think so?" He stifled a laugh, then kept silent—a silence full of innuendos.

The man's eyes widened, "What, do you know something? Something that the authorities would rather keep secret? Obviously, you work in a very important bureau…"

"Pretty important," Rolf gloated. "You want me to tell you?"

The man stepped back, still holding his hand out front, "Oh, don't tell me anything you don't want to. Suppose I assume more than you mean…"

Rolf was still smiling, "Friend," he assured him, "I can see you're like me—dissatisfied. And I can also see that you're too smart to misunderstand my intentions."

He took a deep breath before continuing. "We agree that in an hour it'll be hotter than it is now, right?"

The man nodded, "Certainly."

Rolf's smile grew, "And the Sun is stationary even if it appears to move?"

"Naturally."

"So, it's the world that's revolving around it?"

The man nodded again vehemently.

"These are the official theories," Rolf went on. "But do you feel like you're revolving or do you feel like you're the one that's stationary?"

"Well... I don't know what to say..."

Rolf slapped his own chest, "Me, I'll say so myself. We have to be revolving or else we couldn't explain the temperature and the change in light with such regularity every hour of the day. Which proves that the official theories are right. As long as the Sun isn't in the center of the world..."

The man frowned, "If that's all you want to talk to me about... it's a good thing your logic resulted in this conclusion."

Rolf shook his head and suggested, "You don't see where I'm going with this." He gestured to the Sun, then to space. "The inside is just fine. It's the outside that bothers me."

"You're showing me the outside," the man grumbled.

Rolf lowered his eyelids and shrugged, "I'm showing you the inside of the outside. I call the inside what we see outside and the outside what is beyond the inside."

The man slapped his forehead, "You're making my head spin. I'm going."

Rolf grabbed his sleeve, "Let me explain. Since this world is an egg-shaped bubble and this bubble, inside of the Earth that stretches out in every direction, I can say that the space is inside space even though we say 'I'm going outside' when we leave our house. That's what I mean by saying the inside is just fine."

The man scratched his forehead. "Yes," he said reluctantly. "I see. And what's your problem with the outside?"

"I don't have a problem. What they say bothers me, that's all."

"Seriously, it bothers you?"

Rolf took his cue, "That the Earth is an infinite sphere in which our world is the center, I mean. If there were other bubbles, they would also be the center since the center of something infinite is everywhere inside of that thing…"

"So?"

"So? If the ground I'm on is revolving around the sun we see, the earth and the rocks that fill the infinite are also revolving at the same time."

"Those are the official theories, yes!"

"Oh, yes!" Rolf exclaimed with almost wild ecstasy. "The official theories. What I don't like is that they totally exclude the possibility of other inhabited bubbles."

"They don't talk about them."

"I know! Of course, they don't talk about them because if they did, they'd have to deny it."

"Why's that?"

Rolf snorted. "Don't you see, you big dummy, that if the infinite is full of earths revolving around us and if this infinite contains other bubbles, these bubbles are also revolving around us, which means their land can't be revolving around their sun?"

The man's colorless eyes looked lifeless as well, "In short, the theories are false if there are other bubbles?"

"No," Rolf riposted. "Simply that these other bubbles aren't regulated by the same astronomical system as ours. And ours is necessarily the only one—doesn't that seem to you to be a little… anthropocentric?"

"And if it were?"

"It wouldn't be saying much for its accuracy. But I've got better."

The man's face lit up. He was all ears.

Rolf took a deep breath. "Suppose the Earth didn't fill the infinite. I said suppose."

"Good," the listener huffed, "because it contradicts official theories."

"Okay. So, suppose the world, our world, is like a shell and that space outside it exists, that it's as free as the space inside. Well, we could be revolving around our Sun while other bubbles or rather other shells are also revolving around their

15

own inner suns. Thus, we're not special, which, for me, sounds better."

"That's completely absurd and against the…"

"Against the official theories, yes, but not absurd. I won't go so far as to say that the theories themselves are absurd, but… look, I'm dazzled by the majesty of my idea. I see all these shells revolving around their centers and at the same time around a common sun. Which would mean that our Sun, seeming to move in a certain way, would really have a different movement from what we think. Is this, too, truly absurd seeing that we don't even feel our own movement around it?"

"Pure madness."

"No! And I see this common sun, itself the center of another huge shell revolving around it and embracing all the others I talked about. And this vast shell is nothing but a superworld revolving around a supersun and so on to infinity. Do you know what it would take to find the first proof of my superhuman cosmology?"

The man opened his eyes wide without answering.

"We'd have to search for the existence of little shells between us and our Sun. their existence would weigh heavily in favor of my hypothesis."

"No astronomical observation has ever revealed them."

"But what if they're miniscule, eh? If they're miniscule? They might also be inhabited by tiny men just like the superworlds would have people much bigger than us. No one would notice."

The other guy smiled paternally, "I'm going to tell you something. You notice too much. And since you're naïve and careless, you share your clever conclusions with any old stranger. Any old stranger is me, obviously. And me, I work for the knowledge police. So, you're going to come with me quietly and not make trouble."

He led Rolf, who had turned pale, toward the elevators.

CHAPTER II

Rolf had heard of the knowledge police even though it wasn't official. But he never imagined they would be so ordinary looking, so dull and unremarkable. And since this was the first time he had opened up to anyone about his astronomical concerns, he had never before come up against the repression of deviant ideas.

The man turned out to be talkative on the way. "I'm not upset with you, even though you called me a big dummy. My role is just to bring you in and of course beat you like a wild animal if you resist. But I'll return your compliment—you're too smart to rebel against legal authority. You'll see, you'll get off with a lenient sentence. In my report I'll highlight the fact that you limited yourself to your own ideas without rejecting what is taught officially."

"So," Rolf was trembling, "why not let me go right now, if you believe I'm not really guilty?"

The officer tightened his grip on Rolf's arm, "Watch it! Never say such a thing again or I'll charge you! You think I can just forget my duty? You think I'm ready to violate it by acting as your judge? Don't even think about it!"

He ended his tirade by growling like a dog and he poked Rolf hard to drive home his point. Rolf said nothing. The guy's reactions confused him. Out of the sliding elevators they came to the central police station. There, they buckled a metal plate around his waist and pushed him up against a magnetized wall that he stuck to like a fly in a spider's web.

It was a square cell where other delinquents were stuck against the metal wall like him.

"What did you do?" the closest asked him.

"Don't tell him!" another shouted. "He'll try to earn points by telling the cops that you were propagandizing against them."

"Answer him!" a third guy yelled. "Otherwise, he'll charge you!"

An officer entered with a whip and he lashed the floor. "There's going to be some very heavy sentences..." he almost whispered.

Then he left. All fell silent. Rolf waited, motionless. He was devastated. He wanted to feel sorry for himself. He would've given anything to have a sobbing woman wringing her hands at the door of the station. But he was single and saw how selfish his wish really was. But like the cop said, how could he have been so naïve and so easily provoked?

Thinking about it, he realized that the problem of the structure of the world or the worlds, the cosmology in short, had been on his mind, more or less consciously, for a long time. If he hadn't yet opened up to anyone about it, it wasn't so much that he was cautious, just distracted. And the day these questions finally emerged with all their force in his calm and quiet mind, he talked about them. He talked about them with any old stranger as the officer had said, that stupid brute.

He had no wife but he had an office. His boss would not come looking for him, crying out his name in a fretful voice from cell to cell. No, he would wait for him and cock his head, like always when things were going wrong, and say:

"Rolf, my boy, I understand that you got yourself arrested by the police. All criminals get caught sooner or later. But you must understand that I can't be seen employing a criminal. So, I advise you to look elsewhere for work. Now scram, you lowlife scum!"

But no. It wouldn't happen like that. The officer promised to bear witness in his defense. They'd give him a light sentence and then provide him with a certificate explaining his delay.

His delay? What if they didn't judge him for a month? Would he stay here the whole time, stuck to the wall with these creeps and their incomprehensible conversations?

The officer with the whip came back. This time he was carrying a chain that he hooked onto Rolf's belt.

"Rolf B 40?" he asked.

Rolf nodded.

"Potty," he said curtly. Then he detached him from the wall and dragged him to the door like a dog on a leash.

In front of the toilet he pontificated, "You leave the door open. I don't want to find you hanged."

Rolf shuddered. Hanged! As if he could think of such a thing! He rubbed his neck. He thought he felt a rope. But in the toilets? He wondered why they'd even mentioned it. Did the accused hang themselves like that for no good reason? Maybe they had reasons? Maybe they knew, unlike Rolf, what was awaiting them.

They could unquestionably submit an accused to any treatment whatsoever. Torture, for example. They could stick needles through someone's tongue to make him admit that he'd decided to assassinate the president of the city. Or crush his testicles in a vise to make him say anything. Of course, he'll confess whatever they want.

A wave of horror engulfed him. The wrongdoing didn't matter: when you're caught in the wheels you have to ride it out to the end. And the ride didn't belong to you anymore. What citizen, accused of a harmless mistake, ever came back saying, "I was sentenced to such and such punishment that fit my crime. I did my time and here I am, back among you." Who ever met someone like that? Not Rolf! You only met people whose lives were as transparent as glass. Anyone with a tarnished life, no matter how slightly, either didn't exist or didn't exist any longer. Rolf came out of the toilets with the conviction that he wouldn't escape the hornet's nest. He'd become a disposable human wreck.

"So," the officer snickered on seeing how defeated he looked, "you don't feel better? Well, you've got good reason."

With these comforting words he pulled Rolf in another direction opposite the cell.

He kept talking, "Because you're going to be judged right away. Yeah, there are people who don't have to drag it out. Others, of course, it takes years…"

From the tone of the guy's voice Rolf knew he was lying. No one waited years. So, why lie? Just to talk, no doubt. As if answering this hunch, the officer started whistling an old barracks song. The vulgar tune, the gray light in the windowless corridor, the hunched back of the police officer, all this together gave Rolf the impression that his guard was in the same boat as him. Maybe being a guard was a sentence that he was serving?

They came to a door that the officer pushed open. "Goodbye," he said cheerily.

Rolf heard the door close behind him. He was standing in a small room cluttered with furniture, with a semi-circular table behind which a dozen people sat, facing him, squeezed in shoulder to shoulder. Laughter, insults and whistles rang out along with animal cries. Rolf couldn't believe his ears. But the din was cut short by a gavel banging on the table. The person in the middle spoke up.

"So what," he said, "and the dignity of justice?"

Everything went silent. Rolf stole a glance at the one who seemed to be presiding. He was not shaved, wore a little black hat pulled down to his nose and his dirty shirt collar was open wide.

"Step forward," the president tilted his head back to see Rolf from under his hat.

Rolf went as far as he could, that is to say, half a step. Then he was up against the table.

"So," the president continued, tilting his head farther back, "we're talking nonsense about the Earth and the sky?"

Waiting for a response from Rolf, he pulled a cigar butt out of his pocket, which he lit and chomped on.

"The... officer who arrested me," Rolf said, "is a witness. I only made... conjectures... speculations..."

A storm of laughter broke out. The whistles and animal cries came back and again a gavel banging. Then:

"The police officer repeated what you said," the president informed him. "You declared that all the official theories were a pack of lies, that it ought to be proclaimed loud and clear and that would be enough to topple the head of the country all the way to the equator. 'Topple' is the term you used, isn't it?"

"I never said any of that!" Rolf shouted, horrified.

"Oh, oh," the president said, "we're going to lie now and accuse an upstanding public servant of lying! That's serious, very serious."

Rolf was in despair. He was getting nowhere in this grotesque farce. He decided to shut up.

"Okay," the president went on. "What makes me laugh is that you went off on this story about shells revolving around each other. Most of the delinquents question the immobility of the Sun. Not you. And did you know? The astronomical observations have indeed detected your little shells inside our own world."

With his chin up, puffing out the noxious smoke, he turned his head to the right and left towards his assessors.

"They've sent us a little genius!" he exclaimed while still chomping away.

The ruckus started up again, then quickly abated.

"That's fine," the president concluded. "Let's proceed with the accusation."

He drummed on the table with three fingers.

"Rolf B 40 is accused."

Rolf furrowed his brow and managed to stammer, "Accused of what?"

The president tipped up the brim of his hat, "Quiet, you. You're accused, that's all." He turned to the others again. "And that's the ruling. Do you agree with me?"

"Yes! Yes!" the cramped colleagues cried out.

"Let's move on to the verdict. Rolf B 40 is guilty." He paused, took off his hat and finished, "Here's the sentence: he'll suffer the punishment chosen by the hat."

From a drawer he pulled out a handful of folded papers, which he tossed into the hat.

"Go on, Rolf B 40. Choose."

Rolf reached out. Then he pulled back. Something was starting to boil inside him.

"I demand to be sentenced in a reasonable way. I deny this travesty of a trial and this mockery of sentencing."

Dead silence fell over the room. The president combed his fingers through his greasy hair.

"Listen up, pal, either you pick your punishment out of the hat or we sentence you to death right now."

He raised a shade behind him and with this thumb gestured to Rolf to look out the window. Rolf leaned forward. What he saw froze his blood. In a small courtyard down below a man was hanged by his feet, his hands tied behind his back. It looked almost ludicrous. The shade dropped back down. Rolf chose a piece of paper that the president unfolded.

"Injection 25," he announced.

He emptied the hat on the table and put it back on his head amidst the silence.

"You're really lucky!" he sneered. He nodded his chin toward the right end of the table. "Alby, take B 40 to the infirmary."

Rolf shuddered again. The infirmary! They were going to give him a shot. This was more frightening than anything. He couldn't understand the president's scornful sneer.

Alby got up and squeezed his way around the table, clinging onto binders and piled up chairs and the corner of a sideboard that contained sparkling dishes behind its cracked windows. A minute later Rolf was back in the corridor in which he'd been led down on a leash. This time he was free to move. Alby had unhooked the plate and the chain. He walked next to him, swinging the instruments that clanked annoyingly on the way. Alby was short and fat. He constantly blinked one eye and twitched a shoulder. He addressed Rolf in a tone that he tried to make friendly but reeked of hypocrisy.

"You'll see," he said. "It's not the end of the world…"

The world! There was another side of the Sun and Rolf had never had enough money to take a big trip. He sighed.

Alby pushed Rolf into the infirmary.

CHAPTER III

Rolf stepped into the slider that went to the fourth level. In the end, the whole appalling adventure had happened so quickly that he was not even going to be late for work. But what had come into his head on this fine morning to make him go strolling on the terrace of the grand tower? Truthfully, the shot was not as painful as he'd imagined. A minor accident was more grueling. The worst thing was just the idea of the shot. Well, not to mention the results, which remained a mystery.

Rolf was worried. So worried, in fact, that he wondered if he wouldn't need to use an adapter to get to the office. But no use: he only had to step back to get a better jump.

The other passengers around him acted normally. They were talking to each other, joking around, starting flash flirts. Rolf kept a ready smile on his face and replied without any apparent effort to the young lady who had just proposed a sexual tryst. He made a date with her for lunchtime in the Horizontals Park. He had to keep living normally. To convince himself, he made the same offer to another woman who accepted right off the bat. The second tryst was to take place that night.

But Rolf's anguish grew stronger every minute because he was slowly feeling penetrated by a strange and horrifying fit of something. He felt hot and cold. All of a sudden, he was shaken by a long spasm from head to toe. The guy next to him narrowed his eyes. With the utmost difficulty, Rolf forced a smile.

"Did you feel that jolt?" he tried to look surprised.

"No," the guy said. "These things never even shake."

The passenger glared at him coldly. Rolf dropped it. He had enough problems with the tingling sensation in his nostrils.

Just as suddenly as the tingling came, some other ghastly force threw his head back, then shoved it forward and down even while he sucked in a breath between puckered lips. This made a loud whistling noise that made everyone look at him. And given that Rolf was at the same time feeling a weird chill, he was more confused than ever.

Panic set in along with his stuffy nose. He touched it with the back of his hand and felt it wet. All conversations had stopped by now. You could hear nothing but the whistling wind along the walls. Alone in a six-foot wide circle Rolf fumbled with wiping the liquid running out of his nose. The two women he'd made dates with looked disgusted. He was feeling an unfamiliar and unbearable feeling that was made worse by shame.

Now the conversations were starting up again. But they were all focused on Rolf and ended in outrage. He was seized by another sneezing fit, worse than the first, and sprayed one of his shoes. There was a storm of protests. Someone pulled the alarm. The slider stopped.

When the employee appeared, the passengers all pointed to Rolf without comment. The employee said nothing. He motioned to the open door. Rolf got out, holding his sleeve under his nose.

The slider sped off. Rolf stayed behind on the tiny platform between two stations. He felt really bad. He wanted to go straight to bed, to wash his nose with plenty of water, to do whatever it took to get rid of this intolerable thing. But he couldn't.

He went down by the emergency walkway and came out on the boulevard. His office was not so far. Office? How could he work in the state he was in? And how could he cover it up? Because he'd have to hide it. He imagined the reaction of his colleagues, of his boss… He'd have to leave as soon as he got there and he wouldn't last long in his job. The attitude of the passengers on the slider were just a taste of what was to come.

This was all perfectly normal, logical, expected. Several months ago he himself had seen a man on the street limping and he was not the only one to keep his distance. But it was one thing to avoid someone, it was something else to run away. He had seen sick people before, once in a while. He had never been sick himself.

So, that was it... sickness. An unpleasant heat, pains, spasms that made you look ridiculous. In the end, sickness. Each with its own characteristics. Some worse than this one, maybe. Internal pains as bad as a burn but deep down in the body, in places that couldn't be soothed. Or like lacerations. Or grinding. He was discovering a universe of terror without believing that anything existed more unbearable than what he was going through. Anyway, either something was unbearable or it wasn't. This was.

But whatever the condition might be, it ended up in the same quarantine, the same revulsion from other people. The intensity of the reactions was apparently the same no matter the outward signs of your defect.

Rolf felt his legs wobbling. Was it from fear of the sickness or fear of other people? Another memory came to him: a man in piss-stained pants who was being cornered by people at a railing on the sixth level. Nobody had touched him but he'd been crushed below among the shredders.

Basically, he'd acted like an ostrich. From the moment they'd arrested him, he'd struck his head in the sand. Because even though sickness was rare, at least in the city, everyone knew that there was a Judicial Department of Contamination. For centuries sicknesses had been considered a punishment by God. Since they'd been eradicated, they'd become a punishment by man. Rolf thought that the seriousness of the punishment must've been proportional to the seriousness of the crime. Obviously, the hat of the president of the jury (what a president!) contained papers with the same thing written on them: Injection 25. Why such twisted, vicious methods? It was the custom. Maybe entertainment for the ones who held the reins and who got bored with their power. There were plenty of regular elections, but the same names were always on the ballot, for everything.

Rolf had to act fast. Some people were already getting out of his way. Others were looking daggers at him. He hurried down a side street, then another and another. He was getting farther away from the busy districts with the sliders and entering the zones that were almost deserted. He reached the huge smokestacks of the air purifiers and ducked between their columns. His eyes were full of tears but he couldn't tell if it was the sickness or the stress.

When he was completely alone, he wondered how he was going to get through this.

He could barely breath through his mouth and tried in vain to clear his stuffy nostrils. He started to blow hard out his nose, but this only resulted in disastrous effects for his face and clothes. Nausea came next. He stopped, his heart pounding. This new kind of spasm was particularly weird and scary. He tried to clean himself up, which only made him vomit. He thought he was dying. When he got back on his way, he was a total wreck.

He had to come up with something else. He searched his pockets and found a piece of tissue paper from the office cafeteria. Unconsciously he blew his nose and felt free, almost blissful.

Calmed down, he racked his brains trying to remember the name of this sickness and how they'd fought it in the past. He was no historian. He didn't have the slightest clue.

He kept walking, still moving away from the crowded quarters. The morning mist thinned in the distance, warmed by the approaching Sun… or that they were approaching. Rolf imagined a world where the Sun disappeared completely sometimes. Life would be impossible in such a world. All the creatures would die after the Sun disappeared. But the world would still exist even though there would be no one to talk about the "black day". He shivered. Such ideas made him cold and plunged him back into his sickness just when he had resigned himself to it.

As he approached the suburban zone of hydroponics, a sharp, rasping sound made him turn his head. Hiding in the shadows near a low door, someone was curled up. Rolf sped up at first, then stopped and went back. It was a young woman. When she saw that he was slowly coming back to her, she got up, ready to flee. The effort gave her a coughing fit, which Rolf listened to in wonder. Then his usual reaction kicked in and he backed away, giving the girl a nasty look. He sniffled automatically. The girl likewise backed away from him and coughed again. In Rolf's mind, hope fought against conditioning.

"Hey," he said, "do you know where we can get treated?"

At first the girl didn't answer. She was staring at him with distrust and disgust. Finally she said, "Treated, yes. Cured, no."

He felt his pulse racing, "A doctor?"

"I don't know. A clandie, anyway.

"Far from here?"

"On the other side of the hydros."

Rolf looked north along the long axis of the egg. "What are you doing here?"

"It's abandoned. You know very well we can't stay in the city. There are other sick ones around here."

Rolf realized that these outskirts of the city, the realm of automated machines, provided shelter to a population of people who avoided each other. Exiles like himself, like her, but subject to the same barriers as in the city. One sick person hated another sick person as much as a healthy one hated both of them. He realized this perfectly well but suddenly found something wrong with it.

"What's your name?" he asked. "Me, I'm Rolf."

"Jana. What…" She coughed and spat off to the side. It was red. "What do you care?"

He wanted to stay quiet, to stop the conversation, to flee with his own sickness without having to deal with another's. But he forced himself.

"We're already scorned by… people," he said. "There's no need to make it worse among each other."

She shrugged without answering. He thought for a moment.

"What's the clandie ask for to get treatment?" he asked.

"Money. You got any?"

"Yes," he said. "And you, where do you get food?"

"In the hydros. Is it true, you've got money?"

"Yes. Will you take me to the clandie?"

She shot him a crafty smile. "If you give me money. I don't have any more and it's getting hard."

He figured that money wouldn't be easy to find in this zone. When you run out, there's nothing more you can do, so you die. In his case, it was obviously coming from his nose and stuffing up his head. For Jana, it was the opposite. She would soon have nothing left in her chest from all the coughing.

"I'm going to need it," he said.

"Well, too bad."

But it could take him a long time to find the clandie alone. And his head would keep filling up the whole time.

"Okay, I'll give you some," he agreed reluctantly.

She started laughing, which made her cough. He barely noticed because he was consumed by a burning desire to get treatment.

"We go right now?"

She didn't answer. And then, "Show me your money."

He showed her. Not all of it.

"Good. Give it to me."

"That's stupid, what you're saying. If I give you everything I've got, I won't be able to get my treatment. Then I'd have no reason to follow you and so I'd have no reason to give you any."

She thought about his reasoning. "Well, half then."

"No. A quarter."

She ended up accepting. He counted the bills and gave her a quarter.

"Let's go," he said impatiently.

"Wait until I take my meds. I've got two left. I made them last."

He felt his heart swell. What she just said was something real. Was she messing with him?

"You've got medication?" he gawked.

"The clandie calls them ormedies."

She disappeared in the building and he stepped up to the door to keep an eye on her. She might just as well run out a back door. But he saw the inside of a room in shadows. It was full of old, broken-down machines. Jana had turned it into a makeshift shelter with a pallet and some vegetable provisions. She swallowed the powdered meds in front of him. Then, wrapping herself in her ratty dress, she went out.

"Has it been a long time since you…" Rolf muttered.

"A year." She said nothing more and he followed her.

CHAPTER IV

The industrial buildings thinned out. Now you could see the surface of the ground, close enough, between the cement blocks and the plastic. Also nearby, the slope was unnoticeable. Even though barely seen, however, you knew that the ground was rising. People once believed that the world was flat. They also surmised that it was round like a ball. It took the first serious travels to learn the truth.

Rolf remembered the words of the president of the tribunal: "Most of the delinquents question the immobility of the Sun." There were some really stupid people. With a moving Sun and a motionless shell, how could gravity exist? This gravity which is the effect of centrifugal force. But all kinds of nonsense are in nature.

They walked for 15 minutes without speaking, then Jana suddenly jumped between two huge tanks and hit the ground, gesturing urgently to Rolf. He joined her but kept his distance.

"What's the matter?"

She shushed him and whispered, "A sick guy. I know him. He's looking for money. He's already killed some newcomers."

Rolf felt his hair stand on end. He held his breath. Cautious footsteps approached. In the space between the tanks, he saw a man pass by carrying an iron bar. He had a huge tumor on his neck. Rolf felt like he was about to pass out from fear and disgust. But the man noticed nothing and went his way.

They lay still for many long minutes, then Jana got up and took a peek. She waved to Rolf that all was clear.

In its oblique eclipse, the Sun was coming closer to the ground. The heat became stifling. Jana and Rolf had crossed the hydroponic zone. Now nettles and brambles were slowing them down. They were entering the countryside or rather the empty lands before it. They only came across a few bushes half smothered in parasitical plants.

All of a sudden Jana cut in front of Rolf and went through a thicket where another woman was coming out on crutches. From her wrist hung a chain holding a bunch of open razors. The women said nothing to each other. Rolf also ignored the cripple when she went by.

The thicket was hiding a low house, a small, concrete building that must have housed a transformer. Jana went in first. Rolf stopped in the doorway.

What he saw before him was a genuine, old-time laboratory like in the old, two-dimensional photographs. The light from the unbelievable electric bulbs made the machines sparkle.

"Come in," said a voice coming from behind a stack of trays.

They went over to the bald man busy at some task who glanced up at them.

"Ah," he said, "it's Jana! Long time no see! And you brought me a new client."

"Yes, drugger," Jana replied.

The clandie interrupted his work and looked at Rolf.

"I see," he said. "What you've got is not so bad. It's called a cold and it's caused by a virus. Before they developed the vaccine, they used to treat it, but it could heal all by itself. Yours will never heal, I'll tell you straight off. Its causal agent just laughs at systematic immunization. But I can get rid of the trouble it's causing you. As long as I'm treating you, you'll barely notice that you're sick."

He pointed to Jana.

"For her it's more serious. If I didn't know how to synthesize isoniazid, she'd already be dead. But don't worry, no sickness is contagious. The germs inevitably become parasites of the chosen host. In the past, there were epidemics..."

Rolf noticed the boils on his neck. The other saw him looking.

"Staphylococcus," he said. "Lucky I've got antibiotics, otherwise I'd be one big abscess. Even with my mushroom cultures I can only stabilize its development..."

Rolf was hypnotized by the man, his archaic science, his antediluvian instruments, but one idea, a very important idea, was at the forefront of his mind.

"If I've got medication," he wondered aloud, "will people still know that I'm sick?"

"Not necessarily," the clandie said. "You'll treat yourself when you're alone."

Rolf's heart leapt in his chest. He saw himself pulled out of the nightmare of exile. He imagined going back, leaving behind him the perilous proximity of the pariahs. And if he took care of himself, he could live a normal life.

Jana watched him with a mix of hatred and envy. Her glaring was interrupted by the clandie who grab her arm and pushed her behind a kind of screen. It became dark. Rolf's attention was focused on the screen. His eyes bulged in fear and bewilderment. A green fluorescence lit up the big plate and he saw the shadow of Jana's skeleton take shape.

Rolf had vaguely heard of X-rays and the primitive use they'd made of them. But he had never seen anything like this.

"Hmm," the clandie murmured.

The room lit up again.

"It's time to restart the treatment."

Jana coughed long and hard, as if the comment had aggravated her condition. The clandie stuck a needle in her thigh, which made Rolf step back. But shots could be good or bad. It depends. Then the drugger dumped a bunch of packets into a plastic box. Jana handed him two of the bills Rolf had given her. The box changed hands.

Then the clandie reached for a small, rubber pear on a shelf.

"This is for you," he told Rolf. "Five sprays a day into the nostrils."

He also took a small bottle of white beads the size of a pea.

"And one pill three times a day."

He smiled confidently.

"With this you won't attract any attention."

Rolf showed him a bill. The doctor nodded his assent. Rolf paid, then looked around. "What good is money to you here? You can't use it…"

The clandie's smile reappeared. "I need it for raw materials," he explained. "With the profits I do research on my own condition."

Rolf shook his head, "But how do you make the purchases?"

The clandie slapped Rolf on the shoulder. Rolf jumped back.

"Among my clients there are sick people like you who are my connection to the city. And in the city, they traffic in everything…"

Rolf felt overjoyed. So, it was already arranged with those who were able to get back to their former life. He was suddenly overflowing with gratitude to the clandie.

"I'm ready to help you."

"Be careful, it's frowned upon."

Rolf put on a sly smile, "If you're caught."

They both laughed.

"We'll talk about that during your next visit," the clandie said.

Rolf turned to Jana who he thought was behind him. She had vanished.

"Do you know when she left?" Rolf asked.

"Oh, less than a minute ago. She's kind of a sourpuss, you know."

Rolf turned to go, "I have to find her or I'll get lost. It's a maze out here."

The clandie raised his hand, "Good luck! You can find me without a guide by following the radio signals. I'm on the short-wave."

"But don't you get caught?"

"No one uses those frequencies anymore. You need a special receiver."

Rolf hurried up. He'd spotted Jana disappearing over by the hydroponics. On the way he'd swallowed a pill, which was stuck in his throat. He kept gulping but in vain, so he swore to wash it down with a little water later on. Now it was the rubber pear's turn and he believed it was a miracle—in a few seconds he felt his nose clear up, dry up, become normal again. When he caught up to Jana he didn't dream of any kind of help or partnership. Jana was nothing but a sick person and he was a man in good health.

But she heard his footsteps. She swung around.

"You could please stop prowling around me," she said.

"I don't want to," Rolf replied, "I just don't want to get lost."

She snickered bitterly, "I wonder why you're not so sick!"

"And I wonder why you're so very sick!"

When Jana dove into her hovel he left her without saying a word and went cautiously back to the city.

But he was not used to being cautious. After the first bend he saw the man with the iron bar blocking the road ten yards away.

His fear mingled with anger. Just when the future was looking a little brighter, he had to run into a killer. Jana knew what she was talking about... Jana who had maybe killed someone herself to get such a heavy sentence... even if by accident...

The ground was cluttered with chunks of concrete. Rolf picked one up. Right away the man marched forward. Rolf aimed at the tumor.

CHAPTER V

The man had already taken three steps. When he was closer, Rolf thought he could hit him easily. But on the other hand, there wouldn't be enough time to pick up another chunk. He had to stop him with the first throw. Otherwise, the guy would smash his head in with the iron bar. Not knowing how accurate he might be, or rather knowing full well his inexperience, Rolf tried reasoning.

He stepped back, saying, "You're not going to kill the hen that lays the golden eggs."

The guy stopped. "What?"

Without dropping his weapon, Rolf explained quickly:

"I have very little money, but the clandie got me well enough to go back to the city. I'm going to go back to work. Tomorrow I get paid."

The brute swung his bar. Rolf played his ace.

"You know we can't get treated in the city, so I have to come back here."

"Yeah," his voice had a gauzy tone, eerily inhuman. "And what's that to me?"

"Ten visits for you to the doctor when I come back."

The killer cleared his throat. "And when's that supposed to happen, this fabulous deal of yours?"

Rolf shrugged. "You know we can't last long without treatment, especially in the city where people see you."

The other guy relaxed his scowl. Rolf felt like he was about to scrape through. He added, "The clandie needs products that I'm going to bring him."

"There are others bringing him stuff," the guy sniffled.

"Yes, but he's never got enough. What's he call yours?"

He thought about it for a minute and then, "Anti-mites."

Rolf shook his head, "Never heard of it, but I'll find some."

The guy made a grand gesture with his iron bar and shouted, "Hold on! I'm not done. Anti-miotics, that's it. That's the name."

"Okay," Rolf said, "if I can't find any over there, the clandie will make some here with what I bring him."

The man tucked the iron bar into his belt, then started snickering. "Good thing you didn't toss your concrete block. Others have tried. They're not around to tell what happened." He ducked to the side for a split second, then sprung back. "You see?"

Rolf had to agree that he was right to use diplomacy. He decided to go all the way and get everything he could out of it.

"Okay, but I'm going to ask you for a little something in return."

"What?" the guy suddenly had his hackles up.

"You're tough and you know how to fight. You'll help me out if anyone gives me trouble."

The guy guffawed proudly, "All right, peewee." Then he turned mean again, "But watch out, eh! You walk straight or else!" He slapped his iron bar emphatically.

Rolf nodded in agreement and got ready to go.

The guy pointed an accusing finger at him and said, "Because, you know, I can go into the city at night and search you out anywhere."

"Good,' Rolf tried to sound like he cared. "Oh, another thing. You know Jana, the cougher?"

"There's a bunch of coughers, but I know the one."

"Don't cause her any trouble."

He guffawed again, "Me? Trouble for that wisp of a girl spitting blood?"

He made a wide sweep of his arm and left without saying anything more. Rolf headed back to the city. He wondered why he'd mentioned Jana.

Before reaching the populated zones, he took a second pill, just in case, even though he still had no water. The pill stuck in his throat like the first one. To take his mind off the irritation, he used the little pear again. His nose, which had started to run again, dried up like parchment. He picked some berries off a bush between two rocks and ate them to get down the pill. They were good. He ate all of them that looked sweet, then started off again, his mind floating in a kind of euphoria.

When he arrived at the first elevators that led to the sliders, he didn't attract anybody's attention. He didn't sneeze or blow his nose. His face wasn't even red from the fever.

On the other hand, he felt sleepy, like he hadn't had the good night's sleep he did have. He wondered if the pills didn't have something to do with it. The clandie hadn't told him not to take them all at once. And now he was breathing heavily from all those damned berries he'd eaten. He was so stupid that he acted like a child when he was just about to pull through.

He managed, however, to hide his minor symptoms and he changed sliders to get to the office without any trouble. Too bad that he was late… He would think up an excuse. If he kept living in the city, he'd need an income, so as long as he could do his job as an archivist in the center of exploration coordination, he'd be safe.

Thus, he got to work two hours late. Given what he'd gone through early in the morning, he barely considered his tardiness of any importance. But this lay in the fact that his home and his office were both on the edge of the city near the big tower of the fifth level.

Luckily the boss was absent. Ginou, the typist who shared his office, told him that K 813 must have gone to the main Chiefdom of the Presidency about a dispute over the Incunabula of the land registry that separated V 30, Rolf's area, from the Polygon of Massifs located a few hundred miles toward the point of the Egg.

Rolf blessed the Massifs.

Now he was pretty sure his lateness wouldn't be noticed. Therefore, he got down to work on what had been interrupted the evening before: "Farthest points of exploration carried out by V 30 and interviews with the foreign explorers."

They knew the world only vaguely. Or rather, they knew very well certain survey points whose number increased very slowly over the years. It was vast—the inner surface of the Egg measured 600 miles along its small axis and double that along the other. They had catalogued oceans that covered 600,000,000 square miles and mountains whose peak reached 600 miles whereas the atmospheric layer was no more than 30 miles... They'd flown a supersonic aircraft over forests that took 30 hours to cross and whose fauna remained totally unknown. And all this was revolving around a sun only 6,000 miles in diameter but with a huge density.

Rolf reflected on his personal cosmogony. So, he was right. The wicked magistrate had confirmed it. He was overjoyed thinking of it, even though, basically, such a universe did nothing to increase the possibilities of exploration they worked on: the other worlds were too small or too big and they didn't even know this one. Didn't matter. Rolf gloated.

Just then the chief K 813 came in and sat down in his office, separated from Rolf's by a simple glass partition. They sat there like that, face to face, all day long, trying to avoid looking at each other. The chief gave Rolf an artificial smile through the glass, then dove into his files. He looked nervous. Rolf became so too.

Was it the medication wearing off normally or did his emotions have something to do with it? Rolf felt his nose getting wet.

All his terror came rushing back. Was he really safe and sound for so short a time? He snuck a glance at the chief. He was lost in his files and didn't seem to notice anything. Rolf knocked an eraser off his desk and got down on his knees to pick it up. Under his desk he furtively squirted the pear into his nostril. Then he got up, posed the eraser on his desk and looked up at the ceiling. His eyes had glimpsed the chief looking at him suspiciously. He paid no attention to him and focused on his own files. Three short raps knocked on the glass.

Rolf looked up. The chief was signaling him to come in. His heart raced as he stood up, opened the door between the offices and entered. The other had certainly seen something. He waited, expecting the worst.

"Give me some information," he said sharply.

"Yes, sir," Rolf felt nervous but answered politely.

"What's the relation between the Massifs and the people of the savanna? I mean today. I don't care about their history."

"Yes, sir," Rolf was relieved. "The relation is in favor of the Massifs and overwhelmingly. The people of the savanna are countless but they've only got spears for weapons while the Massifs have catapults."

The chief smirked, "I know all that but I wanted to check your knowledge. Always be ready to answer all questions otherwise it's the boot! Got it?"

"Certainly, sir," Rolf said.

"There's no 'certainly'. That's the way it is and that's all!"

Rolf kept silent.

K 813 went on, "Why am I talking about these people, these races that don't exist?"

"Because it's necessary to act like we're not alone in the universe so that we can comfort ourselves in our solitude with the wonderful stories in which we talk about people like us and different too, but always human beings even though our explorations have never revealed the lowliest lifeform that can compare in the slightest degree with the admirable thinking race that we present to passive nature in a constantly changing, always new spectacle while in the oval sky…"

"Enough!" the chief shouted. "I didn't ask you to recite the Credo by heart! Get into your office and don't spend your day underneath your desk doing who knows what!"

Rolf left the chief's office without saying another word. He went back to his desk, sat down and concentrated on his files of imaginary ethnography. He had to update their Fanciful content with respect to the real discoveries that V 30 made to the geographic map: the fake, foreign explorers couldn't come from regions where they've just learned were converted into magma boiling at 800 degrees…

There were a lot of changes to make. Rolf started cursing the real explorers who left V 30 and discovered something new every day. It was more work for Rolf every time. Work updating, sure, but also inventing: the imaginary parts had to fit with the new and for this Rolf had to transform them, change their recent history, their present state, sometimes their morphological characteristics. With his and his colleagues' instructions they published a weekly bulletin dedicated to the reforms of the official myth. Crazy mental work benefiting no one. Because this history of solitude and comforting was good only for propaganda. Who cared about the existence, real or imaginary, of other men around the world? They just needed to feed the channels of information and since fiction per se was forbidden, they made it mandatory under the title of reality.

CHAPTER VI

Presently, the chief left again but not before flashing a hard look at Rolf through the glass. He pretended not to notice. Finally alone, he got to use the pear. And that was the moment when Ginou decided to enter. She sat on Rolf's desk and raised up her legs.

"Are you free at noon?" she cooed.

Rolf remembered the dates he'd made in the morning on the slider. There was no way he was keeping them after the show he'd put on. But then again, he'd made dates…

"Unfortunately, no," he said tensely.

"Oh. Are you sure?" Ginou straddled his knee and gave him a bear hug.

Rolf was plagued with a feeling he couldn't control—Ginou was attractive. But he almost threw her on the floor. She had just slipped a hand into his coat pocket, the one with the medicine pear.

"What's the matter with you?" she sounded furious.

Rolf knew how to deal with it. "Oh," he forced a smile, "that's fine in the Horizontals Park but not here, see!"

She had gotten off him. "Is that something erotic in your pocket?" she asked, moving closer again.

"No, no. Really, there's nothing…

She gave him a beguiling look, "Sure there is, something round. You can tell me."

He was backed against the wall. She thew herself at him. He instinctively protected his pocket. But she had nimbly slid her hand into the other pocket and pulled out the bottle of pills.

"Aha!" she said, opening it. "I got this at least!"

The pills rained down on the floor, rolling under the desk and under his binders. Ginou stood speechless, the empty bottle in her hand. Rolf turned pale.

"What is this?" she finally asked.

Rolf searched desperately for an answer. "Drugs," he replied half-heartedly. Then more forcefully, "Drugs! You can turn me in now."

She stared at him, scared and impressed. She ended up getting down on her knees and picking up the pills.

"Listen, Rolf," she said submissively, "I never would've thought... So, you lead a double life..." She gave him those puppy dog eyes. "You're a real hard man, you are."

"Yes indeed!" Rolf snapped, not seeing how he was hard by taking poisons that made you crazy, weak and stupid. He showed her the rubber pear and in a dramatic tone that made Ginou shiver he announced, "This one's even worse."

"Will you give me some?" she asked timidly.

He frowned, "You're joking. You've got to get used to them. Me, I've been taking them for years. But you..."

"Just a little, "she begged.

Rolf inspected the floor. He didn't see any pills. "One little pellet," he said gallantly. "But not the pear. You'd be rolling on the ground in front of the boss, screaming like a madwoman."

She accepted the pill with worried gratitude. "What'll it do to me?" she asked.

He nodded and explained, "Neophytes react in different ways. Wait til later when the Sun is farther away."

Her only answer was to stick the pill in her mouth.

Rolf warned her, "Swallow it right away. It tastes horrible."

She grimaced with disgust, trying desperately to gulp it down. "There it goes," she finally said.

Rolf watched her. "I'll keep an eye on you. You might go jump out the window."

She looked fearfully at the window.

"But it might also have a sexual effect."

She plopped down, languidly, in Rolf's chair. "I think it's more like that," she looked ready to drop dead. "Are you coming?"

42

"Poor girl!" Rolf bellowed. "You'll turn frigid. We take drugs alone. You should've waited. But too late now, the harm is done. Don't make it worse."

Ginou looked at him like he was a thousand miles away. Her voice was faint. "Oh, what a strange feeling... like being carried away by flying men..."

"Flying men" Rolf thought—what a stupid idea! He watched her, convinced that she was putting on a show. The medicine did nothing but make you a little sleepy. This crazy girl just needed to believe she was taking a weird, unknown drug to have whatever effect she wanted. Then again, who could say that she really wasn't feeling like being carried away by flying men? He wanted to say "Grab on so you don't fall" but he held back. This was not the moment to make her suspicious of what she'd swallowed.

"And," she added, "I feel my nose all dried up."

Rolf turned pale again. The ormedy works the same on healthy people. If she guessed? But no, she'd never been sick. Rolf didn't even know the name of what they'd given him. How was she going to recognize the signs?

"It's a little uncomfortable," he said, getting closer to her. "But aren't the good effects worth a few minor bad ones?"

"Oh yes," her voice was fading, her eyes wide open.

"Good," Rolf was starting to worry. "Get hold of yourself. The boss is coming back and if he sees you like this... we're both screwed. And for you, with drugs, it's all over!"

She got up from the armchair where she was slipping lower and lower and stood up straight with one eye blinking.

"That's better," she said. "Oh, I feel so much better."

"Right?" Rolf tried not to sound sarcastic.

This gave some relief to his own naïveté, not to mention his stupidity of being conned by this seductress.

Ginou went over to her own chair. She ran her hand through her hair, let out a kind of joyful yelp and started typing the document awaiting her. It was an update signed by Rolf for a few meticulous modifications to some descriptions

43

created from scratch. Between two files she blew hard out her nose. Rolf looked up. She saw him.

"Sorry," she said, "but I've still got my nose feeling like wood. Does it last long?"

Rolf allowed himself to sniffle. "Not too long," he patronized. "Don't complain, you don't have all the problems of an old druggie like me. Well, you'll see if you want to keep going."

"Oh yes," she spurted.

Rolf sprayed the pear in his nose. She watched him do it with a mixture of disgust and respect.

Footsteps echoed in the corridor. He adroitly stashed the pear in his pocket. The chief entered his office, went to the connecting door and threw it open. Ginou was already back to typing away innocently.

"Hey, B 40," the chief glared at Rolf, "you're going to the Presidency this afternoon. I've got a document for them that has to be hand-delivered."

The vertical line he always had between his eyes deepened and his nose wrinkled.

"What's that disgusting smell in your office?" he asked menacingly.

"Sorry, boss," Ginou put on a hangdog face. "It's my new perfume."

The chief looked at her, sniffed the air and turned back to Rolf.

"Well, don't get too close to him," he said. "It's revolting enough for one person."

Ginou shot back, "But I was going to go with him to the park…"

Brave girl, Rolf thought. She's backing me up and how quickly she adapts!

"Figure it out!" the chief shouted, stamping his foot. "I don't want to hear about your libidinous practices, but figure it out, both of you, to get rid of this stench."

"Sir," Ginou said, "the sexual constitution…"

"Don't know it!" he yelled.

44

Ginou stood up. Her eyes were flaring. "Oh, you don't know it!" she yelled back. "And the League for the Promotion of the Redundant? You don't know them either?"

The chief suddenly lost his self-assurance and cautiously inquired, "Why do you ask that?"

She narrowed his eyes. "Because I'm a member of the Marketing Militia. So, my little 813, you're going to walk straight, aren't you? Because, even being the department chief that you are, I can send you to the tribunal, I can! Me, I can accuse you of curbing the expansion! And I can get you contaminated, turn you into a wreck. Understand, creepy little chiefie? Now, get out of this office. And we don't want to see you again unless it's necessary for the work, got it?"

Rolf listened to her in fear and bewilderment. So, Ginou too… Always buried in his files he had never noticed that V 30 was teeming with all kinds of police.

He saw the chief back out of the office, saying, "Okay, okay, Ginou, don't take it so hard. I got it, do what you want…" He turned to Rolf, "Reason with her, pal. Oh, you know how difficult women are to live with…"

He did some kind of gargling that might have passed for a colluding snicker. Rolf just watched him leave without responding. The chief didn't stay in his office.

"Ha, ha," Ginou said, "he's ashamed. He won't stand being seen by us now."

"Right, right, no doubt," Rolf was unsure.

He wondered whether the chief would go find backup from a more influential police officer. He ended up sharing his fears with Ginou. She laughed.

"Someone more influential than the Marketing Militia! I'd like to see that!"

Her eyes drilled into Rolf.

"Nothing escapes us," she said triumphantly.

Rolf was thinking, "And if she's right? What if she knows now that I'm sick and I'm passing off my ormedy for recreational drugs?"

"Like you, B40," she said.

Here we go, he figured.

"I guessed that you were taking drugs." She smiled. "But me too," she confessed. "Didn't you notice that your junk didn't have as strong an effect on me as it would a total beginner?"

Rolf choked back the laugh that was rising in his throat. "I did indeed notice that," he said. "Do you think your reaction could escape an old roadie like me…"

She looked at him sympathetically. "I might be able to find you a covert job in the militia. Because one of these days you might have run-ins with the brigade."

Rolf suddenly matched her words to her behavior. She said too much after doing too much. She didn't belong to any police. She just heard about the one she referred to and bluffed her way through it. Rolf was dealing with a pathological liar. In the meantime, the chief was going to find out from real police just to be sure. His cowardly retreat was a ploy to cover his real intention.

Rolf's face hardened. "Do you know what you did, you whacko?"

She tried to sound haughty, "How's that? Be careful what you say!"

He grabbed her by the shoulders and shook her. "We're both in for it now," he shouted in her face. "The Marketing Militia! What else? The president's favorite mistress? Get your things. We're taking off right now before that bastard comes back."

She wriggled free. "Go if you want. Me, I'm staying. The Militia…"

She was sticking to her lie. She didn't know what the real police were like. Rolf did. But he couldn't tell her. He did, however, give it one last try.

"Ginou," he forced himself to stay calm, "it's you who are going to get contaminated. Come with me, please."

She shook her head stubbornly, "If you don't believe me, wait a while for my colleagues to get here and you'll see."

He glanced out the window. A slider was stopping and five men were jumping out. He almost believed what she was saying. Then he saw the chief with them.

"Goodbye, Ginou," he said. "I tried."

He ran out of the office and jumped on the elevator. He started down while the men were coming up.

CHAPTER VII

On the ground floor the vertical door clicked open. He found himself in the presence of three astonished men and made an absurd movement to scramble back into the elevator. But the men were wearing yellow uniforms with the purple circle like all public service employees. He sent it down when he saw the crates piled up behind them.

"You can go on up," he spoke as if informed. "Everything's ready."

"What?" one of them said. "Now we're not going to the basement?"

Rolf shook his head to get his mind working. "Of course, pal. They've prepared everything up there for you to go down. You didn't let me finish. Go on, boys, and don't talk about the orders because K 813 is no jokester. It's me telling you this."

"Okay, boss!" the warehouseman said. "We're going!" He spat in his hands and turned around to his comrades.

As Rolf stepped into the street he suddenly wondered why he had left the office. What was he guilty of in the eyes of the chief? Letting Ginou get close to him and spreading the secretary's perfume? There was nothing to get worked up about. He started to go back—running away was admitting guilt. Guilt of what? They'd figure it out when they caught him.

He froze. What was Ginou going to do in the hands of the police? She'd accuse him of covering up. She'd declare that he used narcotics. They'd snatch up his medication and get it analyzed. Given the results, they'd alert the contamination service and the watertight walls between the services would come crashing down.

He left. Again the passers-by looked at him. But he walked calmly, steadily. "Joy through work" as the slogan said. Or "You have nothing to fear if you're like everybody else". He wasn't so sure that was right: a mistake is so easily made...

But where to go? He was going to have two or three kinds of police on his tracks. Go back to the outskirts? When he hadn't gotten paid and didn't have a penny for treatment? And forget about the clandie's solution, the one he'd used to snare the killer to save his skin? Stay here and get caught?

He decided to put into action the plan he'd come up with for the evening: get in touch with the underground. There he could both start his indispensable trafficking and find refuge. He took the slider that led to the second level.

In the slider he tried to recall what he knew about the shady places. Not much. Between his files and the park, he'd found a balance that, to maintain it, had no need of any dangerous exotic sustenance. He'd come across or at least heard things in the news. So, he knew what areas were generally the focal points of this occult power that seemed to defy the president and the police. But that was all he knew.

In the distance he saw the massive tower where they had arrested him. He changed at the next station, glad to see that nobody was paying any attention to him. The ormedies were really first class. He took another slider that went downtown. It was there that sin had taken up residence. Funny term. Everyone used it and no one knew why. The same as the tower, which they called "The Watch Out Tower", apparently for no reason. Except for Rolf who was sorry not to have heeded the warning.

The second slider was full of uninhibited cheerfulness. Taking advantage of a little free space, the passengers put on an exhibition of dance, which Rolf recognized as one that he himself had contributed to the description: a pseudo-dance ritual practiced by savage peoples who were said to live on the other side of the sun. Three passengers in business suits were plucking instruments that amazed Rolf: they had obviously been built according to the instructions in magazines. Rolf was in a position to know that the descriptions were purely imaginary, and yet they produced sounds whose harmony his ears could hardly believe.

Once they'd finished the music, which attempted to be barbarous, the passengers took their places with loud applause. All except one, who stood in the open space. It was one of the musicians. He'd kept out his instrument, in the shape of an axe with a string, and he was holding it between his legs to tune it. Rolf approached him.

"You got that down there, eh?" he winked.

The musician looked at him without responding and kept tuning.

"Okay," Rolf said, already worried about the consequences of joking around, "it doesn't matter. What matters is that you did pretty well with it, right?"

The man put his instrument on the floor and faced Rolf, "I didn't do anything," he cast anxious looks around him. "I just copied the drawings I found in the press and I made the instrument. There are no rights reserved. At least it wasn't marked. As for the music, I invented it myself. But I'm not asking for rights either. If that's what you mean, I'm ready to give the music to the presidency…"

He paused, then went on.

"Or I'm okay with throwing it away. I've got no copies, I swear. It was just instinct."

He blushed and sweat beaded on his forehead.

"Obviously not. That's not the word. We can't surrender ourselves to instinct. Let's say I reasoned it out in accordance with the demands, the general interest… Really, in accordance with the interests of the president…"

He dabbed his forehead with his sleeve.

"And the chief, of course… no, not the interest, I mean the sense of the general interest… really, I didn't reason it out, I'm not one of those of snobs who pretend…"

He stopped talking, looking defeated, then in a flat voice:

"I'm ready to follow you… I won't make trouble…"

Rolf was smiling on the inside, telling himself that he wasn't "the only oyster in the soup". Weird expression. Where did it come from? He was about to snap at the musician, even if it meant taking him along as a companion... who knows, an ally? But he needed time. His personality was not used to aggressive replies. Meanwhile, someone jumped in before him.

"What's the problem?" one of the other musicians stood up and stepped in front of the first guy. "This gentleman is a cop and hates music like all cops?"

Rolf backed away and a thought flashed through his mind: I should've known that nothing ever goes right. Why did I open my mouth?

His evil genius, however, whispered that this was the perfect opportunity for him to play the role of those police officers who hold the city under their thumb. But he resisted and said nothing.

The man with the axe instrument regained his self-assurance. With a nervous laugh he said, "Obviously another troublemaker."

The second didn't answer him but spoke to Rolf, "So, what do you have to say, eh?"

Rolf turned around and went to sit in an empty seat. "I don't do politics," he said submissively.

The second musician turned to the first, "Well, do we like troublemakers?"

The first laughed again, tensely, "Not at all!"

The other pulled the alarm. Rolf thought, "Again!" without looking at them.

"Well, I am one and proud of it," the musician crowed behind his back.

The slider stopped. Rolf saw the two men get off on the narrow platform, the one dragging the other. He was submerged in disgust and indignation. As the slider started off again, he shook his fist at the cop, who saw the gesture. Fast as lightning he pulled out his burner and shot at the car without aiming. But Rolf felt the floor give way underneath him. He was jolted out of his seat and into the passenger across from him. Then he passed out. But not before he saw the two men thrown off the platform.

In the thick, dark night where Rolf was floating, a voice was saying:

"It's been almost 30 years you've been alive and you've never seen such a stampede of arrests... Soon you won't be able to move around..."

He realized that the voice was his own. He opened his eyes and made the effort to turn his head in both directions it desired.

He was lying in the wreckage amidst a tangle of motionless bodies. Helmeted men were arriving. They held long, iron hooks. Rolf gathered his energy. He managed to free himself from the pile of bodies and the metal debris and stand up, wobbling, grabbing one of the concrete columns that supported the second level transport. One of the helmeted men came near and pushed him with the end of his hook, using only the round part.

"Are you hurt?" he asked expectantly.

Rolf saw one of his colleagues pulling a man out of the wreckage by planting the hook in his back. He wasn't dead. The pain woke him up and he started screaming. The rescuer dragged him anyway.

"No," Rolf shouted, "nothing wrong. Nothing at all!"

"Run," the rescuer said.

"Got it," Rolf answered and he started limping off. His left knee had swelled to twice its normal size.

"Better than that!" the rescuer moved in easily, hook in air.

"There you go!" Rolf said merrily. He strutted normally. The pain was so bad he saw everything spinning before his eyes.

"Good," the rescuer sounded sorry. "You can go. But I want to see you run."

Rolf ran. He passed the first column, disappeared between two others and fell down in a swoon. Other screams rang out.

CHAPTER VIII

This second fainting fit didn't last long. Rolf woke up lying behind a big chunk of concrete that hid him from view. The screaming had stopped. Rolf risked a peek at the accident.

A potbellied helicopter with small little rotors was hovering three feet off the ground. The rescuers or rather the cleaners were dragging the dead and injured alike with their hooks. It was the first time Rolf had witnessed—let alone been part of—such a disaster. He knew very well that those injured at work or in traffic accidents were never cared for because doctors didn't exist in the city. But he believed that they were sent back home to die or get better as their fate willed. His hair stood on end seeing what they did with them in reality. Undoubtedly, they were now going to take them beyond the countryside and drop them into the void without further ado. Thus, those who were still unduly alive would become as dead as the others.

Rolf cautiously massaged his knee. Doing this he realized that his coat pocket was drenched. He stuck his hand in and pulled out the pear. He shook it apprehensively. It was almost empty. The crash. He quickly checked the other pocket for the other ormedies. They were still there. He swallowed a pill to buck up his courage. At least he could keep the first sickness at bay while waiting for the second one to reappear.

He focused on his knee, which he could barely bend. How was he going to get back to the city in this condition? And how was he going to reach the suburbs to look for the clandie? He tried to get his bearings.

At the end of the concrete block ran a bright yellow, plastic fence. Judging from the noise coming from the other side, it ran long a pedestrian road. Rolf noted the direction of the sun's rays that reached him, remembered the grand tower he'd seen before changing sliders and deduced that he was right in the middle of downtown. He just had to get over the fence and saunter away as if out for a stroll.

He got up, staying vigilant not to be spotted by the cleaners whose helicopter hadn't left. He stood still, leaning against a pillar and trying to put some pressure on his wounded knee. A cry of pain rose in his throat but was held back by his sealed lips. He kept rubbing his knee. At last, he could stand up as long as he didn't put too much pressure on the bad knee. He took a few steps, humming to himself to distract himself from the pain as well as to look casual. "Tra-la-la, la-lira…" What an ordeal!

He reached the fence, which he walked along, peeking through the slats. He saw a street lined with bars whose signs pictured phalluses or hearts pierced with knives. They were lit up even in the daylight that was still bright in these lowlands. Rolf used his temporary solitude to walk slowly, supporting himself on the fence. He didn't want to imagine what he would looked like in public.

He heard a ruckus close by, on the other side of the plastic fence. He peeked. Two men were running down the road, one chasing the other. The second one caught the first and started beating him with an object that Rolf identified as a hammer. The prey fell. The chaser immediately stopped swinging and walked calmly back the other way. He didn't have to finish the job: the passers-by who had stopped to watch were running to the inert body and pummeling it. A woman was smashing its face with a rock. Then she threw the rock over the fence and almost hit Rolf.

When he looked back through the slats the crowd had dispersed. A silent car painted the city colors pulled up to the body. Three men got out, tossed the victim into a kind of small bin in the rear, and then left. Rolf watched them drive off, then he got back to his painful march along the fence.

Soon he ran into another concrete pillar. Between the pillar and the end of the fence was a narrow space he could squeeze through. He was on the street. A perfectly calm street where smiling people passed by. He knew what the calm was hiding and what lay behind those smiles.

He was amazed to realize how long he had lived cut off from the city, buried in his files. Didn't they talk about the violence that reigned between the police and the people, between the isolated inhabitants themselves, between the mobs and the man alone? Or were these things recent? What happened to create such a climate?

"Just a bunch of hot air," Rolf thought. "We know nothing about nothing and what we think we know is a web of lies... I'm in a position to know."

But he had no desire to tell anyone. In fact, he had no desire to meet anyone. Unfortunately, he had to. For two reasons: to find a hideout while his knee became usable again and also to get started on the trafficking that he needed for the clandie in the suburbs, which had two parts as well—one to get money to pay for his medicine and then to get the stuff needed for the killer with a tumor so that he'll be a friend and not an enemy and let him visit the clandie.

Things were not looking too bright. Following through on his thought he found another concern buried deep: help with Jana's treatment. He was very surprised by this. But he had no intention of burdening his mind with such ideas and still less to waste any of his precious time on it. Whatever the case, there were more pressing issues than to ponder this kind of question.

He walked as normally as he could and keep an eye on the people he passed. Ordinary people, it seemed. And how would he react if they lynched someone in front of him? Why would he be the only one to be horrified by the behavior of bloodthirsty dogs? He was thinking things that he'd never even imagined before. Why wouldn't he be carried away by a murderous rage against the victim on the ground? Maybe it was a normal reaction engraved in the needs of the species? He shuddered with fear and disgust like recently in the slider. But no, he felt profoundly differently from these people. But why, then, did he remember always acting the same way as them against the sick? He denied this: of course he felt repulsed by a person debilitated by sickness, by an injury… an injury? Well, this man whom the mob had finished off, he'd been running just before. So, he was in perfect health as far as anyone could tell. And if Rolf were part of the crowd instead of hiding his own physical defect? Would he have taken part in the kill? Honestly, he was sure he wouldn't. And so, he felt reassured. A clear and obvious feeling was worth more than a rational conviction in such matters. He breathed freely.

But his knee held him back and kept him from getting too philosophical. He went into the first bar he came across.

The establishment was below street level. Going down the stairs that led to the counter Rolf's attention was drawn to the lighting system. He'd heard of it but never seen it in action. Cast iron logs were burning in a cutout fireplace under a jet of pure oxygen. A cascade of liquid glass was constantly flowing in the opening and this glass had colors determined by chance alone. In front of this curtain was a tray of liquid air that evaporated for the refrigeration. The whole thing kept the bar at a mild temperature with colorful lights.

Rolf had not yet reached the last step when a naked girl dismounted her wooden horse and came up to him, glass in hand.

"So, pretty boy, are you coming down or what?"

Rolf stared at her, flabbergasted. He'd also heard of this job, so absurd in a world where they made love whenever they wanted with whomever they wanted.

"Well, miss," he said, "personally I…"

"Shut up!" the muse cut him off. "You want to pay or not?"

Rolf was taken aback. "It's just that I…"

He realized that the salt of love in this bar was money. But he figured that love was salty enough for him. He didn't like it pickled. And besides, the money was for the clandie.

"No," he said. "In fact…" But he was afraid of looking ridiculous, stingy, old-fashioned. "I have a bad knee." And right away he corrected himself, "I mean all my eroticism is in my knee. The left one to be precise. So, money or not, right?"

"Queer!" the muse spat out.

She dumped her drink at his feet and went back to straddle the horse. As she was mounting it, a paunchy guy with bushy eyebrows came out from behind a curtain.

He said to Rolf, "If I were you, I…"

"Yes indeed," Rolf said. And he went back up the stairs faster than he thought possible considering the shooting eroticism in his knee. The street was his only option. He took refuge in it.

CHAPTER IX

But the effort he'd made to climb the stairs had worsened his pain. He couldn't help limping and keeping a fearful eye on the reactions of the passers-by.

"I'm sure I've got a sprained knee," he thought. "That's what they used to call it. Now we don't say anything. Either you go as fast as you can… or else you're caught and poof… it's all over, kaput…"

He had no choice but to enter the closest bar, hoping they'd give him a kinder reception.

The second bar was also underground. But the atmosphere was completely different. It was lit by torches that sputtered acrid smoke. A system of ventilation must've sucked it out otherwise they customers would suffocate in minutes. In the middle of the room stood a big, red and green cylinder whose two colors mingled in such a way that they looked like they were moving and you couldn't really tell where the cylinder was.

Rolf gripped the edge of the bar to hop onto a stool that was way too high. He almost fell off when he saw over his shoulder the stacked bunks built into the walls. People were lying there in the darkness. They all had a tube in their mouth that was connected to the central cylinder.

The bartender came over dragging a towel along the bar. "What'll it be, mister?"

"A glass of milk," Rolf said.

The bartender frowned, "With what?"

Rolf realized he had to act like a man, a real man. "Half milk, half alcohol. No flavors."

The bartender gave him an appreciative smile. "Now you're talking. And then the ibogaine?" He nodded toward the cylinder. "Don't worry," he added, "nothing illegal."

Rolf shook his head, "No, I'm waiting for someone."

"Very well," the bartender started mixing the drink. "That'll be six thallers."

Rolf sighed. Another drain on his meager fortune. That much less medicine. He put the bill on the bar and got change. He sipped his drink slowly. The alcohol had precipitated the casein, changing the drink into a kind of soup. While he drank, he felt the pain in his knee getting worse. The way he was sitting didn't help. He was yearning for one of the bunks.

He called over the bartender. "It might take a long time for him to get here. Is it alight if I lay down over there for a bit without taking any…"

"Ibogaine? Look, we can work something out. I'll give you a tube and close the tap. 20 thallers instead of 100. You in?"

Rolf found the price excessive, but the pain in his knee left him no choice. "Very well," he said. "Here you go. I'll take my drink."

"It's okay, I'll bring it over. The third one on the left. The lowest."

Luck. Rolf couldn't see himself climbing up one of those ladders leading to the upper bunks. He gingerly got off the stool and slowly crossed the room without making the bartender too curious. As for the other customers, they were too far sunk in their stupor to notice anything.

Rolf was relieved to lay down and thanked the bartender who brought over his drink and left. He put it on the tray screwed to the edge of the bunk and started thinking. In fact, it was true that he was waiting for someone. Only, he didn't know who and therefore it was hard to recognize who might be useful.

Moreover, no one was coming into the bar.

The bartender came back. "Chew on the tube or else I'll get…"

Rolf put the end of the vile tube between his lips and sucked the hell out of it. He almost puked.

"Alright," he conceded.

And he gave the bartender another thaller since he was standing there for no reason. He wondered how often he was going to have to feed this vampire.

But the vampire went back behind the bar and tortured an adding machine that clicked out musical notes. Thus were born weird tunes that could be traced down the vertical column of numbers. Rolf felt lulled by the musical accounting. The pain in his knee faded. He was just about to fall asleep when he heard a distant noise from the street. It vanished abruptly. What had happened?

The door of the bar had opened. A man had entered and was whispering to the bartender. Rolf opened one eye. Then two because the look of the person reminded him of something or rather someone. The confidential conversation dragged on. Rolf could see only the back of the man. He waited uneasily. In the torch glow Rolf recognized the asymmetrical face, the almost colorless eyes of the police officer who had arrested him that very morning on top of the tower on the fifth level. His head felt squeezed. He wanted to shrink, to melt into the wall. But the cop was already coming over to him. He stopped at the edge of the bunk but looked elsewhere.

He said, "It's been hard to find you. So, you don't want to do business with me?"

Rolf's mouth was dry. "You must be mistaken..."

The cop grabbed his shoulder and pulled him halfway out of the bunk. "I'm never mistaken. Especially not about the identity of criminals whom I've had the pleasure of arresting."

He calmed down and pushed Rolf back against the wall. Then he sat casually on the edge of the bunk. "But the arm of justice is past us, right? We can become good friends."

Rolf wanted to answer: "I never make friends with snakes." But he kept quiet, letting the officer have his say.

"You see," the guy kept his voice down but didn't whisper, "I admit the condition of the condemned is not so comfy, but they've got no one to blame but themselves, right?"

He laughed.

"Plus, they usually find a niche. The little parallel society where they get help, you know what I mean?"

Rolf prudently held his tongue. The other kept going.

"And the little deals, more or less legal, that they get involved in, don't you see yet?"

Rolf's lips were sealed.

"Well," the officer continued, "it's all very nice in theory but you've still got to find merchandise, right? Because without merchandise, no traffic. Without traffic, no survival in the parallel society. And in V 30, eh, no way. You know better than me. Unless you've got the needed products. And you're in business."

He rubbed his hands together and concluded.

"This morning, before arresting you, I told you about a laboratory where I used to work. I told you the truth. It's the lab of the presidency and the police. There's a lot of stuff there, you know... but, you can imagine, it's all pretty expensive..."

Rolf glanced at the person in the next bunk who was up on one elbow to listen to their conversation. The officer noticed his glance. He smiled.

"He's a colleague," he said amiably. "And if he were a snooper, he wouldn't dare say anything—I'm sworn in. I'd have him arrested for slander before he could open his mouth."

Rolf said nothing for a moment and then,, "To tell you the truth, I was hoping to meet someone who could put me in contact with a laboratory. But I didn't imagine it'd be you."

The officer laughed loudly. "Call me Willy. Willy 34. I told you we were going to be friends."

Rolf highly doubted it. The whole chain of events smelled fishy: arrest-injection-forced trafficking-police laboratory. It looked bizarrely like a legal, organized racket. At the start of the chain the troublemakers became bait. There was no telling, if you dug a little, that at the other end the clandie himself wasn't part of the system. Probably he knowingly maintained his dramatic but risk-free malpractice to bolster the confidence of the suckers they sent him. Like the Great Coësre Rolf furrowed his brow. What was this weird name doing in his mind? What did it mean? He didn't linger on this unsolvable puzzle but answered Willy simply.

"I won't say no... but where do you think I'll find money?"

Willy looked sly, "Why do you want treatment? To stay in the city since your sickness isn't dangerous. Just to keep up your habits, your group life. Perhaps your job? But of course, if you work, you earn a salary. A few wages you receive regularly and that allow you to indulge in your little commerce and get treated and therefore keep working and so on."

"I've already thought that out," Rolf replied. "But I don't have a job anymore."

"What do you mean? They fired you?"

"No, I left because I was scared. A pretty little birdbrain screwed me ..."

Willy cut him off, "Ginou 32-34 is not a birdbrain. She got K 813 thrown out the window of his office barely 30 minutes ago."

Rolf rose up.

"Yes, she's part of the Marketing Militia and even I, a cop, don't mess with her."

So, Ginou wasn't lying. Rolf couldn't believe his ears. Well, why had he been so quick to run away for no good reason? He could go back to the office, to his job. He had tender memories of his onerous, absurd and pesty activities.

He asked Willy, "Can you get me antimites?" He corrected himself, "Anti-miotics?"

Willy shrugged, "Yeah! They don't make them but I can get you the basic ingredients. It's in high demand. They inject a cancer into all criminals."

"Aye," Rolf exclaimed without knowing what a cancer was. "I also need something to treat big boils."

"Furunculosis. Yeah, I've got that too."

"And for someone who spits blood."

"Hold on there," Willy said. "How about that! Blood! But I've got what you need."

Nearby them the druggie turned over on his bunk and started sucking the tube, losing interest in their conversation.

"How much would all that cost?" Rolf asked.

Willy stood up. "Come with me. Let's talk."

Rolf limped after him. "See, I'm not sure I have enough money on me."

Willy turned around in the doorway, "That changes everything. You want me to arrest you for attempted corruption of a civil servant?"

Rolf let out a hopeless sigh, "I'll never get through this," he admitted.

They were back in the street. Willy took a moment to think.

"You have to get through it," he declared. "It's in my interest too. Let's go by your office. You can ask for an advance."

Rolf slapped his forehead. "I was supposed to get paid today!" he shouted.

"Well then" Willy concluded, "all's for the best."

They took the transport that led back to the first level. A car was waiting for them there in the parking lot. A uniformed driver was asleep at the wheel.

"Central Bureau of Explorations," the cop said as he sat in the back. "Come on, get in, old B 40."

Rolf sat next to him. It all seemed to be going way too far. Rolf thought: "Willy is the worst kind of bastard. He's not going to do anything to help me. As soon as…"

Willy interrupted his thought, "It looked to me like you were having a little trouble walking."

"No," Rolf said, "the slider…"

"Ah, the accident! You'll get treated… over there. Lucky for you you're in my car. You wouldn't have made it 100 feet. They would've torn you to shreds. But I'll take you all the way to the edge of the suburbs."

In the office he found Ginou gloating excessively. He was careful not to criticize her for fear of getting himself thrown out the window. There was no joking around with this young woman, let alone upsetting her. She reminded him that he had called her a whacko, which ran shivers down Rolf's spine. But she wasn't looking for revenge for something she didn't really consider an insult. She introduced Rolf to the new chief, a lanky fellow with shifty eyes who was called Julius 28 and who did what was needed for Rolf to go to accounting.

Rolf felt relieved to pocket the 5,000 thallers of his monthly salary, all the while harboring doubts about how long he would last in the job. Julius seemed even more unpleasant than K 813. But, then again, maybe he had Ginou's support? The first thing to do, when his injury allowed, would obviously be to take stroll in the park with her. But not yet. He explained that someone very important had need of him for part of the day. If they doubted him, they could call the chiefdom of the police. They accepted his claims with a certain respect.

Willy was waiting for him downstairs in the car. The officer took Rolf to the lab and provided him with the various products he'd asked for. They filled a big bag.

And in exchange he asked for 4,000 thallers.

"But that's impossible!" Rolf protested. "How am I supposed to keep going at such a price?"

"That's not my problem," Willy said. "The law of supply and demand, pal, that's what you should be complaining about."

Rolf shook his despondently. He really doubted that such prices were the accepted norm with people whose income was generally not very high. But the nature of a racket was to keep sentimental feelings out of the trafficking. When the victims were bled dry, oh well, leave them to fend for themselves. It was the worst that could happen.

In a melancholy haze Rolf let Willy take him to the hydroponic zone. They would come back to get him in the evening.

CHAPTER X

After so much stress, so much effort not to show the pain that was gnawing at him constantly, Rolf felt deeply relieved to have no witnesses except the walls of concrete protecting the automatic purifiers and the huge, slanted skylights on top of the hydroponics. He even started wondering why he was so intent on going back to the phony social balance that had grounded his life so far. And particularly why he still needed a city where the slightest physical inferiority resulted in persecution. Maybe it was because, before becoming a cripple himself, he had sided with the persecutors and something of that still lived in him?

But he had to change his view. You survive when you adapt. Basically, maybe it was easier to adapt to an inferior state than to one in which you'd have to harness all possibilities, all aptitudes… at least for Rolf who tended to follow the steepest slope, like a stream of water.

He dropped onto a red, plastic duct that vibrated from its internal flow of water loaded with nutrients. He didn't feel like sitting down but lying down. He stretched out on the duct, his face turned toward the oblique Sun.

Something important was missing. Not peace or safety or security. Not even that ironclad health that characterized the inhabitants of V 30. He'd lost them all. But he felt like it was in light of this loss that he became aware of another emptiness, a lack that had always bored a black hole in the existence that placated him.

What lack? Impossible to say. Would the future answer the question? The future…

"Well, well," a gauzy voice said, "daydreaming, are we?"

Rolf sprang to his feet and cried out in pain. He grabbed his knee with both hands and gazed at the giant who was laughing and shaking his head. The tumor on his neck swung like the red fungal wattle of a turkey. Rolf sneezed hard. The killer stepped back, scared and disgusted.

"Don't tell me you screwed everything up," the brute pulled the iron bar out of his belt.

Rolf dabbed his nose with his sleeve and prolonged the suspense. Pulling the practically empty pear out of his pocket he squirted a cloud into his nostril and breathed in heartily.

"You want some?" he said automatically. "It might do you some good."

The guy twirled his weapon. "And you, you want me to smash your head in for an answer?"

Rolf shrugged, "Smash away and squash it." He lay back down on the water duct.

The guy was baffled and just shuffled his feet without saying a word.

Rolf spoke out, exasperated, "I've got the goods. But I'm not giving them to you. You don't know what to do with them. They're products."

"Products?" the guy gawked.

"Yes," Rolf said protectively. "To make the anti… miotics for you."

He felt he was going too far with the sarcasm. This savage imbecile could kill him and steal everything. He'd take the things to the clandie cutting out the middleman.

He spoke again, wearily, "Got to play the game. I'm the one supplying the drugger. He trusts no one but me. If anyone else brings the products, he'll throw them out, afraid of being poisoned by just touching them. Ask him yourself. Go on."

The guy kept twirling his iron bar as if to prove that he was stronger. Finally, he said, "Alright, don't be a wiseass. Do you really have the products?"

"Yes." He patted the bag and started talking like his tongue had a mind of its own. "But what do you think of what I asked you about Jana?"

The other froze. "On Titanor's honor, I haven't even seen her!"

Who could've given him such a name? Rolf believed him.

"Listen, Titanor," he tried to stay serious, which the pain aided immensely, "you know our deal. You're a man of your word? A man, in short? A real man?"

Titanor grumbled, "There are no men here. Nothing but wimps. And you're one of them."

"Good,' Rolf agreed. "That's what I thought. We need a man here, a tough guy. You want me to spell it out?"

"Spell it."

"You've got to get treatment, alright! We need a chief. Have you ever seen a bunch of scattered wrecks who could keep on living normally without a chief? That's how it is with us. That's partly why I came back."

Titanor was hesitant. Maybe he wasn't as stupid as Rolf thought.

Rolf realized this and added, "Besides, it's in my interest. We can't get treated in the city."

Titanor snickered, "Ah, I was wondering…"

"That's all," Rolf concluded, knowing he'd won him over and the brute wouldn't kill him to steal the medicine. He added, "Now I'm going to ask you for an important favor. Help me walk. A cop demolished the slider I was on. There were a bunch of casualties. I barely got out alive."

Titanor squinted, "Is that true?"

"Sadly, yes," Rolf pulled up his pant leg and showed him his swollen knee.

Titanor whistled in admiration, "Okay, pal." He put the iron bar back in his belt and said, "Maybe you're not the wimp you think you are."

Rolf gave him a cold stare. "When you want something, you want it. And you got to do whatever it takes."

Titanor smiled. "Hang onto my shoulder, pal. No one's ever seen Titanor leave a guy in the lurch."

Rolf limped off hanging onto the shoulder of his new ally.

They went past Jana's hovel before reaching the zone of stunted plants where the clandie's blockhouse was located.

"Okay," Titanor said, "I'll leave you here. I don't get mixed up in business. What counts is that the clandie makes what I need. I don't give a damn about the rest."

He put down the bag he'd been carrying for Rolf.

"By the way," Rolf said, "is he the only one, this clandie, or are there others?"

"In this area, no. No others. Other places, sure, of course. But the customers of a clandie don't like strangers coming to visit. They found out fast, so watch out."

Rolf shook his head. Now the sick are jealous of their drugger. And once again it was the stranger, the loner they distrusted. Or rather they didn't want around. A drugger's customers, if gathered together, could make quite a mob. So again, a mob against an individual. Well, stick to your own territory. Like the hunt for health where the hunters are also the prey. The clandies couldn't care less about the rivalries and probably just laugh at the deaths they cause. They play the role of witchdoctor whose favors people compete for. Rolf didn't dare imagine the fate in store for this little society that would murder a clandie!"

"And the clandies," Rolf asked, "where do they come from? How do they acquire their skills?"

"Well," Titanor said, "they were sentenced like you and me, as you ought to know. But they're guys who dove into the old books you don't find anymore... and maybe also who knew people high up... before taking a fall."

Titanor guffawed. At the sound of his laughter and their conversation the clandie came out.

"Well, well, boys," he said politely. "What are you doing gabbing out here instead of coming into my humble abode and having a drink?"

"A drink of what?" Titanor was still chuckling. "No, thanks. Maybe next time. I'm bringing my friend, drugger. Handle him with kid gloves. He looks harmless but he's a little tough guy. Isn't that right...?"

"My name's Rolf."

"That's it. Right, Rolf?"

"That's right."

And he spit on the ground. Titanor slapped his thighs and walked off laughing.

"That guy," the clandie said, "it's better to have him with you than against you."

"He spotted me right away," Rolf said, "and I did what I had to."

He neglected to say that luck had a lot to do with their new-found friendship. Titanor considered him "a little tough guy" and that was going to his head. He entered the clandie's dwelling with the bag over his shoulder.

"Let's see here," the clandie opened the bag.

He pulled out smaller bags that were labelled. On the labels were inscriptions that were completely incomprehensible to Rolf but made the clandie murmur approvingly.

"Very well, dear boy, how much do you want?"

Rolf didn't dare ask for too much. "4,000," he said timidly.

The drugger swung around, "You're joking! How am I supposed to keep going at such a price? You think people here are rolling in gold and they give me a fortune for every consultation?"

"But I paid 4,000!" Rolf groaned.

The clandie shook his head, "Either you're lying and let me tell you that's no way to start a business relationship… or else you were ripped off. I've got other suppliers, I told you, but we don't work like this. Think about it. Remember how much I asked you for. Multiply that by a reasonable number— I'm not the only one on the fringes of the city, your stalwart friend explained that to you just now, I overheard you—and you can see for yourself that I can't pay more than 3,000 thallers, final offer."

"But you're killing me!" Rolf pleaded. "You realize that instead of boosting my salary, which I was just lucky enough to collect, I'm squandering it with this loss?"

The clandie leaned against a concrete table covered in little varnished tiles that he used as a workbench. "I don't know what rotten network you got yourself hooked up in, but I can only pity you and urge you to reconsider your arrangement and change contacts."

Rolf looked pitiful, "It's the cop who arrested me."

The clandie nodded sympathetically, "I guessed as much. You're not the only one." He tossed up a small bag in his hand like a ball. "I don't want to discourage you, but it's a bad start. Victims of this kind of thing usually come out of it worse for the wear."

"What do you mean?"

"Oh, nothing… you'll know soon enough."

"No," Rolf declared, "you've said too much, or too little."

The clandie scratched his boils. "Some die," he finally admitted. "You'd better watch out. You don't know what the best solution might be? Go back to work. Use your pay to live, find me substances at a normal price and don't try to make a big profit. Let your treatment, which, you have to admit, is not exorbitant, be your means and your end. Any other questions?"

"Yes," Rolf sat down, devastated. "I've got a broken knee."

The clandie laughed, "If that was the case, you wouldn't have made it here. Show me."

Rolf showed him his knee.

"It's a sprain. I have an ointment."

He went to get a small jar from which he dug out a little blackish grease. Rolf watched him nervously.

He asked, "Does it hurt?"

"Why do you ask?"

"Your pear burned someone's nose at the office."

"That person wasn't sick," the drugger shot back. "Stretch out your leg."

Rolf did as he was told. In an instant he saw his knee turn greasy and black. But he felt a kind of heat right away, a tingling sensation, a relief. The clandie put a little ointment in a plastic jar and handed him the medicine.

"Put some on again tonight and it'll be fine. Give me ten thallers."

"My pear is empty," Rolf said.

"Already!"

He told the clandie about the slider accident.

"And you insist on going back into such a city?" the clandie questioned.

"Your activity allows you to support an acceptable existence. A humane existence. I'd even say more humane than what we have in the city where, obviously, you wouldn't be a doctor. It's different for me. I don't want this vegetative life of a sick man."

"But you'll be the king of the sick here! You've got almost nothing—in the land of the blind…"

"In the land of the blind," Rolf repeated. "They grope around and catch the one-eyed man to gouge out his other eye."

The clandie said nothing, just stared at Rolf, undecided. Then, "Maybe you're right. Contrary to what you believe, there are doctors in the city. Only a very few and only working for the leaders. Because even if there's no more sickness, there are still minor troubles and accidents. I was one of them. A tiny mistake on my part sent me here. Obviously, I had a better life over there. Do what you want but be careful. That's all I have to say to you."

Rolf came crashing down. Druggers in the city and entirely tolerated! But could he have guessed? Could anyone reasonably believe that the president or one of his supporters had been dragged by an iron hook when they broke a limb after a fall? Rolf searched his memory: nobody, neither in the press or any media, ever mentioned an accident or its conse-

71

quences. They did talk about murders and sentencing the guilty, but that was all. He had to actually witness a slider accident to learn what they did with the wounded. No doubt there were other witnesses, but they were keeping quiet. How to trust someone when you had two out of three chances of dealing with a police officer? And if you ignored that and found an innocent ear, what would happen to the guy when the news got out, just a little, and was heard by someone wanting to cover it up? And what would happen to you?

The clandie counted out 3,000 thallers and gave it to him. "Look, I'll let the consultation I just gave you slide this time. Tonight, go to the Egg bar. It's a dangerous place, which is why I didn't mention it this morning. But it's also a place for contacts where you won't run into any police. The people who go there pay the police to stay away. I think you'll find someone more reasonable… if you don't get your throat slit."

"Ach!" Rolf said, "The bar where I went was on a road where they hunted down men."

"Good luck," the drugger bid him farewell.

CHAPTER XI

Before Rolf left, the clandie had refilled the pear with medicine. Rolf sprayed it into his nostrils. Now he was on his way back to the city without hurrying. Almost without realizing he was keeping an eye on his surroundings. It was becoming a habit. Even though he had managed to get into this middleman position, he still had the reflexes of a fugitive. According to Titanor he didn't have to worry about being lynched here for being sick, but rather for being in good health. The clandie didn't seem so pessimistic. But he was living among his equipment and products. And for Rolf one lynching was as good as another. Irony or destiny, he only felt safe now with the brute whose homicidal fury scared him.

Two reasons were leading him back to the city: first, he had to go back to the office; then he didn't want Willy—in person or not—to come looking for him. He'd seen enough of that scoundrel who'd taken advantage of the situation to rip him off.

And soon he was quickly among the vats and chimneys, wandering aimlessly. He was thinking that the deserted zone was a maze where you could easily get lost. So, he didn't understand the real reason for his wandering around there until he saw the door to Jana's hovel. He was amazed.

But he knocked on the door.

Jana opened the door wearing a ratty bathrobe with a rusty axe in her hand. "Oh," she looked strangely stressed, "it's you."

"Sorry for disturbing you," Rolf was a little annoyed.

She didn't answer but she opened the door wide. He went in.

Despite the darkness, the signs of poverty were visible everywhere, from the broken utensils to the tattered clothes. Jana saw him looking around.

"I probably don't do enough housework, eh?" she sniped.

Rolf shrugged his shoulders and smiled, "If I were here, you couldn't even get in the door."

Jana put the axe on a wobbly table, within easy reach. Rolf leered at it.

"It cuts just fine," Jana assured him. "I can chop off a hand with it."

He turned his eyes on her, nervously. "You didn't let me in just to cut off my hand, I hope."

What he said next came out involuntarily.

"I need two to hold you in my arms."

She froze. "Say that again, slowly, just to see," she said half in jest.

Rolf said it again. She didn't respond but turned her back and grabbed a bottle that was sitting quietly in the corner. By a surprising fluke, when she bent down to get the bottle, her bathrobe slipped and showed Rolf her cleavage. Seeming not to notice, she picked up two chipped glasses that she put on the table next to the axe.

"What's that?" Rolf said just to say something.

"Bottled alcohol," she said.

Rolf laughed. She frowned at him. He lost his humor.

"I thought you were joking."

Without comment, she poured a blue liquid into the two glasses.

"The clandie forbids me," she said, "but once is not a habit. Not a lot of people come over to my place."

Rolf was surprised. "I guess there's no park around here, but that's no reason... don't men ever get together with women here?"

Jana faced him. "Everyone is disgusted by everyone else. They masturbate."

"Oh," Rolf was appalled. "You too?"

"Me too."

74

He stepped closer to her. "I admit it's not easy to hug a… sick person. But if you're not too… how should I say it… prone to disgust, I think that I could…"

When he took her in his arms he did feel that she flinched, recoiled. He himself had to choke back a little nausea. But they both did their part and the kiss was fairly successful. Lips closed, of course.

They separated right away, avoiding eye contact. Then they started up a pointless conversation without listening to each other. It didn't last long. Soon Rolf took her in his arms again. This time he tried a real kiss. He needed all his self-control to hold the embrace when he tasted blood in his mouth. As for her, she swiftly dried the cheek that Rolf's nose had dripped on.

The third try went farther. But they avoided kissing too intimately, too dangerously. Making love to her, Rolf felt like he had never done it with anyone before. A very strange feeling, sweet and vast, as if they were part of each other and at the same time dissolving into the universe.

When he left Jana's shack, he was sure he'd found something important. Both of them had forgotten to drink the bottled alcohol.

***

The humidity in the air aroused the pain in his knee, but the ointment was so strong and long-lasting that it kept the pain from coming back as hard as before the treatment. Rolf was walking now without showing any signs of an injury. The improvement let him get back to the city and take two gliders without another mishap.

But he'd barely got back to work when Julius called him into his office. Rolf introduced himself again to the chief in a casual manner—thanks to his hypocrisy Julius might bring a friendlier atmosphere into the office than the erstwhile K 813. In reality, Rolf didn't care.

"My dear B 40," Julius began gently, "I know you take an interest in your work."

"Certainly, sir," Rolf replied warmly. Everything had to go smoothly in his paid activity so he could get treated.

Julius tilted his head and looked askance at him, "But exactly what work, that's the question!"

Rolf furrowed his brow, "What do you mean, sir?"

Julius stood up and started pacing the room. "Just what I said."

He halted, turned his back to Rolf and looked at himself in the mirror.

"The police confirmed your explanation for your absence today."

"Ah!" Rolf sighed in relief. "You see!"

"All too clearly."

Rolf's brow wrinkled again.

Julius concluded, "I don't want a cop around here."

Rolf was speechless, then he started laughing nervously. "You think I'm a cop? That's funny!"

"It's not funny at all. They never would've covered for you if you weren't one of them. So, constantly having someone on my heels who pretends to work but is really spying on me and sending reports back to the police—I don't like it. So, you're going to do me the pleasure of clearing out your desk."

He raised his two hands, palms facing out.

"And no threats, please, inspector. I belong to the Marketing Militia. Don't bite off more than you can chew with your little teeth."

Rolf wanted to kill him. "But you're imagining things!" he shouted. "It's false, completely false! Go ask Ginou! She'll tell you…"

"I've already had a talk with her," Julius cut him off. "She told me you were a druggie. I deduced that you belonged, at some time or other, to the antidrug brigade. There are members who use unobtainable products. The only justification for the existence of the brigade is to supply substances to its own members. You see, we in the militia also have our little networks and our little spies…"

He smiled haughtily and finished up.

"Come on, inspector, don't be angry. What I'm doing here is fair game. You'll have no problem finding new hunting grounds."

He shot Rolf a sardonic look and held out his hand.

"Goodbye, pal. We'll meet again, I'm sure, some evening at the presidency, drinking toasts…"

Rolf refused to discuss it any further. It was better to let Julius believe that he, Rolf, was a cop than to risk the possibility of him finding out the truth. He left the office, sick at heart.

At the other end of the corridor the door of his office was open. He went in. His office! A place where he'd never set foot again. How was he going to survive now? And get treated?

Ginou unbuttoned her blouse down to her belt and asked, "When are we going to the park?"

"I don't know," Rolf couldn't help admiring her breasts. "You got me fired. Why did you tell Julius everything?"

She came to rub up against him. "I had to. He'd half-guessed that you were a cop…"

Rolf drew back. "I won't find another job," he said bitterly. "I was completely conditioned to this work. No one will give me anything else to do."

"Oh, please," Ginou was getting agitated. "You've already got your profession. You don't need two!"

Rolf also refused to argue with her. He remembered that he had to keep her off his back. She was touchy and vindictive. He forced a smile.

"Okay, let's not bicker. You want to meet tomorrow in the park?"

She nodded. Rolf grabbed the trench coat he'd left the day before on the coat rack and left.

Quietly pursuing its course, the sun was in the second quarter. Another hour and it would be evening. Followed by the nebula and its universal rest in the almost oblique light. Then, as always, the rising of the star until morning. Rolf had plenty of time—clandestine activities preferred the nebula.

The pain came back. He decided to go back home to take care of it. But he also had a childish desire to curl up and be alone. He would see later about finding a solution to the disastrous firing.

When he got safely inside his apartment, it was high time—the pain was making him limp enough to start attracting attention. He turned on the pulsed-air mattress that had cost him three months salary and felt relieved to lie down. He opened the jar of ointment, massaged his knee for a long time with the cream and was again amazed by the medicinal action. The pain went away as if the vise squeezing his leg had just vanished.

He got up feeling perky, went to the heater where he got a big cup of hot coffee and toast and ate his snack, thinking he'd need it. There was no telling how the nebula would turn out. He had no intention of frittering away his remaining thallers for one of those lousy, overpriced meals they served (as rumor had it) in the semi-legal establishments.

Holding his cup, he went to the window and looked out. He thought he saw someone running across the rooftop across from his. But the impression was so fleeting that he shrugged it off and let his mind wander.

He lay down again on his air mattress. The problem of work arose. For the second time in a single day. It was too much for him, who had always been at the Central Bureau of Explorations.

They took him for a police officer. And what if the police gave him a job? Judging by Willy's behavior, the police department only employed habitual criminals. Why not talk to Willy about it?

He shook his head wearily. He had decided to stay away from Willy who was trying to extort everything he had. Yes, but when the cop found out that Rolf had no job, he would have to admit that it was in his interest as a racketeer to get his victim something. And what would be easier in these conditions than to put in a good word for Rolf with his superiors?

He got off the mattress and strutted back and forth. No more pain but his nose tickled. He sprayed in a little ormedy and followed his train of thought. Even if Willy agreed to help him, he couldn't see himself as a police officer. It was a dangerous job. The underworld knew what was at risk when they got arrested and had to pull out all the stops. Nobody talked about it, but cops must've died every day. Rolf himself had seen one of them fall from the second level. What an idea to shoot at the slider just because someone shook their fist at them! That cop got what he deserved. That's what the murderers would say about Rolf when they took him down. Rolf shuddered.

But on the other hand, how was he going to stay in the city and keep getting treatment? Dejected, he left the apartment and closed the door behind him.

CHAPTER XII

The nebula had fallen. Now, the buildings and ramps were going to completely hide the Sun for hours. Rolf reached the dodgy areas where he kept his guard up. The place he was looking for was on the main street, not far from one of the two café-clubs he had entered before.

The Egg Bar was full. Rolf wondered if its name came from the crowd inside or from the shape of the world. He ordered a milk and rum but the bartender laughed.

"Nettle brandy, like everyone!" he said and he put in front of Rolf a twisted glass that must have been half a pint full of fizzy green alcohol. "100 thallers."

Rolf's jaw jerked. But he had to expect exorbitant prices in an illegal establishment. He lay down the money, which vanished immediately, and tasted the green brandy. His jaw jerked again. He thought his lips had sunk to the bottom of the glass and were going to melt like two cubes of sugar in a cup of boiling water. But no. It was just a feeling. Right after he felt serenity spread throughout his body. He looked around, turned around, leaned back against the bar, glass in hand, gazing blissfully. He took another swig.

The man sitting next to him nudged with him with his elbow, "Not used to it, eh?" and he winked.

"Hell no," Rolf turned to face him.

He almost jumped back. The guy's smile revealed a row of shiny red teeth. The man snapped his teeth like he wanted to bite Rolf, then broke out laughing.

"An accident," he said. "I've got connections. They put on an alloy. Naturally, I only show them here. What are you hiding?"

Rolf thought of the swarm of troublemakers all over the city. He spat out, "Nothing at all!"

The other shrugged. "Whatever, it's none of my business. But you know, you've got nothing to fear here."

Rolf also thought of the absence of police. All the same, he preferred not to reveal his defects.

"I'm here on business," he said in a hushed voice.

The guy nodded, "Like everyone. You need something or you selling?"

"I buy products," Rolf said hesitatingly.

"For ormedies, I bet."

Rolf debated: if he said nothing, he'd get nothing. He had to take a minimum of risks.

"Yes," he drawled, expecting to see the guy slap hand-cuffs on his wrists.

"I've got some. Ormedies, ready-made. Already pre-pared. More expensive, of course."

Rolf considered it. Finally, he said, "I'm not interested. They're for someone who makes them."

"Ah, in that case…" He rose up on tiptoes to see behind a group of revelers and motioned to a woman dressed in black who was wearing a bird's claw in her ear. "Carmina!" he shouted.

The woman turned around, smiled and swished over to them.

He pointed to Rolf with his thumb, "Mister wants to do business. 10 per cent as usual."

"Who gives it?" Rolf asked.

"Me," Carmina affirmed. "Don't worry about it, sugar pie. What do you want?"

Rolf listed the products. To make a comparison he asked for the same ones he'd gotten through Willy and the same amounts. Carmina made a quick calculation.

"That'll be 1,500 thallers," she said. Take it or leave it."

Less than half of what Willy demanded. The clandie had told him the truth. But were the products good? He wanted to make sure.

"Listen, pal," Carmina answered, "the products are al-ways good here. Anyone selling bad stuff does it only once."

"Good," Rolf said. "I guess I have to believe you. You want a drink?"

81

He could very well offer a drink to seal the deal. It was normal, surely. Plus, he was going to save 5,000 thallers thanks to her.

"It's the seller who offers!" she sounded outraged.

She ordered. A second glass of nettle brandy appeared before Rolf. One pint total. And if he didn't drink it, he'd probably insult Carmina. He surrendered and emptied his first glass. He was thinking: "The percentage of the middleman is going to end up being me who pays. She raised her price for that." But it didn't matter. His head was spinning. He ogled Carmina's hips.

"You want to go to the park tomorrow?" he asked.

She smiled, "Sure, but I've already got four rendezvous. It'll have to be the day after."

He came back down to earth. He couldn't miss his rendezvous with Ginou. And the products? He asked Carmina when she would get them to him."

"This nebula. My shop is nearby."

Her shop! It was a real business, barely hidden. Of course! Most of the products, if not all, came from official labs. Whoever was stealing them would get no benefit from seeing the traffic interrupted. And they were also getting paid not to enter the Egg Bar!

"Give me the money," Carmina ordered. "I'll go get them."

"No," Rolf said. "Go get them first."

She shrugged, "It's the same thing. We're regulars here. But I need it to take care of another deal over there…"

She gestured vaguely to another spot in the bar.

"Okay," Rolf said after downing his first drink. "Here it is." He pulled out 1,500 thallers from his pocket and gave them to Carmina.

"You're a sweetie," she said. "See you in a jiffy. Rolf had a bad feeling that he was getting scammed. Why was he trusting all these people?

He told himself that when the wine was poured you had to drink it. This thought reminded him that he still had a full glass on the bar. He swung around to face the bar and started sipping his second drink.

"Oh boy," the middleman said, "Not slowing down on me, are you?"

Rolf took a big swig like all drunks who are praised for their excess and even more for a guy who wasn't used to drinking. "How... how do you like that, eh?" he spluttered. And he proudly downed some more.

Just then they heard someone clapping their hands and shouting, "Quiet, please!"

The conversations faded away.

And the same voice barked, "There's a cop in here."

Complete silence. Rolf's head bobbed in the direction of the voice. At first he didn't see much. Then, struggling to focus, he made out a face that reminded him of someone. And the face was looking straight at him.

"Isn't that B 40?" Julius' voice boomed out.

No one said a word. No one showed the slightest sign of aggression either. But everyone was staring at Rolf, who was the target of Julius' vengeful finger.

Laughter broke out. A little at first, then louder. Soon it was a hailstorm that shook the glasses on the shelves behind the bar.

From the depths of his drunkenness Rolf started to understand that he was the center and the cause of the hilarity. Then he made the connection between this and the ban on police in the bar. Lastly, the link between Julius and the accusation.

And he stammered, "It's not true! I'm not a cop! The best proof is that I've been arrested, judged and sentenced and..."

"And executed, you mean?" Julius smirked.

The laughter had calmed down. But it started up again. Two men entered the circle that had formed around Rolf and dragged the victim of slander to the door.

"Hold on!" Rolf slurred out. "I've got a deal going. Carmina is coming back..."

Carmina surged through the crowd and said, "I don't do business with cops!"

Which caused even more laughter because everyone knew that the police were intimately involved with all trafficking. They threw Rolf out into the street. The door of the bar slammed shut behind him. He just stood there, wobbling, alone in the nebula, and 1,500 thallers poorer.

In Rolf's foggy mind the words of the clandie floated by: "It's a dangerous place..." He'd just had a demonstration of it. But Rolf wasn't expecting this kind of danger. If there ever was such a thing as the irony of fate or the persecution of destiny, he was experiencing it. He leaned against a wall to keep himself up. The cool wind had a double effect on his drunkenness: it cleared his head and at the same time mowed down his legs.

As his thoughts came into focus he realized that another danger threaten: the prowlers and since his legs were failing him, he wondered how he would escape them.

He glanced around uneasily. Nobody. The slider station was a five-minute walk away. He pushed off the wall and got a stumbling start on this new and perilous undertaking.

He'd already gone 50 yards when he noticed that his back was to the station. He turned around. When he came up to an intersection he'd already passed by, a man lurched out in his direction. Rolf stopped, then crossed the street to avoid him. The man did the same. But Rolf was still moving when the man turned back and disappeared down the street he'd come from. Rolf giggled, still very drunk. The other guy was afraid of him. He kept going, braver but still wary.

His legs were getting stronger but the pain in his knee was coming back too. All things considered, he was moving pretty fast. He quickly passed the Egg Bar and kept going toward the station. There was no reason for all his worries because he reached it without incident. But just barely because a gang was coming at him in complete silence when he entered the elevator.

The slider platform was deserted. He waited for what seemed a long time. Sliders were not frequent at this time of the nebula. One came, however, almost empty. Only one man and two women who were heatedly discussing pornosophy. When Rolf got off the first slider, they started undressing.

On the transfer platform, likewise deserted, Rolf suddenly felt overwhelmed by his plight and started crying over his fate with the alligator tears of a drunk. Then, abruptly, the despair was swept away by a flood of aggression. He beat his fists together, swearing vengeance on everyone who was working to sink him deeper and deeper into misery. The slider arrived. He dried his eyes and got on.

He didn't have far to go before getting off the slider after a solitary ride. Moreover, his neighborhood was one of the calmest in V 30. He took the elevator up and went back to his apartment.

Sitting motionless in an armchair in the middle of the living room was individual with an asymmetrical head and almost colorless eyes.

"So," Willy said, "you're being unfaithful to me?"

Rolf's drunkenness had transformed during his trip. Not only did the despair turn into aggression, but his mind was much clearer and his balance improved. A wave of pain in his knee, a kind of light dizziness and a little nausea, that was all. What was brimming over in him now came less from his drinking than from all his setbacks: Fury!

He thought out loud, "You didn't scare me, in spite of sneaking into my apartment and sitting there without moving, waiting to surprise me. This nebula I don't get scared or surprised—I'm a mean drunk."

He was muttering, as if to himself. Willy wasn't surprised by this. He laughed.

"Look at that!" he said. "But me, I don't need to get drunk to be mean. And I don't like your unfaithfulness. You shouldn't have gone home so soon and gone out again."

Rolf remembered the figure he'd seen on the roof across from his apartment. Willy had his place under surveillance not from below but from above. But Rolf had still seen it. He just hadn't realized he was being followed.

"Get out of here," he said calmly.

Willy laughed again. "I like it here. I'll take it. Besides, you've got no job and you can't pay the rent. You can't pay me anymore either for my meager services. Yes, I've already been informed. It's my job."

He stood up.

"It's you who are getting out of here. Go back to the trash. Nobody asks for rent for those squalid shacks."

Rolf marched up to him. "I'll leave when I want. In any case, not for 15 days. Do I have to throw you out?"

Willy wrinkled his brow. "I'm good to you. Like a father. But I can take you in right now for illegal commerce and threatening a police officer. One more word and I'll do it."

Rolf lunged at him.

The fight was messy. Willy was strong but Rolf's anger, amplified by alcohol, evened the score. He ended up cornering Willy against the desk covered in imaginary geographical maps and he knocked him down. Willy got up swearing and holding a gun. Rolf saw the weapon. Before Willy had time to take aim, he snatched the bronze egg he used as a paperweight and threw it as hard as he could. With amazing intuition, he sensed that Willy would duck to avoid it and so he'd thrown it low. The result confirmed his anticipations. Willy got hit hard on the forehead and fell back against the desk, without even a gasp.

Rolf walked around the desk. A fractured skull doesn't bleed a lot, but Willy's heart was racing. It stopped less than a minute later. Rolf stood speechless before the corpse. He had the feeling that he'd just crushed a wasp who'd been trying to sting him.

He also had the feeling that this act was going to bring down a swarm.

CHAPTER XIII

For the time being he had to get rid of the corpse. Rolf wondered whether he should cut it up and carry it away piece by piece. Just thinking about such a solution made him more nauseous. He'd have to drag Willy to the bathtub because of the blood and perform this nightmarish task with tools at hand. No. It wasn't possible.

He could also push him out the window. Hitting the ground would break so many bones that his fractured skull would look like all the others. But they would wonder which apartment he'd fallen from and why. They'd find out in the blink of an eye.

There was no way he would lock him in a closet and let him rot. Or maybe that was a solution if he left his apartment and never came back. But that wasn't what he intended. He was still hoping to work things out, find another job and start his trafficking on different footing. Chances were slim for this but he didn't want to throw in the towel just yet.

There was always the possibility of using the nebula to transport the body to the suburbs where the murder would be blamed on exiles. Or stop on the way if it looked too risky and throw it over the railing of the third level into the shredders.

But he couldn't carry him on his back.

He remembered that on the ground floor of his building there was a big food store. Next to the store was a small warehouse where they kept the carts for customers to use during the day. The warehouse was never closed since nobody cared about what it contained. One of the carts, a good solid one, would do the job.

He listened hard to the silence. Not a peep. Everyone was sleeping. No tenant seemed to have been awakened by the fight he'd just had with Willy. He went to the door, cracked it open and listened again. It was fine. He went back to the corpse and lifted it up. It weighed a ton. Rolf was thinking that

Willy could help him out a little by holding onto his shoulder or something… This dark little joke made him suddenly aware of what he'd done.

Without a doubt, Willy was a creep and Rolf had done the world a favor by killing him. But he was still a man and Rolf was now a murderer. Rolf, a peaceful person who only loved his geographical lies… They had to push him too far.

Now he felt completely sober. Fear didn't paralyze him. He managed to hoist Willy onto the desk and from there onto his shoulders. Then he waddled to the door, went through and had a hard time closing it behind him. Just then the elevator started up.

He'd just dropped his key in his pocket. Sweat beaded on his forehead, both from the physical effort and from this new danger. He pictured himself caught by a neighbor who, with his luck, would step out of the elevator in 30 seconds on this very floor.

Feverishly, he fumbled for his key. It was stuck in a crease or on a thread in his pocket. He pulled violently, almost dropped Willy, but managed to get the key out. Unfortunately, he had pulled so hard that the key jumped out of his pocket, slipped out of his hand and fell on the floor, making a noise that sounded deafening to him.

The elevator was coming up.

He was about to bend down to pick up the key, but he realized that with the weight on his shoulders he would never get back up. His neighbor would find him squatting with a corpse on his back. But he couldn't leave the key. He kicked it against the wall and tried to raise it with his foot. He'd got it about seven or eight inches up when the elevator—as expected—stopped with a menacing click. The door opened. A woman stepped out. He saw her out of the corner of his eye. It was Vera 730, a girl who constantly annoyed him with her machine that made false nails in her little studio. He turned so that she couldn't see Willy's bloody forehead.

"Good evening, Miss Vera," he panted. "Sorry for this lush."

She stood still in front of the elevator. "Good evening Mr. Rolf. What's wrong?"

"Ach! Like I just said. If only I'd known he'd drink so much… I just dropped my key. Can you get it for me?"

Vera 730 bent down and picked up the key. Rolf had to turn a little more to keep Willy's face hidden. His whole body was trembling. He hoped it wasn't obvious. She handed him the key.

"Thank you, Miss Vera," Rolf said politely after catching his breath.

Vera also turned a little. But Rolf imitated her so she could only see Willy's backside.

"Well, good night, Miss Vera," he said, placing himself in front of the elevator. "Whatever you do, don't invite drunks to your place, even when it's their birthday!"

He opened the gate and then the elevator door. He had to turn around when he got in, but he did so at an angle so that Vera still saw nothing that she wasn't supposed to.

"Are you sure that…" she started suspiciously.

The gate and door slammed shut. The elevator went down.

"Goddamn prehistoric elevators," Rolf swore.

He watched Vera's legs disappear. On looking down at the floor he saw a spot of blood. If there was one on the landing, Vera would sound the alarm. Willy kept acting like a bastard, even when dead.

On the ground floor, Rolf got out of the elevator and stood still. No shrieking, no doors flying open. Willy must've kept a little courtesy in the back of his crushed skull—he wasn't bleeding anywhere or anyhow.

Rolf reached the front door of the building. The street was deserted. He slipped into the warehouse and dumped his package into a cart. As he was pushing it out, he realized that he had made a stupid plan and that he would never get out it alive.

Still deserted and silent, the street saw a Rolf only pretending to be drunk stumbling along, belting out an old song about the glory of the divine hen that laid the world. He was pushing a cart in which Willy was sprawled, arms and legs hanging over the edges. He'd covered the forehead with the corpse's hair so that no casual glance would see the wound.

He had to sing to pass for a drunk going back home with his drinking buddy who was even drunker than him. But he was afraid of singing too loudly and attracting the attention of a police patrol. You'd see them sometimes in the quiet neighborhoods. Trying to straddle the fence between two dangers, he headed for the suburbs.

But he quickly figured that he wouldn't have enough nebula to carry out his project, not counting the obstacles he might face on the way. So, he veered off toward the shredders where they threw the garbage every day.

As he was getting off the pedestrian road to take a boulevard reserved for individual sliders, he almost knocked over a guy coming around the corner.

"Hey, buddy, watch where you're going!" the guy said.

Rolf muttered a slurred excuse and tried to keep moving forward. But a slider came speeding down and blocked the boulevard. The man stopped and leaned over to Willy.

"What's with your friend, buddy?" he asked curiously.

"A… a rough night," Rolf said.

The guy stared hard at Rolf, "I'll bet it was a rough night. Did he take a fall or what?"

"No, uh," Rolf stammered, "yes, he can't stand up straight."

He was so scared of getting caught that he forgot to pretend to be drunk. The nervy guy crossed the street at his side.

"Yeah, buddy! He can't stand up straight, right?" While walking he shot a hand out at Willy's forehead and brushed aside the hair. The wound was revealed.

"That's it. He fell down."

He kept walking next to Rolf without saying anything. Rolf was tormented.

He man spoke up, "He must've fallen from high up to smash his face in like that. Your friend doesn't seem to be breathing so easy."

"He's dead,' Rolf barked at him.

The intruder gave him a cold stare. "Hey, look, it happens. There are guys who aren't too strong."

Rolf said nothing, his throat was squeezed by fear.

The other said, "Okay, 2,000 thallers and I keep my mouth shut."

Rolf threw up his arms. "You can scram now, bastard!"

The man smiled, then started yelling, "Police! Police! Help, police!"

Rolf put a hand over the guy's mouth, then took out his wallet. "1,000."

The other shrugged, "I said 2,000 and I'm being generous. It's worth double. In fact, it's worth a lot more."

Rolf had to pluck out 2,000 thallers. He had only 500 left. Since he'd got paid, he'd done nothing but hand out money.

While handing the money over to this new vampire, he wanted to kill him, too, and pile the corpse on top of the other one. But he didn't have a weapon. Besides, the guy didn't look like the type to take it lying down.

"You're a pal," the lowlife said as he pocketed the bills. "If you've got others, I'm at your service. Til next time!"

He sauntered off.

Rolf continued on his way, hoping the shouts of the thief hadn't alerted a police slider. But everything seemed peaceful. He wasn't singing because he didn't feel like it and also so as not to signal his presence.

Now he was starting to hear the sound of the shredders. He hurried his step and was soon in front of the fence that protected the pedestrians from falling.

In a ditch almost 70 feet deep and spread over an acre, the shiny arms of the connecting rods, the teethed gears, the crushers with grinding jaws where the garbage was constantly dumped by the hoppers hooked to cables, all were turning round, going up and down, sliding back and forth. At the bottom of the ditch, under a grill, the big incinerator oven glowed red. Rolf gave Willy one last look. His was face reflected the red glow of the oven. Shifting hues that made the dead man's face look like it was grinning. He estimated the height of the fence. Even if it was lower, he couldn't have hoisted the corpse over it. He just had to take the closest elevator to the third level and push Willy from up there, over the railing. He was about to push the cart to the elevator when he heard the sound of voices.

He turned around. Two men were right behind him. He hadn't heard them come up. They were pointing a paralyzer gun at him, the same kind that Willy had—the weapon that Rolf had left on the desk in his apartment when he was so muddled by the murder.

He leaned back against the fence. One of the men examined the corpse.

"Well, well," he said, "if it isn't old Willy!"

They looked at Rolf.

"So," the other said, "You mean to throw Willy into the shredders?" He flashed his police badge and added, "We're not happy about that. We liked our pal Willy. Come on, you're coming with us."

Rolf pushed off the fence.

The first cop said, "No, no, we can't leave Willy here. You keep pushing him." He turned to his partner, exasperated, "He was going to just leave him here!" Then, back to Rolf, "Get going, little joker. It's right around the corner. And don't try to beat it, I've got the paralyzer on max."

Rolf got back to pushing the cart, one cop in front and the other behind him. He felt caught in a vise.

He knew he'd chosen the stupidest way possible to get rid of Willy and yet when the two cops came, he was about to get in the elevator. 30 seconds more and the plan would've worked.

But now everything had failed. Absolutely everything.

CHAPTER XIV

The slider was just around the corner. The two officers put Willy behind Rolf. At the first turn, he was thrown against him and on the next it was the opposite. Rolf found this situation extremely unpleasant. But the future was promising to be even less pleasant.

For the second time in the day Rolf entered the police station. It was just as busy during the nebula as during the day. But the cell they threw him in was empty. Plastered to the wall by the magnetic plate, he relived the events of the last few hours, trying to invent a story that would be convincing enough to let him go. But his mind was so paralyzed by anxiety that all he could do was brood over the truth, regretful or outraged, neither or which would improve his chances before the tribunal.

Rolf remembered the president, that perverted thug... if he got the same one, he was doomed. But would it be any different if he got another, considering the gravity of his crime? In fact, the only path to safety was escape. But how was he going to escape?

As he was asking himself this question (like all prisoners), they came to get him. But they didn't take him to the tribunal. He was brought directly to the lab. There he started to struggle. They held him fast to give him another shot.

"There you go," said the executioner in the white coat, as friendly as could be. "All done. That wasn't so bad, was it? You might expect something else when you kill a cop!"

Rolf leered at him. Fear was mixed with fury. "I know very well that it's not done. It's just starting." He almost whispered, "What do I have now?"

The punishment tech laughed aloud, "Come on, pal, you'll know soon enough." He turned to the guards and shouted merrily, "Next!"

They left Rolf to himself. One of the guards just pointed to the exit. Rolf headed for it. On the way he passed by a series of glass tubes stopped with cotton. He figured that the clandie might be glad to have one of these tubes. And who knows, the yellow jelly inside might be used for someone's treatment. Rolf's, for example. He snatched a tube, which disappeared into his pocket.

He hadn't gone 100 yards down the street when his teeth started chattering. At the same time, his skin started burning all over his body and he felt an insufferable itching. His nose was running but now his eyes joined in the flood. Everything became fuzzy. He dried his eyes with his sleeve. The contact of the fabric fueled the flames that were consuming his skin. Worried to death he walked faster, slowing down only to see what he looked like in a shop window. He jumped back with a shriek: his face was pocked with small, red spots, so many of them that they looked like a single scarlet coating on his skin.

He took off running. Suffering such a repulsive and visible sickness, it'd be dangerous for him to be around anyone at all. He had to use the end of the nebula to get to the suburbs.

He tried his best not to take any big streets, even though they were empty at this early morning hour. He felt sicker and sicker. The fever burned down to his bones while the rash devoured his skin. And he had to keep dabbing his eyes to see straight. To top it all off, his knee was hurting again from the beating it was taking.

He stopped running so that he wouldn't attract the attention of any passers-by who couldn't see him too closely as well as to give his knee a rest. He didn't have too far to go, but it was going to get harder and harder as the day approached. He walked as quickly as he could.

Time seemed to be stretching out when the first signs of the daily routine appeared. However, he ended up at the edge of the city without any problems. Once there, he took a break. Well hidden between a huge, square chimney and a concrete wall, he sat on a pile of rubble. Was he going to see Jana? No, obviously not. She'd cry out in disgust at first sight. Besides, he felt far too sick to do anything but rest and take care of himself. Care? He had to see the clandie first of all.

He got back on his way, still on the lookout. Here they didn't attack you because you were sick but to rob you to get treated. But the nebula also made the exiles take a break. He saw no one.

He had to knock for a long time at the drugger's door. The clandie finally opened it with his hair a mess and his eyes still swollen from sleep.

"What is it now?" he rasped.

"Let me in," Rolf said.

The clandie drew back and blinked at Rolf. "I see. You were caught again and this time they stuck you with measles."

"Measles?" Rolf's voice rose.

"Yes. It's no worse than the cold you were already given. You must not have done anything too serious…"

Rolf shuddered, "Oh no? I killed a cop."

The clandie shrugged, "There are so many of them," he explained. "They figure it into anticipated losses. If you'd attacked someone really important, you'd have been really punished."

Rolf said nothing. This way of seeing things astonished him. For him every human life was worth the same and he still felt remorse for killing Willy. On the other hand, he thought he'd been punished enough just with that—his sicknesses only made it worse. He shared his feelings with the clandie.

"Listen," the drugger said, "you have to get used to your new face. It'll stay red with the rest of your body. I can only take care of your fever and the rash. I think I can also deal with the watery eyes."

"But that's not possible!" Rolf shouted. "I can't show myself to anyone!"

The clandie nodded, "I admit that the little business you had going got off to a bad start, but concerning your life here, you know that everyone has some kind of physical mark of their sickness. You'll be like the others, that's all."

Rolf scowled and forced himself to say, "She won't want to see me."

"Who's she?" the clandie asked warily.

"Jana," Rolf admitted.

The drugger gave him a concerned look, "I didn't tell you yesterday when you both came to see me," he declared cautiously, "but her condition is very grave."

Rolf knitted his brows, "What do you mean?"

"Well, my examination showed that she had a big lesion that was completely surrounding a pulmonary artery. I don't know what miracle has kept her stabilized for the past year."

Rolf was speechless, crushed. This revelation proved to him how attached he'd become to Jana... in less than 24 hours.

"Are you sure?" his voice was hollow.

"Unfortunately. I may not be able to give the best treatment, but I know the condition of my patients."

Rolf shook his head in despair. Then an idea popped into his head. "I stole a tube from the lab where they injected me. I thought of myself at first, but what if... for Jana?"

He pulled the tube out of his pocket. The clandie jumped on it, examined it against the light.

"It's a virus culture. No one could ever cultivate viruses effectively, but over there they did."

He looked at Rolf.

"No, this culture can't be of any use to Jana. Her sickness is caused by bacilli. They've got nothing to do with each other."

He showed Rolf the tube.

"On the other hand, I wouldn't be surprised if it was the causal agent of your sickness. In this case, who knows what I can get out of it..."

He went off and disappeared into a room adjoining his concrete lair. Rolf heard his muted voice.

"You'd never think I had an electronic microscope," he was saying. "It's because right after my disgrace, I still had some protection... not powerful enough to avoid the punishment, but enough to furnish my retreat with a few little things that make my life easier... like... here you go."

Rolf heard a low rumbling. Electric motors were starting up. The clandie stopped talking. Rolf plopped into a chair. The revelation that he'd just heard about Jana overshadowed everything, even the hope of getting better himself. His eyes were still leaking tears. Now he helped them along.

Clinking of metal and glass in the other room. Then silence. The clandie came back empty-handed.

"The research is begun," he said. "It'll take an hour or so. I mean I'll be able to give you a little more information after that. Real research takes years. Do you have any money left?"

"500 thallers," Rolf said. "It's yours." He took out his wallet.

"I only want ten," the doctor shook his head. "I'm afraid it won't be easy for you to come by it now."

Rolf gave him ten thallers with gratitude. "I have to see Jana. I'll come back."

The doctor let him leave without another word.

Rolf found his way to Jana's hut. Something told him that a disaster was awaiting him. And yet the clandie hadn't gone that far...

Jana was absent and her door was banging in the wind. Rolf looked for a note of some kind. But there was no message. It looked like she'd left in a hurry, not even taking time to shut her door...

He was about to leave when he saw that the light outside was growing dimmer rather than brighter. He stuck his head out the door and looked up at the sky: big, green clouds were rolling in from the horizon like a tidal wave. The closest were already hiding the Sun, which was still low. Soon it was going to be a bad idea to be outside. He closed the door, hoping that Jana, too, had found shelter.

The noise of the hail echoed off the concrete a few minutes later. It was like a rain of pebbles that a truck, as big as the world, had poured over the earth. At the same time, the wind started whistling. The door shook and an icy air leaked through the door. Rolf shivered. The crying wind reminded him of a distant mob of wounded people being dragged by the iron hooks of cleaners. Rolf wrapped his coat more tightly around his body and suffered through it patiently.

His eyes were getting used to the semi-darkness of the place. He had spotted two narrow openings in the concrete that were filled with transparent strips. That was where the gray light from outside was filtering in. It was also where he saw the glare of a purple flash when a loud thunderclap rang out. The sound of the hail got louder, too. Rolf heard it bouncing off the walls of the automatic factories and off the ground. He went to get into Jana's cot, wondering where she could be. But little by little the fatigue from the nebula's adventures got the better of him. He fell into a deep sleep that he couldn't resist.

When he woke up, the storm had passed and the Sun was nuzzling the windows. The nebula was over but Jana had not returned. Her absence confirmed Rolf's forebodings. He rushed outside to go look for her. But he pulled up short.

There were only two options when leaving Jana's place: to the right or to the left—across from it was a wall. Now, the path to the right was being blocked by a guy whose left arm didn't exist, but whose right hand held an iron hook. As for the left, someone was there, too: the woman on crutches whom Rolf had seen by the clandie's hut. On seeing Rolf, she started twirling her five-foot long chain of razors over her head. It was clear that these two had just come across each other and by tacit agreement decided to attack Rolf.

The man started forward, forcing Rolf back towards the woman on crutches. She twirled her weapon faster, started making a figure eight so that Rolf couldn't tell exactly where the razors were whistling by. He stopped. But the other was still advancing. Rolf turned his back to the woman, who was far enough away, and prepared to defend himself against her temporary ally. He kept coming on, sweeping the air before him with the iron hook. Rolf backed up, looking at the ground for a piece of concrete like he'd found before. But there was nothing. He could see his neck being slashed or his chest stabbed. He slipped in a puddle of water that the Sun hadn't evaporated yet. As he fell he heard a familiar, gauzy voice saying:

"Get out of here, vermin, or I'll smash both your heads in!"

He looked up and saw Titanor standing on top of the wall, shaking his inseparable iron bar.

CHAPTER XV

The two cripples had fled, each on their separate paths. With surprising agility for his size, Titanor had leapt off the wall. He took one look at Rolf and backed away.

"Have you seen your face?" his said as decency fought with disgust in his voice.

Rolf dried his eyes. "Yes," he said. "They stuck me with... measles."

"What's that?" Titanor asked guardedly.

"Not too serious, apparently,' Rolf explained. "But it makes you sick, sicko!"

He struggled to keep his teeth from chattering. Why didn't he ask the clandie for some ormedies to start with? He could've gone to Jana's later...

Titanor's brow wrinkled. "It's not like mine. The clandie can't do anything for me. Your meds came too late."

"What do you mean?" Rolf was alarmed.

"It's getting worse... apparently. I've got to stop this. I'm not going to let myself wither away til the end."

Rolf tried to comfort him, "Come on, maybe the clandie's just seeing the dark side."

Titanor shook his head, "He's tough, that clandie. And since he knows I'm no wimp, he doesn't sugarcoat it for me."

Rolf gave up. Titanor was no doubt right.

"In any case, for Jana, I think..."

"It's not true?"

"Sure it is? The clandie told me. He didn't say anything to her."

"Yeah, obviously!" Titanor roared. "What's the use..."

"Have you seen her?" Rolf asked.

"Not this morning. She wasn't home?"

"No. I'm worried."

"You want me to help you look for her?"

Rolf looked at him appreciatively, "You're a real friend. Thanks for that just now…"

"Bah!" Titanor said, "you would've taken those two. I saw that when you pretended to trip so you get them at the turn. By the way, why'd they dump you with the measles?"

"I killed a cop."

Titanor puffed his cheeks and blew them out. "I said you were a hard case! Yeah, well! If you want, we can start looking for your Jana. I'll go over here and you over there."

He left, swinging his iron bar.

"My Jana!" Rolf mused.

Rolf went in the opposite direction. On the way he picked up the chain of razors that the cripple had dropped when she fled. He wrapped the chain around his wrist so the razors wouldn't drag on the ground behind him like a gruesome child's toy. Where did they find these prehistoric things? He didn't care. He just thought it was wise to have a weapon, any kind whatsoever, in this society of reprobates, which seemed poised to become his own.

In the course of his search, he passed several loners who kept their distance—the razor chain that Rolf flaunted made them think twice. He gave himself a pat on the back for picking it up.

The people displayed all kinds of physical defects, which put them in a category apart. A category of subhumans, repulsive and abhorrent. But this was his first reaction. Very quickly he remembered that he, too, was part of this category and that he shouldn't turn his nose up. These people had been like him or more precisely like he had been before they lowered him. Now he was like them. What impression was he making on them with his red face and watery eyes? A devastating impression, naturally. He thought of Jana's poverty. For a rich man, meaning salaried, a poor person was also something foul. It stayed the same when the rich became poor at least until the fallen were absorbed by their condition. Then they tolerated each other, no more. The poor and the sick formed no solidarity except against a common enemy, the one who caused the degradation. And how could they stand up to an enemy as powerful as the presidency of the V 30 supported by the whole, healthy population of the city? The condemned couldn't do anything but wallow in their internal squabbling, their sordid killings, their hopeless selfishness.

Jana's poverty. Her poverty and his terrifying sickness. Where was she now? The girl who had awoken in Rolf a whole universe of sunny feelings that he didn't understand... He kept looking, taking risks.

And he found her.

Jana was lying in a plastic tube, six feet in diameter and ten feet long. She wasn't moving. Fearing the worst, Rolf crawled into the tube, which rolled on the ground until it bumped against something. The movement and the thump woke Jana from her semi-consciousness.

"Oh," she said weakly, "don't look at me!"

He looked at her right away, unintentionally. There was sticky, bloody crud on her blouse. He had to hurry out of the tube to vomit. She saw it. When he came back, she tried to crawl out the other end.

"Sorry," he said.

She turned her thin, pale face toward him, "It's me who's sorry," she gasped.

They kept silent for a long time. She watched him with timid shame. He tried to hide his disgust. He managed it by forcing a smile that held all the attraction he'd ever felt for her. An attraction that he still felt, in spite of everything.

"Don't do a thing," he said. "I'm going to clean you up. Then we'll go back to your place."

She didn't say anything, stupefied by his generosity and by such self-control. She let him take off her blouse and ended up saying, "You're so good to me."

He didn't move, kneeling next to her in the tube, holding the bloody blouse in his hand.

"They say," he said, "that among the people who take care of everything, up there in the higher circles in the palace... there's a feeling, an inclination, I don't know what to call it... there are people who are different."

She shook her head, "No, they're people like us, but they live differently. We're conditioned. We all repress, unconsciously, this feeling you're talking about. It's called love."

Rolf stared stupidly, the cruddy rag in his hand.

"You're the second person to talk to me about that... feeling," she went on. "The first belonged to those very circles. That's why I was sentenced and suffered this punishment. See, I didn't love him."

"Well" Rolf stammered, "me, I'm like him. But where we're at, there's no law stopping me." He turned his head. "Or stopping you..."

"I think this time it's mutual," she said. Then, her voice broke, "But it's too late. You see, I was feeling so bad I went to see the doctor. I was caught in the hailstorm. I took shelter in here and then..."

She broke down in tears. Rolf, whose eyes had almost dried during the search, felt his view getting hazy. He turned away.

"Come on," he forced himself to say, "pull yourself together. I want to see you smiling when I get back."

He left and found a puddle in which he washed the blouse as best he could. Then he went back to Jana. He helped her put it back on.

"I'm going to go with you back to the clandie's," he said. "He'll give you some stronger ormedies right away."

She was shivering in her wet blouse. "You think so?" she asked, struggling to sit up with Rolf's help.

"You'll see... my sweet Jana."

She smiled a little hearing her name like that. Tears returned to both their eyes. He helped her out of the tube. She was so exhausted that she lay down in the sun. The rays were already so strong that steam started coming off the blouse.

"I feel better," she uttered, but her voice was weak.

"You'll see!" Rolf assured her.

He took off his coat, rolled it up and slipped it under Jana's head. Then he had second thoughts, took his coat back and sat on the ground. He laid Jana's head on his knees. He was surprised by his own courage, his magnanimity. But this admiration of self didn't last long faced with Jana's wan features. He caressed her cheek without saying anything. He was thinking of nothing but her, of what the clandie had said. Completely disoriented, his feelings adrift, he held her head in his hands.

"Rolf!" she said with a kind of sad cheerfulness.

"Yes." He found nothing else to say. Now he needed all his strength to hide his anguish from Jana so that she'd believe what he'd just said.

"Otherwise, it's not worth it, is it?" he repeated to himself over and over again. But this kind of absurd purring didn't conceal his thoughts. He knew that Jana was going away, gently, even though she was lying down and he held her head in his hands. He suddenly remembered his own sickness.

"You talked to me, after all," he said softly, following his own thoughts.

"Why after all?" she panted.

"Despite my face... my new sickness."

She smiled without answering. He felt compelled to trust her. "It's because I killed someone," he spoke slowly.

She closed her eyes and replied, "Doesn't matter."

A white bird with a red crest on its head alit on the edge of the plastic tube. It started twittering, then stopped.

"Oh," Jana said without opening her eyes, "I hope it starts up again."

"It will certainly start again," Rolf assured her. "It's always here. Do you want to see it?"

"I don't have the strength." She opened her eyes for an instant, saw the bird and closed them again, though a smile crossed her pale lips.

Rolf lied to her, "I'll let you rest a moment before bringing you to the clandie. It's not far."

"Mmmm…," she murmured without parting her lips.

And she let her head roll to the side. Terrified, Rolf called her name, tapped her cheeks. She'd lost consciousness. He sat there in desperate straits, not daring to move. But soon her breathing stopped, started again, stopped again, started again…

Jana died effortlessly. She never regained consciousness. Rolf watched the bird fly away. Then he got up and put Jana's head gently on the ground. He got on his knees, then lay down next to her, his head on her still chest.

He stifled his screams.

CHAPTER XVI

Rolf had lost all notion of time. When Titanor came up to him and spoke, he felt like he'd been there for hours. Long hours of strange suffering that he seen, several times, as if from outside himself, mystified by his feelings for her. He'd met Jana twice in one day and made love with her once. If he was going to cry over the death of all the girls he'd made love to… But there's the rub: Jana was not just any other girl. Why? Who knows! All that was left was this absurd despair. And also a dark bitterness, a profound hatred for those responsible for her death. Not at all the same feelings he had for his own situation. Something much less passive, much more aggressive.

Titanor repeated what he'd said, "Well, it's a good thing you're the one who found her."

Rolf sat up. He stared at the ridiculous blouse that was almost dry on Jana's skin. What difference did it make to Jana whether her blouse was wet or dry? She wasn't shivering either way now. For her all the little details of life meant nothing anymore. The big problems too. Everything had been razed to the same level of absurdity.

The dead don't understand that we take such pains to get to where they are.

"Yes," Rolf finally said. He stood up, still contemplating Jana. "What are we going to do with her?" he unconsciously included Titanor in the question.

Titanor shrugged, "Leave her here. It she rots here or somewhere else…"

Rolf glared murderously at him.

Titanor grimaced, "Don't get me wrong, I miss her too, the little wisp of a girl. But this isn't her. This is nothing more than a hunk of plastic or concrete. I'll be next and believe or not whatever you do with my body, I really don't care. So, look at Jana, how much do you think she cares. Look, if she could hear us, she'd be laughing."

Titanor's attitude was no different than Rolf's deep down inside. He knew it. As for the idea that Jana was listening and laughing, it gave Rolf odd comfort.

"Let's go," Rolf said. "You're right."

They left. Jana stayed alone in the rubble. But her clean blouse was finally dry.

"I have to go back to the clandie." Rolf said, asked, "You coming?"

"Yeah, just to stay with you," Titanor said.

They walked in silence. Then Rolf spoke. It was a good way not to think.

At first he thought to himself: "Lucky that the sickness turned my eyes into fountains. The more my eyes water, the less I feel like I'm crying."

Then aloud he said, "Someone has to pay for this."

"Good idea. But who?"

"The highest up, therefore the most responsible," Rolf declared.

"Yeah!" Titanor agreed. "Like that I can get revenge before it's too late for me to do anything about it. But I should tell you that if it's the president of the city you're thinking of, it'll be a real bitch getting even within 100 feet of him."

"We'll have to think about it, make preparations for things like that."

One detail crossed his mind that had nothing to do with the subject at hand: Jana had told him that she was going to see the clandie when she got caught in the hail. So, he had missed her by only a few minutes. Maybe she would've tried to reach the doctor with him... he could've helped her along... but no, Jana's time was up. Rolf could've done nothing for her. He shrugged his shoulders bitterly and said nothing until they reached their destination because even if his false tears hid his real ones, he couldn't disguise his voice, which would crack at every word.

"Well now," the clandie rubbed his hands, "if it isn't the two merry men."

"Jana is dead," Rolf stated.

The drugger turned a grave eye on him, "Sorry, I didn't know."

He stuck his hand into his bathrobe pocket and added, "I didn't expect it so soon."

He looked at Titanor, "I have no news for you."

"I figured as much," Titanor confided. "I just came with my pal."

"But for you," the clandie turned to Rolf, "I have something."

Rolf waited expectantly. Just because you suffer a loss doesn't mean you lose interest in your own fate. He who kills himself at night is worried about his health in the morning.

"I have to say right off that it's not a cure. They took very careful precautions." He took his time and then, "You didn't bring me a culture that was in the middle of being prepared. It's resistant to everything I have, but it's so virulent that..." He paused again before finishing, "that the sickness, which is yours, by the way, is transmissible, even by simple contact. I've never seen anything like it. You can't imagine what precautions I had to take just to touch the culture."

"Transmissible?" Rolf repeated, not quite understanding.

"Yes," the clandie explained. "In the past, there were contagious sicknesses. This was one of them. But it needed an agent to be transmitted from one subject to another—drops of saliva sprayed from coughing, for example, or excrements. But the distinction of this strain of virus is that the subject infected will become highly contagious, I'm sure by simple contact."

These details wormed their way into Rolf's mind. He inquired, "And he would be a lot sicker than me, I imagine?"

"Not at all," the clandie responded. "The only difference between you and him would be the alarming contagion."

"I have my vengeance," Rolf declared.

The drugger recoiled.

"Yes, yes," Rolf repeated, "I have my vengeance. Inject me with this damn thing and soon you'll be getting some funny news from the city."

Titanor chuckled, "You're so mean," he said admiringly.

"But you're going to put V 30 into a terrible epidemic!" the clandie exclaimed.

"Listen," Rolf said, "it's not the inhabitants of V 30 in general that I'm targeting. But I won't cry if there's spillover. I have no sympathy for the kind of gang that dreams of nothing but lynching the sick even when they know they're victims of a sentencing. As if that wasn't enough... and even if it was a natural sickness... they used to treat the sick, so they say, instead of killing them off. But in V 30, they kill off those injured in accidents too. I've seen the cleaners in action. So, you get it, me, V 30 and its population..."

"But you were part of it."

"I apologize," Rolf said. "I'm ashamed now. Anyway, I'm not lying when I say that I never participated in a man hunt or any other entertainment of the kind. Perhaps I was always a little different."

The clandie looked very uneasy. "Okay, you think so, but you understand the flood of sick people in this place... and me, after all, I can't tolerate contact with another sick person. Only one is enough for me."

"There won't be a flood of sick," Rolf assured him. "The sick have to go into exile because they're a tiny minority. When they become a vast majority, it'll be the healthy people who will be forced to flee. And then the sick will demand that the presidency treat them in one way of another. And if the presidency turns a deaf ear, V 30 will rise up. The police, all the different police, won't count for much. As for the army, let me tell you that I know about that. The army is down to a few men and even fewer vehicles, if you believe it still exists. But it doesn't exist any more than the enemies they talk about. There are no enemies because there's no one but us. At least, we've never met anyone else. All the discoveries of the explorer are imaginary. I know something about it because I was the one who invented them, along with a few other people. But, yes, I invented them. And I'm not at all upset that I had to give up that noxious work."

The clandie opened his eyes wide, "They didn't even tell me about that when I was the president's doctor."

Rolf started and stared, "What did you say?"

The clandie bit his lip.

"Yes," Rolf said," I knew I heard right. So, if you're a friend, you'll give me and Titanor some information. About the palace, the guards, the president's habits... and a lot of stuff that I haven't thought of yet."

Titanor stepped up to them, "And it's in your interest to help out my friend."

The drugger stared at him coldly, "No threats, please. I'll do as I please."

He turned back to Rolf, but his apparent calm couldn't mask his inner turmoil because his voice trembled slightly.

"You look like you want to embark on an adventure that will be very dangerous for everyone. But me, I've got a little life here and all this upheaval isn't my thing. Yours neither, I might add. You're just as likely to get killed before getting anything started."

"Don't try to talk me out of it," Rolf said. "Jana's death made up my mind and nothing will change it. I never thought about changing the world before. I had reason enough but not the drive. Now I have the drive, too bad... As for your little, personal preoccupations, they're worth nothing compared to what is happening in V 30 and here as well. If you couldn't give up your little habits, you should've figured out how to treat Jana. I would've kept quiet. I, too, would've formed little habits with her and would've stayed harmless."

The clandie raised his arms to the sky, "But you know very well that I can't do anything really serious..."

"Well," Rolf cut in, "if you can't do anything good for the sick, then I'm going to do something bad for the healthy. You'll see that I can be more effective than you."

Like it or not, the clandie had to fulfill his clients' wishes. Since he couldn't really do otherwise, but he wanted to save face, he'd latched onto one of Rolf's arguments, which went as follows: "When everyone's sick," he'd said, "and the president has fallen, the judicial policy will come back. I'm sure the labs have what's needed to cure everyone. They just haven't made it available, that's all. With your past, you'll certainly become the doctor of the new president. And since you'll be cured, just like everyone else, you'll be able to start a new life dedicated to something other than a fruitless quest."

Then Rolf had to ask Titanor's advice. "You'll be risking infection if you go with me. Or rather, you're sure to be contaminated… So?"

Titanor laughed and with all confidence in Rolf replied, "Better to get cured of two diseases than to die of one!"

The clandie had prepared the liquid to inject from the culture. And he had given a shot to Rolf as Titanor watched on in awe. If they'd told Rolf a few hours earlier that he'd be asking for a shot with a third virus, he would've shrugged his shoulders. But what would he have done if they'd added that he'd suddenly he seized by unbearable grief?

They'd discussed waiting for the next nebula to execute the raid on the palace, but the clandie's proposition to get in through the sewers made crowds and traffic a moot point.

Suspiciously, Titanor asked, "How is it you know the sewers? Did you live in them and they brought down the president when he needed to be treated for something?"

"I was also responsible for the hygiene of the palace and I made several inspections. I can draw you a map."

He did draw a map. It was up to Rolf and Titanor to get themselves to the sewers. Rolf chose a path that would avoid passing by Jana's body—he wouldn't leave her again. Therefore, they had to make a long detour. Once done, Rolf's hand inadvertently brushed Titanor's. In less than a minute he was covered in a red rash and started shivering with fever. Right away he swallowed the ormedies that Rolf gave him. With the tumor and now his face the color of fire, he was gruesome to look at, which greatly pleased Rolf.

They had also avoided Jana's shack. Rolf would've gone in and never come out. Thus they arrived at the city limits.

CHAPTER XVII

There was still a reason to delay the raid until the next nebula: the desperadoes had no flashlight. And to get around in the sewers, it was a necessary tool. It was highly unlikely that the sewers—where neither of them had ever set foot—had lights on all the time. The nebula, when the city became deserted, would make it easy to break into a shop. Now they just had to find one. Rolf told Titanor his plan before entering the first inhabited district.

"Okay…" Titanor was perplexed.

Rolf took matters into his own hands. If they waited, he feared seeing his determination wane. Not that he was afraid of forgetting Jana and his vengeance, but he knew his natural apathy and his tendency to get discouraged. For the moment, he was boiling over with hatred. For him, vengeance was a plate that had to be served hot. As hot as his hatred.

They started by locating the closest sewage drain. No problem—they were all around the fringes of the suburbs.

The first one they saw was like a square hole 30 feet across and whose true depth couldn't be estimated. They could only see maybe 20 feet down, the surface being constantly stirred up by a blackish cesspool that flowed through the drainage holes towards sone porous ground. The reservoir, a conduit located halfway between the edge of the hole and the surface of the liquid, fed it constantly. A foul juice flowed out of it with the sound of a waterfall. All kinds of stuff drifted by, which they'd figured were worthy of becoming waste but not good enough for the crushers.

As Rolf and Titanor wondered at all this, a human corpse sprang out of the conduit and fell into the hole with a big splash. It was so completely covered in a kind of black grease that they couldn't tell if it was a man or woman. A moot point for Rolf who backed away.

"But," Titanor said, "how's it going to get through the other pipes?"

The answer had already come. Something huge was breaking the surface, snatching the prey. The jaws snapped shut. Everything disappeared. This thing was living in the cesspool. A living crusher. Rolf thought that Jana was lucky to be rotting in the sun.

"Should we go?" Titanor asked.

His question made Rolf shudder. But he was stuck now with the image that Titanor had of him.

"The flashlights first," he tried to sound assertive. But such resolve confused the brute.

"No point," Titanor said, "but you're the boss."

Rolf noted the presence of an iron ladder giving access to the drainpipe and two walkways with railings that led into the conduit at each end of the horizontal diameter.

"That'll do," he said.

At the same time, he was aware of the fact that their endeavor was kind of crazy. But there hadn't been any insane people for a long time. Or was it the opposite and everybody had become crazy? How to tell?

They went to look for flashlights.

A row of parallel alleys opened onto a big boulevard on the first level. The alleys were deserted while the traffic on the boulevard was getting busier 100 yards away. They took the first one to the corner where they could see the shops. Nothing useful. They stepped away from the wall they were hiding behind and went back to take the second alley, leading to the same boulevard. They got lucky.

A small bazaar was open almost directly in front of them. They saw some pedestrians and a few sliders, but the shop looked empty at this early hour. They could see some plasma lights in the window.

"Obviously," Titanor whispered, "no weapons…"

"Obviously," Rolf concurred, wishing he still had Willy's paralyzer. "But if you look a little to the left in the window, you'll see some tools I've seen used by builders. They might prove useful to us."

"I see. You deal with the flashlights and I'll take care of those tools."

They ran across the boulevard. A slider stopped a few feet from them. The driver jumped out and ran away. A crowd was already forming and screaming. Titanor veered off towards the group waving his iron bar and roaring in his gauzy voice. The crowd dispersed. Titanor rejoined Rolf who had entered the shop and was ransacking the window trying to reach the flashlights. They left together amongst the cries of fear and fury from the shopkeeper. Titanor was holding two objects that did not look light but that he handled like feathers.

They beat a retreat down the alleyway where no one dared pursue them.

They didn't stop running until they had returned to the drainpipe. Not a soul in sight. Rolf gave a flashlight to Titanor who, in exchange, offered Rolf one of the tools.

"So that's what it is," Rolf explained. The object he was holding was used to inject different substances into a block of something, even concrete. It looked a little like a big paralyzer fitted with a tank.

"The tank's empty," Rolf observed, "but it doesn't matter. What counts is the strength of the air jet that it spits out."

He turned on the pressurizer, aimed at a two-foot cube of concrete and pulled the trigger. The cube lifted off the ground, rolled a few feet back and stopped. There was a small, round hole in it. Titanor whistled.

"Just wait," Rolf said. "Let's see what you've got there."

He grabbed Titanor's tool. It looked a little like the other but its sides were longer and held 20 or so different compartments, each containing a small, black cube. Rolf put one of the cubes into what looked like a grip and aimed at a scrawny bush 30 feet away. He pulled the side lever and watched a blinding jet ravaged the bush, which went up in flames instantly. Titanor whistled louder this time.

"What's it used for?" he asked.

"Distance welding," Rolf said, "for hard-to-reach places. I had to learn a bunch of technical stuff when I worked in the Bureau of Explorations."

He gave him back the tool.

"I like this better than a paralyzer!" Titanor boasted.

"Mine's not too bad either," Rolf said humbly.

Titanor agreed. But he preferred his. Still, he refused to give up his iron bar.

Thus equipped, they went down the little iron ladder that plunged into the cesspool. The stench was unbearable. When they reached the drainpipe, the black mush was stirred up again and the jaws shot out, snapping at the empty air. Titanor brandished his flamethrower.

"No!" Rolf shouted.

Titanor glared at him, "Why not? You like this critter?"

"No," Rolf said, "but there are always... things falling down there. If they're not crushed, they'll clog up the pipes, the level will rise, flow back into the drainpipe and we'll be drowned before we're halfway there."

Titanor reflected on this silently. Then he said, "Okay, pal."

They went down the tunnel single file. They turned on the plasma lights and lit up the tunnel as bright as day. The iron walkway shook under their feet. It seemed solid, however. Titanor noticed a sign near the entrance that read "Small diameter".

"What's that mean?" he asked.

Rolf was almost overjoyed, despite his grief. "That means the drainpipe leads to the small diameter of the egg. It leads to the center of V 30."

They disappeared into the tunnel.

They walked for long enough to have gone half the distance. Rolf had turned off his light to save energy. Titanor's alone was enough. There was a ventilation system that created a strong and noxious wind. At least they wouldn't suffocate.

Rolf glanced behind them and noticed that the drainpipe was not straight.

117

"We have to turn back. We're heading away from the center."

They went back and passed by a perpendicular pipe that they'd paid no attention to before because iron bars closed it off. But behind the grill was a sign reading "Small diameter".

"It's this way," Rolf said. "We'll have to use your flamethrower. Melt the bars."

"I don't have enough ammo," Titanor said. "Wait."

He put down his flashlight and his weapon on the walkway, then grabbed two of the bars and strained his muscles. Sweat beaded on his red forehead. The bars bent, then one of them gave way and tore out from the bottom. Titanor bent it up, then gave Rolf a triumphant smile. Anybody other than Rolf would've run screaming from such a smile.

Rolf just said, "Good job, pal."

They slipped through the grill and entered a pipe that was smaller than the last one where the torrent raged.

"The stuff carried down this tube," Rolf said, "would get stopped by the bars and clog it up. So, there must be a creature down here too."

Hearing this, Titanor stepped away from the railing and skirted the curved wall. At that very moment, a white thing, three times bigger than a man, surged up and snapped its jaws on the iron ramp. It dropped back into the black water with a hideous noise. A chunk of the ramp was missing. Titanor refrained from commenting but turned to Rolf and gave him a little salute. They went on their way, sticking close to the wall.

Soon after, Titanor, who was in the lead, suddenly stopped. He didn't have time to put down his flashlight or to ready his flamethrower. The flashlight rolled into the current where its red glare turned into a faint glow that faded away as the current dragged it off. But Rolf saw a creature identical to the last one—maybe the same one—that leapt over the railing and lunged at Titanor. He lit his own flashlight and aimed his injector. But he couldn't shoot without hitting Titanor. He could just make out a mushy thing without eyes. And in a split second Titanor had his iron bar in hand and was thrashing away with all his might. The thing exploded, spraying both men with a geyser of black blood. But it was still hanging on. Titanor broke its feet and fins, stabbed it and pushed it back into the pipe current where it sank immediately.

Titanor gave Rolf a big smile; "What was that beastie thinking?"

Luckily, the flamethrower wasn't lost. But there was only one flashlight. While keeping his weapon at hand, Titanor tore three strips off the thick tissue covering his huge chest, braided them in record time and gave Rolf the line.

"Tie the light onto your belt."

Rolf obeyed. He was still trembling but didn't let Titanor see. They got back on their way. Rolf had fastened the flashlight so well that he had both hands free and kept his injector ready. Titanor was still in the lead, brandishing his flamethrower, which he'd recharged.

It was then, as they came upon another grill, that they were attacked for the third time. The thing was mowed down before it'd barely broke the surface. It sank, half-burned, while the stench of charred decay wafted through the drainpipe.

"Okay," Rolf said, "you go at the bars and I'll cover you."

Titanor broke off two bars and went through. Rolf backed through after him. As they were squeezing through, another creature sprang up and buckled the walkway when it dropped. Rolf fired. The thing rolled around, broke the walkway, scratched at the metal wall, shaving off slivers of it and creating sparks. Then it went flying over what remained of the railing and dove into the black water where it disappeared.

The two men kept going, turning at the first junction of the drainpipe: a new sign was on the wall of the side passage.

Here the lifeforms seemed different. The water was teeming with tiny creatures that were hard to see but whose function must've been the same as the giant larvae. It would not have been a good idea to go swimming among them but at least they couldn't attack.

119

Thus, they reached a huge, round chamber with a walkway running all the way around it. Drainpipes without grills emptied into it but the toxic dumping produced a slower current.

"The map," Rolf said.

The round chamber was noted on the map. It was almost under the big tower of the fifth level. The drainpipe of the palace bore the number 8. Rolf and Titanor started searching for it.

They found it easily and went in. First, however, they took a few precautions, like turning down the light.

The tunnel was straight. The light was too faint to see the end. Unconsciously Rolf tried to muffle his footsteps, but Titanor continued making his personal noises.

Rolf called softly, "Do you think it's a good idea to announce our arrival?"

"Bah!" Titanor shot back. "The clandie made a map that's supposed to lead us to his old apartment. We won't be going by any guard posts."

"So why turn down the light?"

"Well, like that…"

Rolf already knew that there was no point arguing with him. Logic was not one of Titanor's strong points. And yet he had proven that he wasn't stupid.

"Do me this favor," Rolf said.

"Okay…"

Titanor walked more softly. Now they were both going as quietly as they could. But the iron walkway would rattle and creak, which echoed through the shadows. Rolf kept his weapon aimed at the darkness that sprawled beyond the railing. He was expecting, at any moment, to see some nightmarish creature spring up. But nothing troubled the serenity of the drainpipe. And they came to another round chamber. Turning up the light, they saw that it was a dead-end. They also saw the rungs of a ladder bolted to the wall.

CHAPTER XVIII

Still in the lead, Titanor went up the ladder first. Rolf followed with the flashlight in his belt. Not a sound, nobody around. They climbed for a few minutes without the light of day coming to compete with the flashlight. Soon, however, they could see the upper opening. They higher they climbed, the clearer it got. Titanor reached it and stepped into a corridor and disappeared under the vaulted ceiling that Rolf could see. He followed right after.

Titanor was on his knees on the ground, trying to get up. Several uniformed men were aiming paralyzers at him. Rolf raised his weapon but didn't have time to shoot. He was hit by the paralyzers and dropped to the ground, unable to move.

Their passage led to a square room, furnished sparsely with cots, tables and shelves with bottles. The playing cards were still on the tables along with open bottles and half-filled glasses. From the looks of things, it was a guard post.

One of the men turned up the flashlight that hung from the ceiling. The flashlight that they'd dimmed while waiting for the intruders.

Even though paralyzed, Rolf felt enraged: so, the clandie had betrayed them! His map led them straight into a trap. They'd made all that effort for nothing. No, not for nothing—just to get caught.

Three guards bound Titanor's arms and legs with an iron chain, then started on Rolf. Their fear and disgust made them careful not to touch the prisoners. Rolf was raging inside: if they hadn't been paralyzed, it'd only take a tiny movement to touch their enemies. And then something really marvelous would've happened. But it didn't, even though the guards had no idea how close they'd come.

"Did you see their faces?" one of them asked.

"It's madness!" another said.

Their dialogue stopped there. They were too stunned, too disgusted, too terrified to go on. A third guy, however, spoke up.

"The... ugh! The sick aren't only in the zone. Here they are in the sewers now! There could be thousands of them. What are we going to do if they all come up together?"

Rolf remarked how absurd his fear was. How could thousands of people come up one ladder together?

"We should demand something more than the paralyzers!"

"Yeah, we need blowers."

Rolf examined them. There were eight. All of them had glassy eyes in alcoholic faces. Their uniforms were stained by the wet concrete they were leaning against. Poor bastards, really. But malicious, nevertheless.

He felt his strength slowly coming back. They claimed that at full power the paralyzers could stop the heart. They claimed a lot of things...

"When they're recovered, we'll haul them upstairs."

"And if they refuse to go? Me, I'm not touching them."

"Me neither. We'll whip them and drag them."

Rolf noticed that they had refills for the paralyzers in their belts. He also noticed that some of them had decided to put their weapons away. Of course, the prisoners might break out of their chains but running away would only drive them deeper into the jaws of the death. What choice did they have?

"Instead," Rolf thought, "we could just touch their faces, for example."

They prodded them off the ground using bottles as batons to avoid contact. Rolf managed to stand but Titanor fell to the floor again, which provoked an outburst of laughter.

"Look at that mountain crumbling!"

"We'll teach him how to walk!"

Three guards took off their coats and threw them over Titanor. Six of them now grabbed him through the fabric and heaved him up.

"He weighs as much as three men."

122

"No wonder he crumbled—it's all fat!"

Titanor wobbled on his feet, blank-eyed. Rolf looked on, stupefied. How could this brute be so devastated by the paralyzers while he, Rolf, felt practically no effect anymore?

There was a loud snap. Titanor's chains had just broken, all of them at the same time. Simultaneously, the giant swung one of them and pulled out his iron bar, which they'd failed to take away from him. Three men went down screaming, skulls and collar bones crushed. The five others fled or tried to fumble refills into their paralyzers. Roaring like a wild animal, Titanor threw one of them into the hole. They heard his yells fade away down the drainpipe.

Against the rays of two paralyzers, Titanor lumbered towards the four other guards. His movements slowed down but not enough to put him out of action. He grabbed the arms holding the weapons and snapped them. The paralyzers fell to the ground. Calmly and dexterously, Titanor kicked in the chests of the two guards. But last two came up behind him, wielding broken bottles.

Rolf shouted, "Watch out!"

Titanor swung around. One of the shards sliced the tumor on his neck. Blood spurted out and blinded the two guards. Titanor quickly tossed them down into the drainpipe. Then the giant plodded back to Rolf.

"They got me," he gargled. "Come here quick. I won't have enough strength after."

Rolf, confused, walked over to him. Titanor seized the chains imprisoning his friend and pulled. The first chain broke immediately. The second took longer. But it yielded—two links twisted, then snapped. Rolf was free. Titanor backed up and leaned against the wall.

"You know," he struggled to catch his breath, "the one with the key for these is the hole. You could… never take him… and you'd stay here… like a jerk…"

He slid down the wall in a puddle of blood. The blood Rolf was covered in.

"Get out," Titanor panted. "Too bad the clandie wasn't... straight. I'd loved to have... healed with you."

Like Jana. A bloodbath. Friendship, love? Dead leaves. And him, Rolf, a poor guy too mild to attack a huge, oppressive system on his own.

Too mild?

"You"ll see," he told Titanor, choking back sobs, "the president counts on his guards. But there aren't any guards. You've taken them out. And if there are others, I'll have a word with them. Then with their president. Trust me. I'll avenge you both, you and Jana. You've got my word."

A smile grew on Titanor's face, then froze, as if chiseled into red stone.

Rolf picked up the two paralyzers and an ammunition belt. Then the grabbed the flamethrower that had rolled to the edge of the hole. He turned and strode down the corridor. A bright corridor where he had no need of his flashlight.

At first he walked like in a fog. Titanor had become a friend. Rolf remembered, without believing it, the terror he'd felt when they'd first met. A killer. And this killer had just saved his life by giving up his own. That's how things were in the race of men where nothing was ever entirely black or entirely white.

But how could anything positive exist in a social system like this? In a man who supported this system, what could humanity, what tenderness could be left? That was a mystery. And Rolf could only think of three solutions to this mystery: either die of it or get rid of it or clarify it.

The third possibility seemed the least likely. The most likely was the first.

The corridor ended in a stairway that he started to climb in silence. He was expecting to come across another guard post at any moment. But he came out, instead, in a small, deserted courtyard, which he crossed unhindered. He followed the path laid out on the map—there was no other.

Another stairway led to another corridor, then a series of rooms: the clandie's old apartment. He entered cautiously and got ready to confront the new drugger of the president.

Laughter rang out behind him.

CHAPTER XIX

Rolf swiveled around. He didn't have time to finish his movement. Men came rushing silently out of another room and pinned his arms, snatching away his weapons. The man who had just laughed stood off to the side. Rolf recognized the president himself like in the pictures seen everywhere.

"So," the president said, "the convicts make it all the way to the palace. Someone will have to pay for this. In the meantime, take him to door T, I'll deal with him personally."

They dragged Rolf, against his will, to a door that they forced him through. He was expecting to fall into a pit of carnivorous beasts. But he was just in another corridor. The door closed behind him. He heard footsteps behind him. The president came up and casually put his hand on Rolf's arm. A surge of hatred boiled Rolf's blood and he grabbed the president's hand.

He forced a laugh and said, "There's something you don't know, but I'm going to tell you…"

"Quiet down for a second," the president cut him off. "I know you're contagious. That's the least of my worries. I've been vaccinated. I got you to come here by gambling on this idea of vengeance."

Rolf stared at him, puzzled. The president smiled and led him to the end of the corridor.

"I couldn't summon you. You had to come here of your own free will and, if possible, with malicious intent."

Rolf stayed silent. He was understanding less and less.

"I couldn't minimize the dangers of the trip either, but something told me you'd survive. And you did."

They came to a dark opening in which an iridescent, shadowy curtain rippled.

"Have no fear. Follow me."

The president walked through the curtain and disappeared. Rolf hesitated, then did the same. All these mysteries were too much for him. He had to clear things up. There would be plenty of time for action later. And if the man was immune to the contagion, Rolf could always fight, pure and simple.

Rolf entered a dark space with no visible limits. Nearby he could make out the president's outline. Bright objects danced before him, twirling around each other. He heard the president's voice:

"You're in the topology lab. This is our universe. In this place where we are endowed with special properties: it encompasses the universe and expands us beyond its scale. It's a finite universe. We're outside of it."

"How is that possible?" Rolf stammered.

"Let's get this straight," the president said, "it's not a real topological transformation. It's the elevation of a certain point of view in which we encompass everything. Well, not everything, obviously... but in simplest terms. Sit down."

Rolf felt for an armchair and sat down. The president did the same. The glowing objects kept spinning in the space. Rolf thought: "A clever model but why?"

"You'll soon understand why we're staying in this weird place instead of talking in my office over a drink," the president said.

He said nothing for a moment, figuring out where to start. The strangeness of this welcome had completely taken the wind out of Rolf's violent sails.

"First of all," the voice said in the dark, "if you had acted differently, I would've adapted. So, in case you hadn't spoken up at first, Willy—poor thing—would've figured out how to loosen your tongue. You had to be sentenced and exiled. There, if you'd made contact with another 'clandie', we would've found some way to send you to the other. I'd given specific instructions."

"You'd also given instructions to save Jana, I guess?" Rolf interrupted. "They weren't followed."

"That's regrettable, but I couldn't do anything about that. Believe it or not, this is the only place where we can make free decisions. The tragedy is that once we're outside, we can't do anything to implement them. You need not be in the same case. But you yourself are a case."

Rolf waited for what would follow.

"A long time ago, the research started. It started with meaningless words and false memories. The meaningless words first. Words like 'sin' or expressions like 'The Watch Out Tower. Impossible to say where they came from. But things got worse with the false memories. I say 'false' because no written or recorded document can verify them. And they belong to everyone. We don't, generally, try to verify a childhood memory, not to mention what are called historical facts. Except for specialists. It so happens that at the instigation of my predecessors and myself, work was undertaken along these lines. No results. And it's not because of a huge upheaval, a war or a cataclysm—when details disappear, the important achievements don't survive either. But our technological achievements have survived so well that it can only be the result of thousands of generations. But we have no past."

Rolf kept listening without seeing where the president was going with all this.

"Onto this was added an opinion that was certainly more significant to the echelons of power than to the citizens: the impossibility, both psychologically and physically, of making free decisions. The attempts made to repeal the law of sickness-sentencing were never put into effect. And yet, we all kept trying. The same for the intervention of the brigades after an accident and a lot of other intolerable practices. By the way, the epoch when we became defenseless against sickness also belongs to that mythic past that left only traces in oral tradition. An oral tradition in a world dominated by audio-visual."

"And you can't do anything about it?" Rolf tried to sound sarcastic.

"Nothing, like it or not. We don't feel like we're moving but rather being moved."

He paused and then went on.

"So, the researchers challenged these opinions with what we found materially. No rock was datable by carbon-14. Using this method they were all newborn rocks. And yet, their structure and their chemical composition fit into a natural cycle that should date back billions of years. But they're probably no more than 30 years old. But that's not the worst. The results of our biological research done over the past 20 years all converge on you."

Rolf jumped, "What do you mean, on me?"

"You are present everywhere in the universe in certain gene configurations that belong to you alone and that are more or less deformed in all other living beings. This is the very latest discovery, which explains why you weren't brought here earlier."

"Me!" Rolf was flabbergasted.

"You. Believe me, the president is not the important one here. It's you. We need to pursue this further."

"Yes," Rolf said, "but how?"

"There's a contradiction in this world between its history and our logic. Our logic which is, nevertheless, part of this world. And there's your omnipresence for which we must find the cause. These two points, which might appear unrelated, cannot be separated. It's this very link that we must find."

"And if it's the universe that's outsmarting us? If it's your logic that doesn't fit with it?"

"Then we have to find out why our logic is like this. It'll be our second trial if the first fails."

"The first? You have a way?"

"Being without freedom, we have to begin by searching for a way to search. Meaning, a situation where the researcher can be protected from the hold on us that I mentioned."

"But to remove it would mean to be removed from it!"

"No. There are cracks, a kind of corridor of freedom that we've taken full advantage of. The corridor widened, so to speak, and we got the topology lab, then this observation space that puts us outside the universe."

Abruptly, Rolf realized that the president was telling the truth. Now in the presence of what he'd taken for a clever model, he became dizzy. Was he really outside, bigger even than the world and embracing everything in a single glance? What was that shimmering, rippling curtain they'd come through? Was it really a gateway to the infinite and a multiplier of dimensions on a cosmic scale?

"But how can we be alive... outside the universe?" he forced himself to ask.

"That's where a kind of topology comes in," the president said. "We're still inside. This observation chamber is inside, but it contains it. It's an incomplete reversal."

"Ah!" Rolf said.

"Yes, a complete reversal would be like an inside-out finger of a glove. Get it?"

"Vaguely," Rolf admitted.

"Well, its importance is like an airlock in a submarine or the successive stages in a spaceship. Here we're free to make decisions and also to implement them if the implementation doesn't require us to leave. And these decisions can go a lot further than we've ever gone."

"How's that?"

"By making a complete reversal with respect to us, without damaging it more than we do right now, I'm sure we'll find an all-embracing explanation for all the anomalies I told you about. With this explanation we imagine we can rectify all the absurdities and cruelties of this world."

Rolf tried to see his face. The president's words made so little sense that he was almost hoping to see a smile on his face. But the shadows were too thick to see anything.

The president concluded, "It's you who has to make the voyage, of course."

All the old indecisions and fears of Rolf came rushing back. As if nothing had happened and he'd never faced a zillion perils in a day.

"Me!" he squawked.

"You. I told you that you were present everywhere here. Without a doubt you must be, in one way or another, in this elsewhere we have to go."

Rolf laughed out loud. "But you're saying, you're affirming… I'm not the beginning of a proof!"

"You want me to show you your chromosomes as they're recorded in the civil registry and then the atomic structure of anyone else's body? Or of any other living thing? Do you want me, finally, to introduce you to the biologists dealing with all this?"

"No," Rolf said after a moment. "I believe you." But then he added, "You talk about a voyage and you claim we're going to reverse the universe. That's how you put it. What's going to move, me or the universe?"

"I wasn't clear enough. You know, I'm not a specialist. I'm explaining according to the physic-mathematicians. I think I remember now what they used as a research hypothesis: for there to exist a universal equilibrium, they think the world has to have topological symmetry. And they have a way to send a subject into this symmetrical world. Again, it's you that the dangerous honor falls upon. Remember that you'll come back armed with information that will allow us to change what you rebelled against."

"If that's the case…" Rolf said.

CHAPTER XX

Rolf passed through the first laboratory where they gave him a speed treatment. He left cured of both his cold and the measles. Despite his joy, one last surge of revolt jolted him.

"And why not hand out these doses?" he asked the president. "What's stopping you?"

"Try it," the president replied. "You'll see. There's some kind of paralysis of movement and of the tongue that seizes you when you try to act against the system of sickness sentencing. It's like conditioning imprinted before birth."

"But me!" Rolf said. "I did revolt against the system! I wasn't paralyzed."

"You proved to be totally ineffective. If you'd really been effective, you'd have run up against the same thing, believe me. As for me, I wouldn't have been able to keep forcing you onward. Let's go, the method we've conceived is the best."

They went into another lab that was just off the observatory where Rolf had gazed upon the world from the outside.

"Where's the vehicle?" Rolf asked.

"There is no vehicle," a physicist in a white lab coat smiled at him. "Here, behind that screen, is a special place, a node of lines of force."

Rolf saw a screen like the curtain in the entrance of the observatory.

"To come back," the physicist explained, "you orient yourself along the lines of force where you'll always be positioned. You'll easily feel how to harmonize yourself with the lines of force for both directions of the roundtrip."

He stepped aside to let Rolf through.

"Good luck!" the president said.

At the last minute, Rolf wondered whether all this was not just another setup and they were simply going to electrocute him amidst roars of laughter.

"Might as well", he thought to himself.

And he stepped through the ethereal curtain.

He swiveled around, as if orienting himself involuntarily. And right away, he felt stretched out, torn apart. It wasn't painful. Just the feeling of exploding, of being reduced to tiny particles that shot off in every direction at breakneck speed. And yet, he remained himself, a thinking being scattered over the borders of what was no longer a universe.

It was impossible for him to know how long it lasted. Time, also, had lost its smooth flow, cut into sections by seconds and minutes. He felt like time was no longer a river but an ocean. He was floating in time, a duration that couldn't be cut up. Just like space where he was everywhere at once.

And then everything was reorganized. Rolf remained shattered, but no longer like some random mote of dust. He had become like some huge architecture ceaselessly reforming. Immense and complex chains made up its fragments. They broke up and reassembled in different ways. A distant flux brought in other chains while the debris from the former ended up being carried away. This, too, lasted a duration of countless directions. And there was a condensation of Rolf in a single pace in space and time.

He was floating in the void, a black space sparkling with luminous points. He remembered the observatory back where he'd come from. But the closest celestial bodies were fundamentally different from those that inhabited his world. He saw a blinding sun, but it wasn't a round sun like his. I was surrounded by lumps and flames that gushed out as far as its diameter. However, the strangest thing was not the sun. It was the round worlds that it shined on and Rolf saw two specimens in the distance.

He really had arrived in a reverse world where the suns didn't revolve inside of hollow planets but the opposite.

And then he wasn't so sure. What if he was inside a big planet? How would he know? After thinking about it, he decided on the reality of the fist hypothesis. He remembered the comparison between his voyage and the exploration of a finger glove turned inside out. When you reverse a world made up of hollow planets that contain suns within, you get a universe of full planets revolving around suns that are outside of them. Startling but true. Rolf let himself drift in the void.

He doubted that he had become himself again. This was but one stage of the voyage like those long chains perpetually reforming.

The duration, however, felt more familiar, just like the space. As he was thinking this, he tilted suddenly and headed towards a monstrous, black body that he hadn't seen before. He scattered again into a million pieces before reaching it and recomposing right away.

He was standing in a bright light near a bed on which a man was lying. He looked at the face of the man.

It was himself.

This was an illumination. His mind suddenly put the pieces of the puzzle together. He had been dreamed by this man, along with his whole universe. The meaningless words meant something to the dreamer. The false memories belonged to him. Rolf's world was recent only because he'd just started dreaming it, taking into account the difference in the passage of time between the course of the dream and that of his concrete projection. And this feeling of being moved instead of moving? And omnipresence of Rolf, of this sleeping Rolf who had created the other with all his characteristics without knowing it?

Even the voyage is explained, with its passing through the constantly moving chains—these chains were nothing but the long molecules present in the cerebral cells of the dreamer, the physical foundations of the world they were projecting elsewhere, an elsewhere where Rolf had come from directly.

"But why this dream or rather this nightmare?"

"Who are you?" a voice behind Rolf asked.

Rofl turned around. A man in a white lab coat—again!— had just entered the room. He spoke the same language they used on V 30, naturally. Rolf motioned to the man on the bed. Just then, he took notice of the tubes and bottles. The man was sick… And on and on.

"I…" He found what he thought best to say. "I'm his brother."

The lab coat glanced at the man on the bed, then at Rolf, "I admit there's a striking resemblance. But it doesn't explain how you got through the barriers."

"What barriers?" Rolf asked absently.

The man considered this without saying a word. Then, "Where are you coming from?"

Rolf couldn't answer. He evaded the question. "I wanted to see him."

The other kept silent again before saying, "Rolf Leber has no brother. He'll tell you that himself. He's saved. We've beat the coma."

Other men in white coats came into the room. The first one spoke again.

"We're going to proceed with the resuscitation."

Resuscitation … The word sounded to Rolf's ears like a threat. If they awakened the sleeping sick man, they'd interrupt his dream. They'd annihilate a universe. But if they let him die, the same thing would happen. He had to keep him sleeping forever. But also divert the dream so that everything would go better in the world he'd brought to life.

"He… must be having nightmares…," Rolf said haltingly. "Can't you give him… happy dreams?"

The men in white were grouped around Rolf. They stared at him, then looked at each other.

"Happy dreams?" the first one repeated slowly. "No, we can't give him happy dreams. We're in a biological war and he was contaminated. That doesn't make for happy dreams. And, really, we can't do anything but save him. Don't you want us to save… your brother?"

Biological war? Of course. This explained everything in the dream, all Rolf's hardships.

"Yes, sure," Rolf said, searching desperately for something reasonable to say. "But… that's not a reason, is it?"

Everyone looked at him.

"The barriers," the first one said, "are there to keep spies out…" He looked at the others and went on, "And to keep out the mentally disturbed. There are a lot of them around with this war."

"They've infiltrated everywhere," one of the newcomers said.

The first one took one of the syringes lying on the bedside table.

"Would you mind leaving," he asked Rolf flatly.

Rolf grabbed the syringe and threw it on the floor. Then he stomped on it. The plastic broke. Murmuring outrage ensued.

"You don't realize!" Rolf shouted. "You're going to kill off millions of people in the hollow earth!"

"Take him to the manic ward and give him some Thorazine. And bring me another dose of insulin when you come back."

They dragged Rolf down the glossy corridor.

He wouldn't stop yelling, "You've already killed Jana with your damned war and your damned dreams… My little Jana… My little Jana!"

His voice was lost down the corridors of the hospital.

KURT STEINER

LES ENFANTS
DE L'HISTOIRE

FLEUVE NOIR

THE CHILDREN OF HISTORY

CHAPTER I

Iona turned slowly on the bed of pulsed-air to face Silas.

"He's not the only one like this," she said. "If we decided to fight them all, the police wouldn't take long to make the connection. In my opinion, each of us defends himself perfectly well individually when attacked and this give us the advantage of minimizing the investigations."

Silas shook his head and said coldly, "I've every reason in the world to believe that he represents a more general danger. If you refuse, I won't hold it against you. I'd simply get someone else to execute the plan."

"Execute is the right word," Iona replied without smiling. "Can I know these reasons you're talking about?"

Silas thought for a moment. "Nothing really clear," he finally said. "A vague feeling as a result of several confused images. But a feeling strong enough that a serious warning was given to me."

This time Iona smiled. "You know that your 'warnings' (she articulated the word) are not always, how should I put it... genuine."

Silas shrugged his shoulders, "Many of them are. That's enough for me to heed them every time."

She gazed on him without answering. When Silas half-closed his eyelids, he went totally unnoticed in a crowd, any kind of gathering. An unassuming man with no distinguishing features. Now he had his eyes wide open, which he never did in public. The entire room seemed transformed. Iona herself didn't feel completely at ease. And yet, Iona, too, had to conceal her eyes. To react against the kind of spell she was under, she glared at Silas. It was like the battle of two flaming swords.

Silas ended up smiling, "Come here."

She moved closer to him. In this movement, her black hair crackled with tiny red sparks. Deep in the dark of the room, her parted lips revealed her faintly phosphorescent teeth. But Iona turned away.

"Tell me about him," she said.

Over Iona's shoulder Silas was slowly surveying the wall.

"At this moment he's on Boulevard 12. He's wearing a black, very traditional suit: pants tight at the ankles, a single-breasted, baggy coat with black epaulettes. He's also carrying a radiant in his left armpit... and knows how to use it. Don't ask me where his astonishing skill to detect us comes from. He's stopping in front of the Gillis store window. You know the one—Fireworks at Gillis!"

"I know it," Iona said. "What kind of idiot designer came up a slogan like that?"

"It was the director himself. But our man is walking away from the window. He's crossing the street by the underground."

"In fact, what's his name?"

"Alberg."

"What kind of person is he?"

"The worst. A cold and determined man, totally lacking emotion. If you take on the mission, take every precaution possible so that he doesn't catch on to you. He'll snuff you without a moment's hesitation, without giving you the slightest chance."

"Oh," Iona said, "it's not just my teeth... and you know that except in certain circumstances..." She caressed her hip and finished, "...they're nothing special."

"Watch out. His track record is impressive."

"Where does he live?"

"He has no fixed address. He goes from hotel to hotel, always luxurious palaces."

"There's nothing but palaces."

"On Venus I agree with you. And particularly in Aphros. But still, in the suburbs there are some seedy joints where you have to take baths in water. You'll never see him there."

"Tell me about his past."

"I don't know much. He studied business like most people. Then he got into a firm specialized in manipulating other firms where he wrote long reports on the motivations of the seller. His personality didn't fit with the job so he signed up for two years in the *Gun and Murder* training camps. He came out a changed man."

"And since then?"

"Since then, he's been a hunter. It's been three years. He's only been wounded twice. And he's never missed his prey."

Iona turned lazily on the air bed. "So, are you trying to get me to kill him?" she asked ironically.

"That's it," Silas responded. "You guessed it."

He turned her cheek so she would look at him.

"I'm worried," he spoke seriously. "Alberg, with absolute certainty, represents a huge danger. I can't send just anybody after him. And he knows me. You, you've got charm in addition to your... skills as a killer. You know how I'd feel if I lost you. But we're not the only ones involved."

"The air-conditioning's on the blink," Iona said indifferently. "You could suffocate in here."

Despite the blinds that completely covered the big bay window, a little of the hard, Venusian light leaked through. A light that made the clouds green along with the stratospheric shield against ultraviolet and infrared. The gammas were blocked by a forcefield even higher up.

Silas bounded out of bed and went into the electrostatic shower stall. Iona heard his voice crack with controlled irritation.

"I'll take it that you accept. If you decide otherwise, call me. But do it quickly. Right now Alberg's left the underground and is heading to Avenue 34. I'm almost certain he's going to pass by the Temple of Scales. Maybe he'll go in, maybe push on all the way to the Grand Clothes Counter. Either way, there's a good chance that some major event will guide you to him. See you later."

While talking, Silas had dressed. He left the room as silent as a cat. Iona stayed still for a moment, then she got up and took her turn in the electrostatic shower stall.

CHAPTER II

Alberg was walking in the crowd. He was on the look-out. He had detected nothing for two months and his funds were running low. Poverty was frowned upon on Venus. Just like everywhere else, on Mars or on Earth. There was a time when you could adjust your needs to fit your income. It wasn't always nice, it could cause suspicions, but in the end, no one would really find reason to complain. Unlike now when everybody always had substantial needs and had to adjust their incomes accordingly. By hook or by crook.

In fact, this didn't bother Alberg. At other times, his needs had been as great as now, relatively speaking. He'd always had his sights set high. This was partly why he'd so quickly given up the traditional profession of three planets—business. Certainly, they almost always made a fortune, but it took too long. Besides, Alberg found it absurd that entire planets spent their lives circulating products that came from somewhere else. Even more absurd that this activity required theoretical knowledge of the highest order, that he'd made the effort to acquire it but had never had the desire to use it. Completely different was his time spent at *Gun and Murder*. There he had the opportunity to develop his natural talents, perfect them and polish them. When the training was over, some went into space. Alberg became a hired killer.

As he passed by the Temple of Scales, he noticed a man lifting his head and looking into the green sky. It only lasted a second and the man got back on his way. But, after a few steps, he took out of his coat pocket a raincoat, thin as a cloud, and hastily put in on. Alberg followed him, glancing up at the sky. It didn't tell him anything: the sky of Venus was always the same. A green screen, as flat and unbroken as the underside of a lid.

Avenue 34 was full of people who were certainly not just out for a stroll, but who weren't in a hurry either. None of

143

them were wearing raincoats. There, at the end of the street, blazed the sign for the Grand Clothes Counter. The man Albert was following walked quickly along the high walls of the buildings, stretching his back.

The trail lasted a few minutes. The Counter was close now. But before the two men had reached it, a huge, mauve flash of lightning, spectacularly long, streaked across the sky while a deafening roll of thunder reverberated between the buildings. Immediately, drops of burning water, as big as a fist, came crashing down, sounding like a torrent on the streets of Aphros. Such a flood would have turned the city into a lake if it had been built haphazardly. But an extensive system of drainage and runoff had been designed so that the tons of water disappeared accordingly through the countless holes in the sidewalks and roadways. Nevertheless, the storm did have a prompt and deleterious effect on the magnetic motors of the vehicles that broke down by the dozens.

Well protected by his raincoat, the man continued on his way. Alberg took shelter under one of the ugly awnings of fake bronze that are stuck on so many buildings. He threw on his own raincoat, which took up the space of a lighter in his pocket, and got back on the trail. In the meantime, the man had turned around and gotten lost in the crowd.

Alberg hurried his step, unrolling a black hat that he put on his head. His hair was already wet. His whole body was steaming. The warm steam drifting off the sidewalks was shrouding the street in a fog that made it harder and harder to see.

He pushed through a group huddled together under an awning. Just expensively dressed men talking and gesticulating about the variations of the ratings of the scented flabella of Uranus. They cursed him. Alberg turned around momentarily and looked daggers at them. They fell silent.

He was off again, even faster, with his light and springy step, and reached the end of the window of the Counter exactly when the man entered the store. Albert went in after him.

A lighted sign inside lured the attention of the customers: *Here no surprises in the cut, no fraud in the fabric. All our mannequins are catatons!*

Despite his ice-cold, hard-set temperament, Alberg felt a little shiver run through him. Everyone knew what a cataton was. A convict who had gone through the schizotron. The schizotron used radiation to cause a mental illness: schizophrenia. But this illness, appearing instantly, developed to its final stage during the radiation treatment. Which made them catatonic in less than an hour. Muscular rigidity with total loss of communication between the subject and the outside world. A cataton made a perfect mannequin: it struck any pose desired by the buyer or seller and it didn't move. Moreover, it was still a human being with a beating heart and breathing lungs, in short, ideal for displaying clothes.

What made Alberg jittery was that the sentence could very well be carried out on him some day. In fact, this kind of punishment had been designed for hunters who missed their prey. Of course, if he made such a mistake and an order was given to bring him in, he'd be informed in advance—and there'd better be plenty of police coming to arrest him. He'd leave a massacre before being brought down. But, in the end, they'd take him alive and send him through the schizotron. Bah! He'd never made a mistake and the more experience he got, the less likely were his chances of doing so.

Unfortunately, his prey here had melted into the crowd that was milling around inside the store. Alberg went down the middle, keeping an eye on the other aisles. Halfway down he glanced between two displays, one of them with a pile of flower wigs, the other with transistorized shoes that would put themselves away in a closet as soon as the owner took them off. They were also selling the transmitters tuned to the shoes' wavelengths—heavy, bulky devices that you couldn't put anywhere but without which the shoes were useless.

Between these displays, Alberg saw a man with a slightly curved back who was fiddling with the objects on a third stand. The individual was not wearing a raincoat, so he must have taken it off when he entered the store. Alberg was sure it was the guy he was following on the street. Something put all his senses on alert: the objects he was examining were working radiants.

The radiants were sold openly, but no one ever used them. It was a step too far. Except in the case of Alberg who was paid handsomely for his head count.

The man looked disinterested, didn't seem to realize that he was being watched. But Alberg wasn't fooled. Something told him that he was dealing with someone on high alert. There wasn't one second that went by without the guy having a radiant in his hand, pretending to examine it. If Albert made a move toward his left shoulder, the guy would take him down instantly. The hunt was not easy because he was always after a formidable prey. This one hadn't looked at him even once, but Alberg was sure that the guy saw every movement he made.

Alberg continued down the aisle and turned quickly to get to the next and go back. When he got to the radiant display, the man had vanished.

Had he stolen a radiant before leaving? Highly unlikely. The police had the right to search anyone on the street and no one was allowed to carry weapons except certain people like Alberg. When someone was caught carrying a radiant, they were slapped with exile without bothering even to go through the courts. And life on the three planets was too cushy for anyone to want to leave them... especially for a destination in exile. It was, however, to this destination that a lot of brains went and voluntarily. But the brains were a very special fraction of the population just like the natural men and the children. Alberg was dealing with another category altogether— they were seldom sent away.

Temporarily thwarted, Alberg wandered around for a little while. He was counting on his intuition to pick up the trail again.

He was familiar with the Clothes Counter. He knew it had no other exit than the main entrance. He was prepared, as a last resort, to watch the entrance until closing. Calculating the time he'd taken to get back to the radiant display, he figured it was impossible for the man to have left without him seeing.

Alberg briefly reflected on the age when stores needed emergency exits in case of a fire. Today, everyone had oxidant pills in case of accidental suffocation. A fire broke out? They sucked out all the oxygen in the place with powerful reducers while the crowd dealt with the lack of oxygen by taking a pill. In an instant, the flames were extinguished and the reducers were retracted into their housing. Then they blew in hyperbaric oxygen.

The hunter turned his back to the giant doors and fixed his attention on the people crowding around the aisles in the back of the store. The bright light made everything visible—even distant faces could be seen clearly, though the distance didn't bother Alberg since he had very sharp eyes.

He located the man who was trying to hide behind a stack of canned goods. In front of the pyramid was a sign: *Buy Earth air. Price based on locale and quantity. Be careful of the pressure in the cans!*

He sauntered over toward the special display but made a detour that brought him behind the man. He didn't turn around. Alberg watched him scrutinizing the can and took note of the gloves with abnormally thick fingers. He stepped up and slipped his hand under his coat. The guy still had his back turned.

As Albert was pulling out his radiant, the man swung around, lightning-quick. He was holding a can, which he popped open as he leaned back against a pillar. The jet of air struck Alberg full in the chest, lifting him off the ground. Alberg fell on his back, rolled over and fired just as the guy was running away. Hit between two strides, the prey fell without a sound.

Alberg got up calmly amidst the crowd that was gathering. A few outcries from some women, but most of them just looked at Alberg inquisitively. He went over to his victim, whose heart was stopped dead by the radiant. Before the curious eyes of the circle of spectators, he pulled off one of the gloves of the corpse. A murmur of astonishment ran through the crowd: the fingers were stuffed so they'd all have the same thickness, except for the first, which had two index fingers.

Alberg walked through the crowd that parted before him. A mixture of revulsion and respect enveloped him. He picked out an axe from the tool section nearby, came back and chopped off the hand with six fingers. Someone turned their back and threw up. But the hunter had already taken the rain-coat out of the victim's pocket and was using it to wrap up the evidence.

At that very moment, a man in an orange and black uni-form appeared. His boots were the first thing that Albert, still on his knees, saw. He looked up and without a word showed him the open raincoat.

"Yes," the police officer said, "I believe it's unquestion-able. But please come with me to the Commandery to proceed with the required chromosomic verification... Mr.? "Alberg."

The officer smiled ambiguously, "Oh, it's you, Mr. Al-berg? Congratulations! Your reputation travels far. Will you come?"

"After you," Alberg said.

They headed for the exit. The crowd dispersed from around the corpse. A robot coffin slid up to the inert body, evaporated the blood and enclosed the corpse. Then it left.

"What happened?" asked someone who had not seen anything.

"Oh, nothing. Another one of those filthy mutants was shot down," another responded.

CHAPTER III

As they left, Alberg asked the police officer to make a detour through the main part of the store since the area around the entrance had only a few things on the annex shelves.

Thus, they went between two rows of catatons dressed in different outfits from a simple sex sack to a pressured suit. Some mannequins wore evening clothes made of glittering fabric, others mesh resistant to hard radiation for working on asteroids deprived of oxygen, but without particle shields. The mesh was only for resale because no inhabitant of the three planets ever worked on the surface of asteroids, needless to say…

Alberg also passed a row of catatons whose customers were lifting their arms or shifting their legs to see how the fabric looked while moving. Some of the unconscious female bodies wore night gowns that covered only their limbs. There were more men than women in this arae, some of whom were picking up the catatons and moving them around to see the ethereal fabric in better light, or so they claimed. The department managers were at their beck and call. Alberg didn't slow down. His eyes were staring ahead, empty and cold. He just wanted to comfort himself with the grim sight of a state that he would not be sentenced to… at least not this time.

Once the detour was made, he left the store with the police officer. Outside, the storm had moved away. The green sky of Venus was serene again. A few clouds of steam were still floating over the sidewalks but that was all. Alberg thought of the mutant he'd just killed and completely ignored the gorgeous girl with brown hair whom everyone seemed to know and who crossed his path.

What luck that the guy had made the mistake of showing his gift of divination in meteorology or rather his electrical sensitivity of the approaching clouds. And double luck that the finger malformation corroborated his first impression. In the

149

past, surely, you could've seen such malformations on people who were not mutants in any way, but things had changed. Structured biology had eliminated all congenital malformations and those that appeared now were always a result of transmissible mutation linked to the existence of other mutational characteristics: in the present case it was a matter of sensing electricity.

"It was also a matter of something else," Alberg thought. It was obvious that the prey picked up on his tail. It was also obvious that he realized what was happening behind his back: that can of air had almost saved his life. Alberg wondered whether the official propaganda might not be right in proclaiming that the mutants are becoming more and more dangerous, more and more inhuman. If so, the chase would be riskier every day and the younger mutants would be more menacing.

The Commandery sat in the center of Aphros. To reach it Alberg and the officer got in a police car painted black and orange —the colors of Venus. Behind them the pretty brunette got into her own car as a crowd of admirers blew her kisses and waved.

But Iona took a different route to get to the Commandery. Even if Alberg had not acknowledged her existence— though he knew her like everyone did—the police officer hadn't failed to notice her. And she knew where they were going.

At the Commandery Albert was immediately taken to the captain who supervised the extermination department. The trophy was sent by magnetic tube to the microcellular biological labs where an automatic examination was going to be made in short order.

"Mr. Alberg," the captain said, "while waiting for the results I have to warn you that even though our department is still called 'Extermination', this name is less and less representative of reality. Our investigating teams, following the directives of the Senate, will henceforth endeavor to capture mutants alive for study and material use. In addition, and with all due respect to your talents, I have to bring to your attention the reduction of the premium on corpses and the increase for live captures."

Alberg furrowed his brow. "That wasn't communicated anywhere," he said coldly. "I keep well enough up-to-date on the laws concerning my profession to know."

"No doubt, no doubt," the captain sounded a little uneasy, "but political reasons are preventing us from publishing these decisions. Let's keep this between us and say I'm telling you as a personal favor. Of course, and for this time only, the premium..."

He broke off. A piece of paper had just slid out of a slot in his desk. He took it and skimmed over it. The lab results. Despite his certainty, Alberg felt a new shiver run down his back.

But the captain nodded and put the paper down to continue, "... will be paid at the regular rate."

He pressed a button and a file came out of the wall.

"Here's the sum total of the premium in Venusian sollars plus the fees calculated for an average two weeks of research minus the senatorial taxes. So, 42,800 sollars."

"The taxes have gone up," Alberg remarked as coldly as ever.

"You're complaining," the captain forced a smile, "my pay is 3,500 sollars."

"But you get that every month," Alberg was unmoved.

"Fortunately," the captain replied. "Otherwise I'd be working on trade promotion with Mars, even though I'm not very fond of the people you meet there."

"I don't know Mars," Alberg said indifferently.

"It's a very hard planet," the captain explained.

"Everyone knows that."

"Yes, but what you probably don't know is that the capture of a live mutant is not all appreciated there but the premiums paid for killing them are triple what they pay here."

Alberg pricked up his ears. "I thought it was on Earth that they paid the highest."

"In between," the captain said. "We're all influenced by the Senate on Earth, but Venus is more liberal than Earth whereas Mars is more... how should I put it..."

"Tyrannical," Alberg offered flatly.

The captain made a gesture as if to push away the too harsh word, "Come now, Mr. Alberg, no bad words."

"We're already not on the best of terms with Mars..." Alberg stood up to show that the conversation was over.

"I'll get you a ride back. You can get your premium in accounting. You know the way."

He showed Alberg to the door of his office and shook his hand. The handshake of a businessman, an administrator. Alberg wanted nothing more to do with him.

After pocketing his pay Alberg left the Commandery. He had no intention of depositing his money in the General Bank of Venus where the money was used for the most unpredictable investments. He had no need of interest, which would involve him, in one way or another, in commercial activities that he'd learned to hate during his brief engagement at The Firm for Manipulating Firms. On the contrary, he had no fear of carrying big sums on his person. He smiled on thinking of the fate in store for anyone planning to relieve him of his money.

The light turned to emerald—evening was coming. Alberg decided to relax a little by catching a quick show. Three blocks from the Commandery, slender plasma lettering danced brightly on a façade: "The Saga of Soap". It was the Aphros Opera. He headed for it.

Parked 50 feet away, Iona's magnetocar drove off slowly. She had polarized the windows to attract as little attention as possible. But she didn't have far to go. On seeing Alberg enter the theater she parked again, got out and bought a ticket.

The show had already started. She pretended to choose a seat at random, which happened to be right next to Alberg. And she sat down.

CHAPTER IV

Big bubbles were bouncing off the stage to the sound of synthetic music that sounded like splashing water. Inside each bubble was a naked girl sprinkled with glitter. Backstage a chorus of men dressed in gold suits was chanting the story of soap.

The phosphorescent program they had given the audience placed the ballet in the second scene. The subject of the first apparently covered the black soap and the mineral soap. At cleverly variable intervals, old production curves were projected onto the actors, along with images of balance sheets and invoices.

The third scene came on, dedicated to washing detergents with and without foam. A transparent wall rose up on the forestage, enclosing a huge aquarium that was filled in an instant. Other naked girls swam in it without oxygen equipment—they'd swallowed a few oxidant pills, which allowed them to stay underwater without breathing for a long time.

A discharge of foam overflowed down to the first rows. Then big blades started rotating in the back of the aquarium, each carrying its obligatory naiad and the foam sank like a cold soufflé. A quartet of electronic trumpets started the grand finale that ended in a massive din of drainage.

During the fourth scene, which sang the praises of the modern electrostatic shower and showed a man covered in mud who was cleaned in the blink of an eye by a sheet of fragrant emissions, Iona's foot brushed against Alberg's leg. He glowered at her.

"Oh, sorry," she whispered.

He looked at her more closely when the shower lit up the hall and his eyes flickered a little.

"Haven't I seen you on the 3-D TV?" he asked blandly.

"But of course," Iona smiled without showing her teeth.

"What show was it now?"

"Scary stories for children," she said. "I host it, tell stories, illustrate them and such."

"Oh, yes, I remember. I saw one episode." He finally smiled and added, "I was almost scared."

"Everyone gets scared," she said even more softly because people were starting to complain. "Only the children laugh."

"That's true," Alberg admitted. "Children are really disturbing."

"And we're not talking about those filthy mutants," Iona said. "Just normal children."

"Right," Alberg agreed. "We're not talking about those filthy mutants."

He felt no hatred against mutants. They were just a healthy source of income for him. But he didn't like talking about work in a place meant for entertainment.

The show ended with a ballet of multicolored emissions accompanied by a piece of astral music, the latest and trendiest. The Opera emptied out slowly. Alberg left with Iona.

Night had fallen. Onto the ever-present clouds powerful projectors cast publicity slogans by the hundreds. But one warning was bigger than all: "Watch out, mutants!"

On reading this, Iona thought she saw "Watch out, hunters!" Why had she been so careful not to reveal her teeth when she had smiled in the darkness of the hall? Usually she acted ice-cold with everyone. This more often caused amusement among her admirers, for whom she was inaccessible and who used this to build a personality fitting the stories she told on the 3-D. It was only with Silas that she stepped out of her coldness. Only with him did she feel those emotional troubles that caused her teeth to glow like other girls blushed. She was a mutant and three planets were intimately familiar with her face and her voice, taking her for a normal human. What would happen to her if the first hunter she met aroused something inside her to the point that she was afraid she'd give herself away?

This mission had to wrap up quickly. Otherwise, Alberg would unmask her before she eliminated him. In point of fact, he wasn't the first hunter she'd met but he might be the most dangerous. Even before her fear of revealing her true nature, she had already made the mistake of showing herself near him in public. She started wondering if her anxiety wasn't a sign of something else: it was certain that this merciless killer had made her slip not from fear but from attraction. Being attracted to the most sworn enemy of her race! She repressed a shudder and started forming a plan.

Alberg looked up and chuckled, "Between us, do you think the filthy mutants are as dangerous as they say?"

"Be careful of what you say," she answered without turning her head. "They could accuse you of aiding and abetting."

Albert chuckled again. He suddenly felt cheerful. This girl really knew what you're not supposed to say.

"Do you know who you're talking to?"

"I've probably seen your 3-D somewhere," she tried not to compromise herself.

"Certainly. I believe I'm almost as famous as you. In fact, I'm a hunter."

"Oh!" she sounded scared.

"So, you see why this idea of aiding and abetting is funny to me."

She laughed in turn, but a little forced as befit a weak woman frightened by a bloodthirsty profession. "I understand..."

"No, you don't really understand. I'll go back to what I asked before: are mutants as dangerous as they claim? This means that although, on the one hand, they might be enemies strong enough to take me down some day, they might not necessarily be enemies of the human race like everybody's shouting from the rooftops. The only reason it's hard to believe I could be their accomplice is that, from that point on, I'd cut myself off from my income. That's all."

"You like money a lot..." she said.

"And you, do you hate it. How much do you earn per show?"

"You're being indiscreet, Mr..."

"Alberg, Ms..."

"Iona. Seven million sollars."

"And you do how many shows per month?"

"Two, often three."

"Well, well. That's not so bad. A mutant head brings me around 40,000 sollars. And it's my head on the line."

"Alberg!" Iona spurted out. "Of course, Alberg!"

"At your service. Do you know that I'm prepared to ask you to dinner? I just took down a guy who could forecast the weather. In my opinion, that didn't deserve a death sentence, but now my wallet is fat."

Iona hesitated a moment. First of all, she'd already been seen with Alberg, so a dinner wouldn't change anything. Then again, getting him to spend the earnings from killing a mutant was repulsive to her. But it was to cleanse Venus of this mob of hunters.

"All right," she said.

Deep down she thought of Silas like a stranger. For some time now she was pulling away from him. Physically, sure, she was still attracted, but her heart, so to speak, not so much. This didn't mean that her heart was at the mercy of a ruthless enemy—or only money, which came to the same thing. She convinced herself that she wasn't putting the mission at risk. Whatever her relationship with Silas, he was right to entrust her with it.

"Do you want to go to the Tower Spindles?"

"Oh, but Alberg, it's exorbitant."

"Nah, it's a celebration."

This person was kind of hideous with his cynicism and vulgarity, Iona told herself. But, really, was he any worse than the rest of the people who lived off of endless, scientific haggling over the goods and commodities dropped off by the space cargoes? Of course, there were also natural men, disturbingly pure, and children, no less disturbingly depraved.

Iona decided that the only pleasant social category was that of the mutants, which she was part of.

And then, really, you could see that behind Alberg's cynicism was a certain lack of moral comfort. He repeated too often that the mutants didn't deserve their fate for him not to feel a vague sense of guilt every time he killed one of them. "No one is as bad as you think," she mused inwardly. And also, "No one is as good as he believes himself to be..."

The restaurant was located at the top of a 2,500 foot tower. Access was by a magnetic elevator that passed through magnetized rings—each ring passed thrust the cage up to the next ring that pulled it just as strongly. To go down only the repellant poles were activated. This produced a very fast, steady movement whose acceleration at the start and deceleration at the end was not unreasonably jerky.

The elevator brought them to a big, dark hall whose walls were decorated with sparse lighting and many mirrors. In one mirror Iona saw her teeth glowing very faintly. She forced herself to think of Alberg as a monster with a heart of stone, but this only brightened the glow. So, she let herself be washed over with a wave of pity for him, the irresponsible and tortured product of an aggressive society. In an instant she saw in the mirror just an ordinary face, although sublimely beautiful. A smile revealed white teeth, no sign of a glimmer. From now on she knew what she had to do to fight against the outward expression of her emotions.

Alberg let her enter the restaurant first. A round room where three curved glass walls looked out upon the dark clouds in the night. The rest of the walls were full of constantly changing slogans and the tables were arranged to face a central platform reserved for the 3-D TV.

"Let's sit there," Alberg chose a particularly well exposed table.

As they were heading for the table, the very formal maître d', wearing a cold and haughty look on his face, blocked their way.

"This table is taken, sir," he sneered. "Please follow me, I'll take you to a table."

Alberg turned to Iona and said aloud, "Don't you think this maître d' is a little funny looking?"

"Oh, do you think so?" Iona answered in a sharp and snobbish voice. "It's true that you see them everywhere, those filthy…"

"Come now," Alberg cut her off, "we can't prove anything. Let's be reasonable… Only, I just killed one, so…"

Half the room was staring at the maître d' who had abruptly lost his pompous attitude and was peering around like a hunted animal. Without saying anything more, Alberg stepped in front of him and sat Iona at the table. Then he sat down himself. Just then the platform lit up and the 3-D image of a garish character appeared, drawing everybody's attention. The maître d' leaned over the table:

"If that was a joke, sir," he spoke moderately, "I think it was going a little far…"

Alberg regarded him dubiously, "I'm still not sure. You know, I know them well. I'll keep an eye on you. Give me the menu in the meantime."

No one talked about the table reservation after that and the dinner began: dragonfly fritters, filet of giant lobster, pterix liver in its ink, mango sorbet. Everything washed down with wine that had aged a long time in space.

On the 3-D TV they were showing the election of the new Ludocrat of Venus, replacing the one who had just died.

"I wonder why there are always two Ludocrats per planet," Alberg said. "There could be 50 of them and they'd have no more influence on the politics of the Senate."

"Hm," Iona said. "Don't forget that they're elected by the children, whom they speak for, and they have the power to dissolve the Senate. The children regularly send me a lot of mail that I have to read and answer. You were saying before that they're disturbing. They're worse than that. They're powerful. And since the Ludocrats are their direct agents…"

"It's funny, everyone considers the Ludocrats as unimportant…"

"You know I'm a terrian. They know me everywhere only because of the interplanetary broadcasts, of course. Well, believe me, the children of Earth are not the same as here. Nor are the Ludocrats. Everything is different, starting with the Senate. Is there here on Venus a head of the Senate as violent as Dorf? And the opposition, is it led by a man of Garon's stature?"

"I've heard that on Mars…"

"Mars is in the hands of the army," Iona cut him off, feeling warm from the wine. "Senate and Ludocrats are just puppets and they recruit children starting at eight years old. Even over there they're weird and dangerous."

Alberg stayed quiet, watching her. Usually, he paid as much attention to a woman as to a chair or a table. "This woman," he told himself, "knows about everything and she has personal opinions."

The 3-D TV was showing only part of the election, which took place over several days. The candidates came one by one in front of the cameras. They included entertainers, teachers, parents, gang leaders, soldiers and police officers. Some of them, bold and provocative, played the mutant, the natural man or the brain because they claimed that the children were particularly interested in these elements. Of course, those who played the mutant had to go through a chromosomic test to prove that they were really human.

Thus the election was going through round after round until only one candidate remained. He would become Ludocrat! Alberg knew all this, basically. But Iona riddled the broadcast with comparisons with the habits and reactions of Earth, which ended up making him uncomfortable. Alberg was glad he didn't have to chase terrian children.

The show was interrupted shortly before the end by a special interplanetary message followed by a brief report on an attack: someone had tried to kill the terrian opposition leader.

"Again!" Iona said.

"Yes, I've heard something about them trying to kill Garon a few times already."

"More than ten times! He always survives. He says its justice and righteousness that deflects the assassin's hand…"

"Yeah," Alberg said, "He has something."

"No one knows… Anyway, Dorf uses it to say the opposition doesn't represent the will of the people and Garon insinuates that it's Dorf who's arming the fanatics."

"Birds of a feather," Alberg commented, "and the people too. First of all, where are the people? All the fattened businessmen? The ones who pay me to kill mutants because they don't have the courage to do it themselves? Is that the people?"

"No," Iona said, "they exist but nobody talks about them. They're not here."

Alberg shrugged his shoulders, "Well done. You just have to scrape by to get everyone talking about you."

"It's not that easy. A lot of people don't react like a single individual."

"And the natural men? Now there's a name! What does it mean? These guys in beards preaching to give up technology and go back to a normal life?"

"That's all they can think of to react."

"React against what? Against an easy life, free-flowing money, luxurious apartments and six months of vacation a year for everyone?"

"They say the human race has degenerated, that the mutants are going to take their place."

"Bah, there's still the brains. Some of them could stand up to the mutants."

"The brains are leaving. They're as fed up with the lifestyle on the three planets as the children and the natural men."

"Good, let them go. As long as there are mutants around, I'll manage. I'm not a degenerate."

Iona looked at him with horror. Alberg's eyes crossed hers and he stared at her curiously. Then his expression froze.

"Why are your teeth glowing?" he asked in a flat voice.

CHAPTER V

Iona felt a chill down her back. Why hadn't she killed him in the street, when she saw him at the entrance to the Clothes Counter? It would've been so easy! No, she had to devise a complicated plan to meet him so they could be alone when she struck, so she could bid him farewell from Silas, whom he had once tried to kill but failed. Why did Silas matter? Now she was going to have to kill him here in the middle of a restaurant. If not, he was going to strike her down without incurring the wrath of the law. And he would get another 40,000 sollars to boot.

But something was blocking his decision. And yet, it was so simple. No. She heard herself muttering:

"It's my toothpaste."

She took courage looking at his stony face.

"You know the spray 'Fire' from Arnold's? It leaves a shiny trace on your teeth."

"The spray 'Fire' from Arnold's?" he repeated. His voice sounded like a hushed croak. He had put both hands on the table. Iona knew that he could grab his radiant in a split second. She also knew that she could kill him even faster. She could... No, actually, she couldn't.

He leaned over to her and whispered, "Close your mouth. Other people might notice this anomaly."

More than just leaning back, she collapsed against the back of the chair. However, she managed to pant, "Oh, I'm not afraid of anything from anybody…"

"Let's get out of here," he said, paying no mind to her pathetic response. "The maître d' might be vindictive."

He tossed a 1,000 sollar bill on the table and stood up. Iona did the same. The intangible image of a game show host twitched on the platform. No one noticed the couple leaving.

They said nothing to each other in the elevator. Alberg hailed a magnetocab at the foot of the tower and they both got in. Iona didn't mention her own magnetocar. She was giving up.

The taxi took quite a long time to get from the Spindles to Alberg's hotel. They stayed silent, gazing distractedly at the busy, evening traffic made heavier by the carnival of advertisers that cluttered the streets of Aphros. It was a special promotion for Lease-Sell Week. Bellboys, gofers, traveling salesmen, reps and sandwich boards were running around the magnetocab and throwing colorful leaflets into the car. Contract peddlers were waving their merchandise on the corners in front of improvised orchestras that drown the streets in fanfares of astral music. On the sidewalks the pedestrians bustled around with happy faces. Business was booming.

Alberg got out first, paid the taxi and opened the sliding door for Iona. Her mind was so muddled that she was unsurprised by Alberg's courtesy. She got out and followed him into the hotel. When they got into his darkened room, her teeth reflected brightly in the window, which was shut off from the exterior by shutters.

With a wave of Alberg's hand the room lit up. He turned to Iona and spoke very softly.

"They sent you to kill me, didn't they?" The question was rhetorical.

"Yes," Iona had completely lost her self-control.

"Now I vaguely remember having seen you in front of the Counter. I guess you couldn't do anything there. But, coming out of the Opera, we passed by a dark, deserted-looking alley. That was your chance."

She managed to hide from him the fact that she could have easily killed him on the busy street in front of the Counter and it would have been impossible to pin the murder on her.

"I don't know," she said, "I balked."

Alberg's face darkened, "Me too, I balked. It's the first time. I have to say I just got paid and I don't like to work when I've got money."

A thin smile crossed his angular face. His pale eyes narrowed. "Not bad, us as a couple, in the restaurant. A cat sleeping with a trapped mouse. It must be pretty rare for a hunter to go out strolling with a mutant."

He started to laugh heartily. "What really kills me is that the people on the three planets applaud you all the time. If the adults found out what you are, some of them would drop dead on the spot. As for the children, half of them would help the hunted mutants..."

He shook his head. "...which wouldn't make my job any easier."

He looked her over from head to toe and put an arm around her waist. Only one, the left. His right hand stayed poised for the radiant. Instantly, red sparks starting crackling in Iona's hair.

"Look at that," he said. "You never know what to expect. There aren't two of you who are alike. I wonder what else you have in store."

Iona closed her eyes and let herself fall into his arms. She whispered very softly, "That's for you find out."

She shivered. Alberg raised his hand to her black hair. The red sparks jumped at his fingers and he felt a little tingling. But he kept his guard up. "Do you think I'm going to bring you in bound hand and foot?" he said.

She drew back, narrowed her eyes, clenched her fists and raised her voice, "You still don't understand." Then more slowly, "If I haven't killed you yet, it's because I can't do it. I want you alive, not your corpse."

Behind his cold mask Alberg felt his apathy crumbling to dust. After all, he'd taken so many risks but not just to get hold of a volcanic female. Women, obviously, were of no great interest, but his one here!

He started to undress her. She had a brown body, slender and shapely with long muscles. Naked, it became obvious that she didn't belong to the human species. He led her to the air bed. On the way he tossed his radiant on the low table and went all in.

163

CHAPTER VI

Lying on the air bed, Iona gazed at Alberg. She remembered times when, like this very afternoon, she was with Silas. Obviously, Alberg didn't have the resources of Silas, but she excused him for a certain clumsiness resulting from his constant solitude because it was this solitary characteristic, not too prone to emotional outbursts, that attracted her.

"What are you going to do now?" Alberg asked.

She made something up on the spot. "I've still got a few days free before my next show and I have to go to Mars to research the reactions of the children over there."

In truth, she really wanted to leave Venus for a while to put off her next meeting with Silas, which was bound to be stormy. Alberg, whose ears pricked up at the name of Mars—like in the Extermination Department—thought he might take the trip with her. Time was nothing with the Spaceless Tunnel and she'd be gone before he started searching for another prey. That was better…

"Look here," he said, "I mean to come with you."

She glanced at him. She had no desire to leave tonight. On the other hand, it was awkward and dangerous to walk around with a man who could bring out, just by his presence, her mutant features. She thought about it. Then again, on a planet as hard as Mars, it might be helpful for her to have a hunter at her side. It would divert suspicions. She searched for more reasons to justify a trip together but couldn't find any. She decided that what she had was enough.

"All right," she said, "if you don't see any problems…"

"We'll go together," Alberg decided.

He knew that what he was doing was as wrong as could be, but his habit of living dangerously kept him unconcerned. Iona, too, could be cold and calculating, but the present moment was rushing her toward a future that she didn't want to imagine.

"How long has the Spaceless been in service on the solar lines?" Alberg asked.

"Oh, 50 earth years or so," Iona said. "Before, it was already used on interstellar routes but it consumed so much energy that it was never used for freight."

"Oh, right, I remember. Faster-than-light cargo took years. It's strange how we forget things we don't use and don't think much about."

Iona refrained from telling him that she never forgot anything and that she sometimes found things in her memory that she could swear she'd never learned. This thought reminded her that Silas could track the movements of people miles away. The next meeting would be stormy because he would know everything she did and everywhere she went, every minute of the day and night.

"Yes," she said, "it's like personal memories..."

"Oh, that's even worse," Alberg said. "Except from your childhood..."

"That was a good memory for you?"

"There were 15 of us. We fought. In eight years, three of us were dead. On my tenth birthday, I broke my father's nose with an iron bar. He tried to get me executed but the Ludocrat vetoed it and he was the one put in prison. It's true, in fact, that the Ludocrats do serve a purpose."

"I see," Iona replied. "Among the mutants, the family is artificial. We have a lot fewer children and we put them together under the supervision of a few couples to look like a human family and not attract attention. But mutant children are as dangerous as others. I myself sowed terror."

"How did you all end up so calm?" Alberg asked without realizing the scope of his question.

"We're not calm. You spend your time murdering my race and even though I'm with you tonight, I started out to kill you. And your father, who was hoping to execute you because you'd hit him? Do you think adults are calm?"

"Well, I don't know. I see all the businessmen, the retailers, the traders, the developers, the publicists and marketers... okay, they're sharks, but they don't kill each other."

"They kill through a third party. They're children who put on gloves as they get older."

Alberg considered this for a moment. He wasn't used to talking about such subjects. Finally, he said, "What madness to have so many children!"

"And the colonization of foreign planets? Who would do it? You know we have to pass a series of terribly difficult tests to stay on one of the three planets and become a cog in the wheels of commerce. You have to go through that to be able to branch out later. Everyone who's been washed up here had to head out at 15 years old for foreign worlds..."

"According to my tests, it seems I could've become a brain. But I didn't want to spend ten years in the monasteries of physics and biology."

"It would've been better for you than becoming an assassin. Okay, let's talk about something else."

"Yes, it'd be better."

They kept silent for a long time, keeping their distance as well. It was Alberg who spoke again first.

"Bah, we're going to leave each other soon. No bickering. It's been so long since I met a girl like you. In fact, I've never met a girl like you. Too bad it hadn't been earlier..."

Iona shook her head, "I don't understand myself... How could I have acted like that? I deserve to die."

Alberg put his arm under her head. "I won't be the one to do it," he smiled nervously. "I'll let your brother mutants do it. To hell with the money."

She snuggled into his arms without answering. Outside, the carnival was raging. Through the shutters filtered the multi-colored lights from the glowing balloons they let fly over Aphros and they heard the shrill cries of the magnetic birds launched from the ground against the balloons. Every time a balloon popped, it released a small parachute holding a microphone and a giant voice boasting the merits of a food preservative by radiation or maybe the effectiveness of a rejuvenating cream.

Iona fell asleep in Alberg's arms as he lay for a long time with his eyes open in the darkness striped by rainbows.

CHAPTER VII

The buildings of the Spaceless stood on the edge of the Aphros Astroport. When Alberg and Iona got out of the magnetocab (Iona thought it better to cancel her magnetocar rental) a huge cargo ship was crossing the cloud cover and drifting towards the runway, slowed down by its magnetic circuits. It had obviously stopped the faster-than-light propulsion long before entering the solar system. Alberg imagined the hundreds of thousands of tons of merchandise it was going to dump on the land. All this merchandise would be bought and resold several times before they consumed part of it and destroyed the rest.

On the tree-lined avenue that led to the Spaceless, they ran into a group of Martian tourists who had just come through the tunnel. They were all dressed in identical outfits, with flattops, and walked in close formation behind a Venusian guide who gave them long-winded explanations with the help of a mini throat microphone.

Alberg and Iona made no comment as they passed by and went straight to the entrance office of the Spaceless where a clerk stamped their passports and handed them the gravity soles they would be needing on Mars.

"I don't think you'll be staying long," he told them, "but the visa doesn't expire, mind you."

They thanked him. The ticket booths were nearby. The trip cost 3,000 sollars, but Iona insisted on paying for her own ticket.

The cabin was around 40 feet long and half as wide. It was already full of chatty Venusians and silent Martians. Two Venusian businessmen—pioneers in trade with Mars—were discussing the respective merits, profitwise, of both the Spaceless network and the development of imports resulting from the extension of the cargo lines.

"My friend," one of them said, "the tunnel beyond space speeds up communications so much that without it nothing we know could ever see the light of day."

"No doubt," the other responded, "but the investments needed for such a network and the immobilization of energy it required put a stop to the expansion of lightweight consumption for three centuries…"

"There's some truth to that, but with these two opposing factors, the solution to the problem was found by stimulating scientific technology, which had stalled for centuries."

"Obviously. The hemorrhaging of the brains."

"Yes, Venus trained a bunch of them, but let them leave. The Earth trains fewer, but tries to keep them, without much success. And Mars trains practically none. We're headed for disaster. Our governments lack both determination and discernment."

He lowered his voice but Alberg listened carefully.

"I'm not sure it all doesn't come from the sabotage perpetrated by the filthy mutants."

"Right, I don't think the economy is healthy, but the word is that there are a lot of mutants among the brains. You know about the right to asylum in the science monasteries. Some mutants take refuge there, churn up their minds and urge them to leave."

"That's certainly true. But they should crack down on the natural men, too, who have got a lot bigger audience than you'd believe among the feeble minds. In trade they're bringing in resistance, sliminess, contempt and disinterest… It's serious…"

He was interrupted by the loudspeaker:

"Attention! Stay clear of the doors. Prepare for departure."

A red light turned on in the ceiling of the cabin and a bell started ringing. The walls seemed to vanish. 50 men were as still as statues, suspended in the middle of a dark void. Only the red light over their heads was a reminder of their contact with the universe. But this contact was tangible so dramatically that it looked more like a threat. A few muffled conversations restarted among the regulars of the Spaceless. The others couldn't help thinking of the accidents—rare, it's true—that happened on other lines. Three quarters of the passengers could simply just disappear. The others would make it to their destination, but they were missing parts of their bodies. The descriptions they'd given of the blood-stained cabins were enough to give you nightmares.

What made it worse was that the cabin had become like a bubble outside of space and time was disrupted, undergoing variations in the regularity of its flow, which resulted in a sudden acceleration of speech or a slowing down of watches whose second hands stood almost motionless. Besides this, no sensation of movement, no tremors. The cabin, in reality, was going nowhere because it was passing through non-space, but it rematerialized at the end of the line, which could be hundreds of light years away after being dematerialized at the departure. Once again, these terms, materialization and dematerialization, only meant something to an outside observer. Inside, the red light was enough to show that matter and energy still existed for anyone who might doubt the reality of their body.

With this disturbance of time, it was obviously impossible to understand how long the trip took. What mattered was the measure of it by an outside observer. The Independent Company of the Spaceless (whose budget alone was as much as a planet's) gave it an equivalent of two earth hours, no matter what stations it departed from or arrived at.

The red light soon turned to orange, then yellow, then green. Just then the bell rang again, followed by the speaker. The voice seemed to come from nowhere.

"Attention, keep away from the doors… Arrival is imminent…"

The walls became visible, but the passengers remained motionless. A few were leaning on one leg or the other, but, truthfully, the trip had not been tiring. No more than if it had lasted only a minute or two. That's why the Company saved on seats, tables, flight attendants and snacks…

The doors slid open. The passengers stepped casually onto the spongy cement of the Arespolis Astroport. It was a dark night but something bright was lighting up the vicinity.

At the exit, Alberg and Iona heard screams. They stopped to see where they came from.

50 yards away stood a column on top of which a bluish white, infernally bright spotlight was slowly turned round. At the moment it was lighting up a big, white wall with narrow windows—the wall of the annex buildings. At the foot of this wall four men in black uniforms trimmed with silver were savagely beating a fifth man lying on the ground. They looked like they were hitting him with cables. The man was writhing on the ground, trying to get away from the lashes that whistled through the cold, thin air before ripping through his clothes and flesh.

"Charming welcome," Alberg said.

"Hey now," a gravelly voice spoke nearby, "you've barely arrived and you're starting with the subversion. Another word like that and you'll get a thrashing, too, before being tossed back on the Spaceless."

Alberg looked over. Stepping out of the darkness, a giant dressed in the same morose uniform was glaring at him. He was holding a 3-foot long cable in his hand.

Alberg gave the giant a look as soft as a shard of glass, "And you're the one who's going to give it to me?" he shot back in his icy voice. "You're too small."

The giant took a step back. He looked stunned. He blinked, then looked over at the uniforms still beating the man on the ground.

"Hey, you guys!" he yelled. "Come over here and see this!"

Most of the passengers had hurried into the visa office. A few, who had stayed out of curiosity, took off when the four torturers walked over, leaving their victim passed out. Only Iona stayed by Alberg.

"Look at this guy," the giant said. "Let's set him straight."

All five of them started for Alberg, raising their cables. As fast as lightning Alberg pulled out his radiant.

"I kill the first one to move," he said calmly. "And if you all move, I'll kill you all."

"Ah!" the giant was petrified.

The spotlight had turned and was throwing huge, dark shadows onto the ground and the white wall. They all stood still for a few long moments.

"Good," Alberg said. "I'm going to put this away. Then I'm going to turn around and go into the Company office there. Don't try anything cute. I can turn around and shoot before you've lifted a finger."

Slowly, he put his radiant under his arm and added, "I'm a hunter."

The giant started swinging his cable, visibly impressed. "A hunter? Well, then, I get it. Why didn't you say so first? Us, we like hunters." Then a second later, "Listen, as fellow hunters, we won't say anything about this to Captain Corlis. But my advice is, be careful. You're not on Venus here. The less you say, the better it'll be. The police and the regular troops are not too fond of hunters. We're the Voluntary Militia of Order."

"No problem," Alberg replied. "Greetings, boys."

"Greetings, friend," the giant grinned.

Alberg pushed Iona toward the office. On the way Iona spoke in a trembling voice, "Your new friends are super. Bravo, you really know how to choose them."

Alberg didn't answer at first. But before entering the office he spoke up, exasperated, "If I didn't tell them I'm a hunter, I would've had to shoot one or more of them to keep from getting lashed. Then I'd have become the prey. And I'd be leaving Mars feet first."

It was Iona's turn to say nothing. But she looked tense.

172

From the duty officer at the entrance to the building Alberg asked, "That guy they were pulverizing over there, what'd he do?"

The officer looked dubious. Stationed at his post, he'd missed the ruckus.

"He helped an injured mutant," he said warily. "If you've come here to do the same, the same thing will happen to you."

Alberg smiled at him and the man looked away.

"Take out your passports."

But Iona already had hers in hand. She went in first. It was not a counter but a long desk behind which sat five men in green and black uniforms. Three of them wore colored ribbons on their chest.

"Decorations," Alberg thought, stupefied. "Medals like two centuries ago! For what feat of arms? The planets haven't fought for 500 years."

The man sitting in the middle had a gold stripe on his left shoulder. He took Iona's passport and glanced at it. Then he stood up.

"Captain Corlis," he said, bowing. "Miss, I must tell you that although the visas, in theory, are issued with no expiration date, there are still a number of exceptions. Unfortunately, you are one of them and you can only stay on Mars for four days."

"Can I know why?" Iona asked.

"No. We don't like to give out information. Nevertheless, not to make your stay here too unpleasant, I can tell you that your activity in the field of interplanetary television doesn't correspond to what we desire here. Children are not encouraged to watch your shows and I advise you not to try to prolong your stay."

"Thank you," Iona said. "I believe I'll make it an even shorter stay."

Alberg gave his passport. As soon as Corliss saw it, he frowned.

"Mr. Alberg, you have an honorable profession. No one can stop you from practicing it on our planet. However, we have here incomparable organizations that are more efficient

173

than on Venus and these organizations are rather jealous of their privileges. So, I advise you, in the relations you might have with them, to be particularly accommodating. That said, the premium is 240,000 Martian sollars, or around 120,000 Venusian sollars. But you have the right to kill only one a month for budgetary reasons."

He bowed again to Iona, then to Alberg and gave them back their passports.

"You're free to go."

They left, crossed a courtyard, down a hallway and came out on a brightly lit but deserted sidewalk. A patrol passed by them in quick step.

"You should be happy," Iona said. "On this hospitable planet, you'll have the right to kill once a month. And if I help an injured mutant, I'll be beaten with steel cables. But it won't be your victim I'll be helping. You never miss a target. You're a real hunter. You said so yourself to the Voluntary Militia."

The slap echoed down the street.

"There's the first lash you'll get on Mars," Alberg said.

Iona walked away. "I wouldn't spend the night with you for all the money on the three planets."

There was no magnetocab in sight. She left alone, aimlessly.

CHAPTER VIII

Half to protect her from any harm, half to know her address in Arespolis, Alberg followed Iona—keeping to the shadows to preserve his self-respect. With the bright streetlights it wasn't easy. But Alberg was used to the hunt, even in the worst conditions.

After half a mile of tailing her, they came to a district that was a little less gloomy with a few vehicles passing by. On the sidewalks they ran into groups of drunken soldiers singing outdated war songs, all to the glory of Mars. From the start, the inhabitants of this planet must have been influenced by its name. Silent and quick, Iona skirted around the groups so deftly that the soldiers didn't turn around until she was out of their reach.

This went on for a few minutes after which she stopped at a big building on the corner of two avenues. Plasma lettering quivered on the façade: Ares Hotel. Iona climbed the opulent front steps and entered the hotel. Alberg noted the street numbers, the general layout of the neighborhood and left. He planned to get back in touch with Iona when her anger had cooled off.

The best solution was to find a hotel nearby. He went in search of one, all the while wondering why he attached so much importance to her. He usually just went off with a prostitute once in a while and his emotional life stopped there. Now he had to have his mind cluttered by a mutant. He, Alberg! Softened up by a girl whom he just had to kill for her to earn him 120,000 sollars on the spot. Something was wrong. He'd known it before he took the Spaceless.

Another hotel. More white letters on the façade: Argyre Palace. This should work. He went in.

In the lobby, several Venusian travelers, holding drinks, were talking with some Martians recognizable from their clothing. Even the traders on Mars looked military. The Venu-

sians glanced over at Alberg with surprise. They had obviously seen the start of the altercation at the astroport and they
were no doubt expecting to hear that he'd been thrown in prison. In any case, they would have been less surprised to see
him arrive in bloody rags.

Alberg gave them a little wave and a wry smile before
going to the front desk. Two of the Venusians returned his
greeting sheepishly. They others looked away abruptly.

When Alberg had gotten the number of his room—6480,
turn right, then a half-turn left— he leaned over toward the
clerk.

"Are there mutants around her?" he tossed off casually.

The man jumped back, "Surely not in our hotel, sir," he
was offended.

"I'm not accusing you of harboring mutants," Alberg
was quick to say, "I just want to know where I might find
them. I'm a hunter."

The man's face lit up, "Oh, very well, sir, that's different."

He looked over Alberg' shoulder, who turned around just
in time to see someone leaving the hotel.

"Who's that?" Alberg was curious.

"Oh, the police chief. To get back to your question. I believe there are mutants everywhere. But you're pretty sure to
find some in the libraries, bookstores and bars. All those places are surveilled by the police and the militia and army make
regular raids, but they keep going back even when one of
them's caught. They never get more than one at a time. But be
careful. The mutants on Mars are extremely well organized."

"Thanks," Alberg said.

He left the hotel. He hadn't slept since after the Venusian
night—a restless night but he'd still got some sleep—the
Spaceless had dropped him in the middle of the Martian night.
He headed to downtown Arespolis in search of bars. So, the
mutants of Mars were organized. Obviously, this was a consequence of the Martian politics, more savage than on Venus.
This state of things was cause for concern. But Alberg was

preoccupied with another feeling he had. A vague feeling, formless and nameless. As if danger was dogging him, a danger already on its way, something he could deal with if he knew what it was about. In fact, he was certain the peril was real but his cluttered mind, after the scene with Iona, was keeping him from identifying it.

He put his trust in his reactions and hurried up. He didn't like the idea of staying too long on this dismal planet, especially since he knew that he couldn't hunt at will. The best solution was to bag one huge prize and take off. He didn't admit to himself that leaving with Iona was figuring into his decision.

He got a whiff of the first bar. Here, too, it was hard to tell on first sight the difference between businessmen and soldiers. But he could see right away that the crowd was split almost evenly between the two social categories.

The omnipresent 3D TV sat a little far back. As Alberg entered the bar, a fervent speaker was winding up an introduction:

"... that we all know. But here's someone who will give you a livelier picture, more fitting to the behavior of such a scandalous character. I give you His Excellency the Senator-General Farel."

There was some clapping in the bar while the image of His Excellency appeared in place of the speaker. He was a tall, thin man with eyes like coal.

"Martians!" he said gruffly, "They consider you people of a minor planet. Venus smirks when it talks about our necessary investments in the military. But on Venus, the mutants roam freely, waiting to take over. As for Earth, with its high potential but also strong and ridiculous pride based on its long history, the majority of the Senate supports, nay, encourages the minority of senators sold out to that vile Garon."

They whistled when the still photo of Garon appeared beside Farel's gesticulations. The head of the terrian opposition had a little potbelly and a paternal smile.

"Here's Garon's platform," Farel went on. "Improvement of the relations with Venus. Utilization of the mutants. Simple exile for natural men. Independence of foreign worlds. Freedom of research for the brains. And last but not least, what he wants for you: pure and simple destruction of the military Senate, by any means necessary, whose spying and aggression are its two pillars to be replaced by a suicidal regime like on Venus."

The whistles turned into a tempest. Just then Alberg looked over at the door where a man had just entered the bar. But the newcomer must have sat down right away because Alberg couldn't find him.

"Fortunately," Farel continued, "there are still sensible people on Earth. In regard to the different points I just mentioned, they know that we have at our disposal a considerable armed force. They also know that the freedom of research for the brains will inevitably lead to the infiltration of mutants among them and to the creation of a caste of technocrats with powerful means of offense at their disposal. They are fully aware that the independence of foreign worlds will lead to a feeding frenzy on the three planets. They want to set an example of punishment for natural men and they think that the only good mutant is a dead mutant. As for relations with Venus, they agree with us."

Feral laced his fingers and made a gesture with his crossed hands as if he were hitting someone's neck.

"I haven't mentioned children. Do we have the same problems here as on Venus or above all on Earth? No. Thanks to what? Thanks to discipline. Need I say more?"

He took a deep breath and concluded.

"Dorf is head of the majority on Earth. He aggressively defied the demands of Garon and his cohorts. But what else has he done? Nothing. I'm telling you, Martians, we have to prepare ourselves for an inevitable confrontation. We still need more space cruisers, more commando units to guard the Spaceless, more men, more weapons. Our security depends on our strength."

The applause made the walls shake as the image of Farel faded out along with Garon's.

"He's a deranged lunatic," Alberg thought.

But the deranged lunatic seemed very popular on Mars. Or else the crowd here was packed with cops who wrote down the names of anyone not showing their enthusiastic support. As for the Venusians and Terrians, they were conspicuous by their absence. Alberg would have recognized them immediately. He was Venusian himself and he had met enough Terrians to identify their antiquated, tailored clothes, their strict etiquette and their refined language. The accent, too, never failed—thick and drawling on Venus, hard and nasal on Mars, explosive but half-swallowed on Earth. Thus, the artificial language, created out of a mixture of old Earth languages, had adopted its various tones before the simplification of communication.

A man leaned over to Alberg, "You're not from around here?" he asked.

Alberg looked at him, "And you?" he said sullenly. "Where did you come from? Were you under the table?"

The guy looked surprised, "Me? I was sitting here next to you. No one's ever under the table. What a weird idea!"

"It's okay. Drop it. What do you want?"

The man looked baffled but quickly pulled himself together. "Please give me your name," he said coldly.

Alberg turned to face him directly. "I'll keep it," he said. "I only have one."

Silence. Then:

"I don't understand what you mean," the guy barked.

Alberg gave him a grin, "Obviously. I don't mean anything."

"Aha!" the other gloated. "You don't mean anything! But you're going to answer, that's for sure."

Alberg turned his back to him and focused on the orchestra of electronic cymbals whose members were setting up on the 3D platform.

A waiter came over and he ordered, "Bring me a milk and get this piece of human trash off my back."

The waiter looked behind Alberg and froze. Alberg turned his head. There were three of them now, standing behind him. He stood up.

"Speak up," he said. The three men looked at one another, then the first guy spoke up, "We're plainclothes militia." He turned up the edge of his sleeve to show his badge.

Alberg sighed and pulled out his passport. "It never ends," he said. "I'm going to paint my name on my forehead."

Handing over his passport, he spoke to the still frozen waiter, "And my milk? You waiting for it to curdle?"

The waiter shook his head and left.

The man gave him back his passport, "We didn't know you were a hunter."

He signaled to the others and all three went over to the bar. The cymbals rang out. The milk arrived. Alberg looked around. A new guy came over and sat at his table as friendly as could be.

"I heard," he said.

"You heard what?" Alberg was annoyed.

"I heard that you were a hunter. I can give you a good lead but it's 10 percent."

Alberg scrutinized him. Something in his attitude, in the way he cocked his head, reminded him vaguely of someone.

"It'd be 100 percent if you did the work yourself," he answered.

The middleman smiled, "I like living. I prefer to earn less and die older."

"And if I get killed," Alberg asked, "how much do you get?"

The other raised his eyebrows, "You mean, do I work for the mutants? Are you crazy? That'd be even more dangerous!"

Alberg thought about it. On Venus there were death speculators. But they were rare. Here, organizations showed up on every side. It was not impossible that this guy really did belong to a group of mutants specialized in counter-attacks, traps and ambushes. But for a Venusian, this seemed so far-fetched, given the fanatical individualism of mutants, that the idea didn't even enter his mind. He calculated that 120,000 minus 12,000 was still more than 100,000 sollars, two and half times as much as he got on Venus. Besides, he wasn't scared of ambushes. He was wired enough to spot them at a distance.

"So, this lead?"

"Not so fast. The 10 percent up front. I don't like taking risks when it comes to money either. After all, whether you get killed or not, it's no business of mine. My tip is good. It's worth the price. It's your job not to screw it up."

"Look at this little shark!" Alberg said with half a smile.

CHAPTER IX

They had compromised at 6,000 cash plus 6,000 in the same place after the success of the operation. The scout, then, pointed out a person drinking alone at the bar. The hunter had waited for him to leave and trailed him, always watching his back. He couldn't strike without being absolutely sure that he was dealing with a mutant.

Alberg was heading away from the busy district now. Something in the silhouette, in the gait of the prey told him visually that he hadn't been led astray. But he needed to be totally sure. Although there were no catatons on Mars, the Martians could very well have invented another punishment for aberrations.

Phobos had risen and was drifting over Arespolis like a big balloon. It was a welcome replacement for the rarer and rarer streetlights. When the prey turned around, Alberg barely had time to jump behind the wall of a gray, cubic villa. But in a flash he was grappled and disarmed. They dragged him into the villa before he could open his mouth.

There were four of them as far as Alberg could judge in the dark. Four nyctalopic mutants whose eyes glowed dimly. A fifth arrived, the one Alberg had been following. The pieces of the puzzle were falling into place. This was the formless danger that was looming, that Alberg had picked up on the moment the front desk clerk had glanced at the entrance. The captain was also the scout. That's why he reminded Alberg of someone. And all of them, the clerk, the captain, they were all mutants. The Argyre Palace was a mutant lair. And the militia in the bar had given the scout an opening to talk to Alberg for whom the trap had already been set.

He had to face the facts: the mutants on Mars were waging an organized fight. Corlis was either a liar or an idiot in claiming that the extermination organizations were more effective on Mars than anywhere else. Or else, if it were true, the mutants had just as many on their side.

"It's due," one of the invisible people said, "to that fact that Mars was populated first."

Telepathy to boot, Alberg mused to himself.

"Yes," the mutant said. "Telepathy to boot. We don't need to use interrogations."

Alberg suddenly felt cold. The mutants of Venus had all kinds of abnormal traits, but only a tiny minority had really superhuman powers. He had fallen into the hands of a gang of monsters and he wasn'st going to last long. He started to understand the official propaganda, even though he kept thinking that extermination was only a solution of fear, a solution that burned the bridges for the future. The natural men were right: these people were going to replace the human race. And remembering what men had put them through, there would be no possible coexistence. The mutants would also turn to extermination and they would succeed where the men had failed, more and more. The human species was truly doomed. It was only a matter of time.

"No, the mutant said, "vengeance doesn't interest us. It's only for the feeble-minded."

"Ach!" Alberg was angry. "Now you're really pissing me off, listening to all my thoughts."

There was a laugh. "You think, therefore you are. And you're complaining."

A magnetocar passed by on the street. It was absolutely silent, but its radar-headlights had lit up the room for a second. Alberg had time to see the five mutants encircling him. Martians from their militant clothes, absolutely impossible to tell them apart from the Martians who were hunting them.

The one who had spoken was talking again.

"I could communicate with you silently, but we're not all telepaths. So, we're going to talk."

Alberg felt a chair being pushed behind his legs. He sat down. He was starting to think he might get out of this dilemma alive.

"But you won't mind if I stay in the shadows. You must understand that we don't like to attract attention."

All this was said very casually, with a sense of restrained cheerfulness. From someone whom it was not only legal but recommended to kill, such a tone was disorienting. Especially when you were a professional killer. But Alberg was not easily disoriented.

"I'm all ears," he said.

"First of all, I want you to understand that we don't want to kill you. Outside our special capacities, which are physiological, we're no different from you intellectually. We're not 'superhumans' as you fear. We are... let's call it 'alternative men'. The lemurs gave birth to both men and monkeys. You may have given birth to us, but you might give birth later to another race with even higher capacities. This possibility alone forbids us the right to exterminate you. It would be like the selective genocide of pregnant women."

He paused before continuing.

"First you conquered your two nearest planets. You furnished them with oxygen and water thanks to plants. Then you colonized a certain number of stars. It was during these voyages that you were exposed to the penetrating rays that produced mutations among you. They continue to appear everywhere except on Earth more and more frequently. On Earth itself, they don't exist, but the earth people travel. And thus, they are starting to pop up. Even from trips on the Spaceless where other factors than the radiation might be in play."

Alberg's eyes were getting used to the dark. He could see the outline of the one speaking as well as his silent partners.

"The first of us were born less than two centuries ago. You've only been hunting us for 50 years and your efforts increased in line with the frequency of mutations among you and by our own multiplying in which our heredity preserves the mutated characteristics. This process is a little like the spread and eventual victory of Christianity in ancient Rome, if we weren't convinced of the current trial and error character of mutations. In reality, we're probably not 'alternative men' and neither are we one of the distinct races you will give birth to. We are the result of blind biological experiments some of which will prove viable to give birth to one or more other races. Some of your brains talk about this. I know they talk about it in secret."

"And besides this morale of the future, this preservation of races to come," Alberg asked, "don't you have more practical reasons, for the present, to spare us?"

"Yes. There are a lot more of you than us. If, by any chance, we decided and managed to eliminate you, we'd be utterly incapable of maintaining the technological civilization you've developed. Not for want of intellect—most of us are your equals, even though we have our share of idiots and mentally disabled—some of us surpass you not in intellectual superiority but because their gifts of calculation, memory or quick thinking put them ahead. Intelligence is something else. It's the capacity that we have to see the links.

"But we couldn't maintain the civilization for the simple reason of numbers. At a higher level, the calculation of probabilities shows that it takes a large population to sustain an infrastructure. Otherwise, everything collapses and it's decadence, then extinction."

He wrapped up.

"We've decided to spare our murderers in order to stay alive."

"Yeah," Alberg grumbled. "There's some truth to what you say. Maybe a lot of truth. But me, a mutant hunter, what should I do? You think I'm going to lock myself up again in one of those cells where they talk about nothing but balance sheets? I'd rather die right now."

"No, you'll still be a hunter, but you won't hunt. You'll keep your profession in the eyes of the authorities and we'll pay you."

Alberg thought about the offer.

"Suppose that works here," he said. "This planet is unlivable. In two days I could take down half a dozen of these

185

puppets. It's not the police I'd have to deal with, it's the army."

"Our organization stretches across the three planets and beyond. We'll pay you on Venus just like here. Anyway, you won't be alone. The authorities don't know that some hunters are paid by the prey to stand down. They don't know that a lot of investigations are cut short because we have our people in the police, either men we pay or mutants themselves."

"And where does the money come from?" Alberg asked.

"Dues. A lot of us handle huge capital."

Alberg pondered. Getting money not to work. It wasn't unappealing. He could still do something. Something that let him travel, that required self-control... space, hunting pirates who plundered intra-solar vessels...

"And if I return to Venus and your network shut down? I'll be broke."

"We have many networks. Generally speaking, you can trust us. We're reliable in business because our lives depend on it."

Alberg looked at the situation from every angle. For the first time, he thought of Iona. She'd have to swallow her anger and insults."

"Well," he said, "okay. When's the first installment?"

"Right now. And then 50,000 Venusian sollars a month."

There was the sound of paper shuffling in the dark. Alberg felt around for the wad of bills. He didn't try to count it or thumb through it. Nothing of this felt fake. They could have killed him quietly.

"And on Venus?"

"We'll be in touch. Don't you worry about a thing."

A faint rustling and a current of air. Alberg was alone. He stood up and brushed his foot against the radiant, which they had left on the ground.

CHAPTER X

In the Ares Hotel, Iona had entered boiling with fury. That lowlife Alberg, that mutant killer had dared to lay a hand on her. Because she'd made love to him, he considered her an object, a jumpy dame you could slap around to make her walk straight. He was going to see how wrong he was.

But deep down inside she couldn't find the courage to fulfill the mission Silas had given her. Alberg had made too big of an impression for her to get over him so soon. For the present, her anger and resentment were covering up her hesitation and confusion. She was going to get a few hours rest and think about it before taking the Spaceless back to Venus. She would also like to get back to Earth, but she had to clear up the situation with Silas first. She couldn't run away like a coward, which would only delay the inevitable. Silas never got sidetracked by events.

At the front desk, she showed her passport and they told her the room number. She asked them to send up a snack and refreshments. Then she took the elevator. In the 10th floor hallway she heard a child's voice behind one of the doors. A muffled voice that screamed something she couldn't understand. She stopped but the voice went quiet. She went on, frustrated. What were the children on Mars really like? She was interested enough in her job to ask this question. But her anger against Alberg had not entirely subsided. She entered her room and jumped back.

A man in a black and green uniform, radiant in his belt, was staring hard at her, fists balled on his hips.

"One mutant is as worthless as another," he said unequivocally. "These enemies of our race should be exterminated to the last one, male and female alike."

He grabbed his radiant. Iona fell flat on the carpet. But she saw him take aim, but then put it back in his belt. "Martians," he went on, "it's our only path to salvation;"

Iona stood up, heart racing, just when the bellboy came around the corner and almost ran into her. The tray he was carrying almost fell out of his hands.

"What's wrong, miss?" he asked, alarmed.

"Oh, nothing," Iona muttered. "I tripped."

She went into the room where the 3D TV kept up its call for murder.

"Maybe you were a little surprised," the bellboy wondered. "The hotel is the only one in all of Arespolis where opening the door automatically turns on the 3D—in all the rooms, regardless of price. Isn't that something to be proud of?"

"Oh, sure," Iona answered warmly. Her lower jaw was still trembling a little. "Put the try over there. Thank you."

"Goodbye, miss. And death to the mutants."

"Death to the mutants!" Iona repeated earnestly.

The door closed. Iona found the switch and swept the fuming officer out of the room. She ate sluggishly. The food was bland. The drink tasted like plaster. Afterward she lay down on the pulsed-air bed.

She felt both calmer and more distraught. Go back to the Spaceless? There were plenty of flights both ways.

She started dozing off to escape her problems. It lasted maybe half an hour, an hour, then she was yanked out her lethargy by a row of bright purple lights flashing on the headboard. She pushed a button next to the lights.

On the 3D platform in the middle of the room, a black and silver uniformed militia materialized.

"Long live Mars! Miss, are you the one who landed here with the hunter Alberg?"

"Uh... yes," she said.

"We'd like to inform you because the police won't do it. Your friend made a contact in a bar and took off on a hunt. Unfortunately, we couldn't follow him or lend a hand because it's not within our jurisdiction. We just wanted to inform you since he went to the Argyre Palace."

"Thank you," she said coldly.

"Good evening and long live Mars!"

The man disappeared.

Iona thought: "So, that's it. Barely off the Spaceless and he slaps me and starts killing again!"

Her anger came rushing back along with loathing. What kind of man was he to arouse the sympathy of these savage brutes? Why hadn't she killed him in the darkness of the Aphros Opera? Or on the street? Her mind was made up right away. She got off the bed, left the room, went down to the front desk and paid the bill for one night and the meal. She felt totally detached from everything. Complete callousness possessed her.

She returned to the Spaceless where she waited less than 15 minutes, not far from a child who was watching her. She got into the cabin just when a militia man came marching up to her.

"Alberg is really a mutant!" he said as the doors were closing.

The child was still nearby but went skipping off.

CHAPTER XI

On his way back Alberg got lost. It was one thing to follow someone, another thing entirely to get back to the city on your own. There were several intersections where the streets looked exactly the same. At one he took a street that seemed to head towards the lights of Arespolis but soon it veered off. He had to go back, which made him lose a lot of time.

When he reached the edge of the city his flagging vigilance suddenly went on alert. There were some vague shapes wandering around. He backed up warily and took a different street. His mind started working fast.

"The police already know about it. Or else there was a cop among those five mutants. Or else the scout was no mutant at all but a spy and they were all cops. In that case, they're going to try to get their hands on me and when I'm caught, they'll bring out the recorded conversation from the villa. They'll search me and find the 50,000 sollars as supporting evidence. Should I get rid of the dough? That wouldn't do any good. The rest is enough to arrest me. Arrest me for what? For switching sides. Even if they're all spies, they'll say there was at least one guy from the gang of genuine filthy mutants, which will turn the crime of intent into a crime plain and simple. This planet is truly the worst of the worst."

He made a detour to get closer to the hotel.

"Yes, I figured as much. There, too. They think I'm going to try to hide out with Iona. I hope she hasn't been arrested already. Why would she be? There's no reason. They have no proof against her. They don't like the work she does, that's all. How could they imagine that she's a mutant?"

He kept moving. He knew that the hunt was on, but not in the usual way. And he, when he tracked a mutant, he was alone. Whereas now, he had the police, the militia and the army of an entire planet against him. Starting with the forces in Arespolis. They could easily identify him from his Venusian clothes.

"Ach!" he scowled. "That's it. I'm going to snatch one of these plainclothes spies and switch clothes in some dark alley. Then I'll blend in and head for the Spaceless. It shouldn't be too hot for me there."

He approached two men standing 50 yards from Iona's hotel. "Hey!" he shouted. "Are you looking for me?"

The two men ran at him. When they were six feet away he brought them down with a fan of his radiant. After a rapid estimate of their weight, he dragged one of them into a small garden where crystals were growing and he started to undress him.

But others were on the lookout and came bounding over—they had taken off their gravity soles. Alberg knew he didn't have time to put his plan into action. He in turn took off his gravity soles and jumped over the garden wall. Then he went hopping by a short, little guy on the sidewalk whom he paid no attention to. He leapt into a courtyard, went up some stairs that came out on a terrace, crossed it and jumped down into a side street. And he bumped into the little guy he'd barely glimpsed before.

"Follow me," said the high-pitched voice.

It was a child holding a radiant in his right hand.

Alberg looked stupefied at him. But the child, who might have been 12 years old, had already crossed the street and was disappearing down an alley that was barely visible from where Alberg was standing. He obeyed and turned into the alley just when his pursuers showed up in the street and on the terrace at the same time.

The child was running with astonishing speed and seemed to know the neighborhood like the back of his hand. Alberg ran after him through a maze of darker and darker streets and caught up to him in front of a big, black door stuck in a huge wall. The police were starting to swarm into the surrounding streets. He heard them calling out. But the child was talking through a slot. The big door cracked open and he slipped inside, waving to Alberg to follow him. He did so. The door closed with a dull thud followed by the click of a magnetic lock.

It was a vast hall with a vaulted ceiling that led into a dimly lit inner courtyard where a few trees could be seen. A man in a black robe, tied at the waist with a red cord, stood before them.

"I don't want to know your business," he said. "This is the only science monastery of the province and every person in dire straits has the right, in theory, to asylum. But the authorities have already violated this right on several occasions, either by the militia wearing the robe and cord of disciples here or directly by breaking in. They've gone so far as to use wingers to land in the courtyard when they couldn't break down the door, which is made of yterbium steel."

He shook his head worriedly.

"I don't know if the adjutor will approve," he added. "For me, as the elder censor, the traditions are sacred. However, you're going to meet someone who's been waiting for you and you can't stay here."

Alberg only half-listened to this speech. He also heard the noise the police were making outside. He barely retained one piece of information: he was among the brains. The elder censor brought them into the courtyard, which was surrounded by a huge, glass gallery where blue lights revealed the shapes of gigantic machines. Above were brightly lit, archaic windows—the disciples were hard at work.

When they started across the courtyard, shouting broke out behind the front door, which shook under the pounding of gun butts and steel cables.

"Hurry up," the elder censor urged. "We have to get to the nuclear crypt before the adjutor wakes up."

On the other side of the courtyard, the elevator cage opened. All three of them jumped in. The cabin dropped like a stone and stopped after a few seconds.

"Go on," their guide said. "Me, I have to go back up."

He closed the door after they got out. The cabin shot back up. Alberg looked around. The crypt was a good 300 feet square and 30 feet high. Other machines were humming along here, but very quietly.

"It's this way," the child said, coldly, no longer skipping.

He started running between the machines. Alberg shrugged his shoulders and followed. What choice did he have?

Presently, they came to a door that the child pushed open with his foot. Alberg stood petrified.

They were in the doorway of a small room lit by… candles or chandelles… anyway some kind of prehistoric lighting. Sitting at a table, a man was looking at them.

Alberg first saw his white beard, silky, lavish, fluvial. Then his hair, likewise white, that fell to his waist in undulating waves. The man was wearing a white robe and wore a cord around his head that wound around the middle of his forehead. Under the table, you could see his bare feet. On the table, you could admire his hands. Knotty hands with very long fingers whose tendons bulged out of his leathery skin.

"Enter, Mr. Alberg. Enter, Little Paul. Allow me to introduce myself," the man spoke in a very deep voice. "I am Del Padre, a natural man. I have divided my life into two parts: one in which I preach the return to the fundamental values of altruism and simplicity; in the other I sculpt mountains."

Alberg flinched, like he'd just been pinched. "You think that's simple?" he gasped. "To sculpt mountains?"

"It's simple when you see the scale of man, meaning the scale of the universe."

Alberg said nothing. He had already met natural men but not of this caliber. He emanated safety, serenity, so complete that it was like turmoil and danger.

After a moment he asked, "How do you know me?"

Del Padre smiled, "I've had you watched since you missed that mutant named Silas. You see, it goes back a ways."

"Oh," Alberg groaned. "A tough one, that guy. You know him?"

"Of course. And you, do you know Little Paul?"

Alberg looked at the child. Of course, he'd heard of Little Paul. Little Paul was a Terrian child whom some people believed was just a legend. They said he was the son of a VIP and head of a gang that branched out everywhere. For more than a year they've racked up horror stories of thefts, kidnappings and murder of adults. Many people watch what they say when a child's around for feat that he might belong to or have links to Little Paul and they'd get chosen as the next victim.

"I know the name," Alberg gave nothing away.

He looked at the child again. Little Paul stood in the middle of the room. The flickering flames danced in his blue eyes. His blonde hair was a mess. He was missing an incisor. When the radiant jumped into his hand, his clear eyes fixed on Alberg, who suddenly felt a chill and had to muster all his self-control to keep a smile on his face.

"I see," he said. "A little tough guy."

The child had a shrill laugh and spit on the floor. "You're lucky," he said, "that you switched sides. I was going to deal with you myself."

Alberg knew he was joking. "So, you're with the mutants?"

Little Paul shrugged his shoulders and in a reedy, mocking voice said, "Maybe you'd like me to be with the Senate? With the Senate who sends us out into foreign worlds at 15 years old instead of letting us slack off like all the bastard adults? The Senate is in our sights. The whole Senate. And the enemies of the Senate are our friends. Mutants, natural men and brains."

Alberg thought: "That's what you get for sending kids out to foreign worlds like manufactured goods. People forget that each of them has an individual existence and they'll remind you of it the day they stick a radiant in your face."

At the same time, a very old memory came back to him. When he was still a child himself, he belonged to a gang, but he had very weird friends who sometimes went on expeditions to nobody knew where. One of them talked sometimes about Del Padre. The memory became clearer. A big scandal broke out about offloading some cargo in Aphros. Natural men led by Del Padre had tried to block the robot dockers and were hacked up, but not before burning a bunch of machines. The scandal had been double-sided. He'd shared the Venusian opinion, those people who were outraged by the sabotage, which they considered absurd, of material and goods and time and money. Others spoke out against the massacre of natural men who had earned some respect among the people. The natural men impressed people by their courage, their philosophical jargon and their crazy clothes.

"I also remember you," Alberg turned back to Del Padre. "The scandal with the Venusian cargo."

"Ah!" Del Padre said. "Yes. There were many others on the three planets. That expedition cost us dearly. I only survived thanks to a crew member from the ship. He burned a robot that was about to crush me."

He grinned, barely visible behind his huge beard.

"You know," he added, "if our ideal wins out, we'll keep a few machines. Don't believe we only want fire that's got by striking two rocks together. In that case, why not take purity and privation to the limit and refuse fire altogether?"

"How did you know and you, too, Little Paul, that I was wanted?"

Del Padre blinked. "It's a long story. I don't have time to tell you right now. Listen!"

A dull explosion echoed through the rock.

"They're forcing their way into the monastery."

Little Paul had another one of his shrill laughs. "Oh, they're sly. They're going to destroy the monastery, imprison the disciples and exile the brains! And they want to set up a powerful army! If they keep this up, they'll have to attack Venus with crossbows!"

Alberg watched him with a kind of fear. Little Paul was too thoughtful for his age. Was he a mutant? But no. The mutants themselves had told Alberg during their conversation that they were no smarter than humans. No, this was just a very intelligent child.

"We're going to leave," Del Padre said. "Each of us separately. Because they'll come down here into the crypt."

He turned to Alberg: "I was already on Mars. Little Paul had to meet me here by passing through Venus. It was the mutants who told me about your arrival and your meeting with them. As for Little Paul, he was contacted by militia when he got off the Spaceless and made his way to the place where they'd laid the trap for you. Then he brought you to me."

"But my meeting with the mutants was just a short time ago."

"There's a video network on Mars."

He stood up. He was huge. More than 6'2". He went to the back wall and put his hand on it. The wall opened, unveiling a black hole that exhaled dry, cold air.

"Take the candelabra," he said.

"The what?"

"The thing with the flames. Bring them all. There's no need to leave behind any traces of our presence. If the adjutor manages to appease them up there, at least they won't find any proof against the elder censor down here."

Alberg took the candelabra. "Thanks, Little Paul," he said.

"Don't mention it," Little Paul answered with his squeaky laugh.

"Thanks, Del Padre."

"Goodbye."

Alberg entered the underground tunnel wondering why he was being so gracious. The wall closed behind him.

Left alone, Del Padre and the child said nothing for a moment. The room was dimly lit by the luminous ramps of the crypt that glowed around the doorway.

"You were right to stay quiet," Del Padre said to Little Paul. "He thinks the police are looking for him because he defected. There was no need bring up what Iona said at the Spaceless. How were you able to videophone me?"

"Oh, a booth by the hotels."

"I also avoided telling him that Iona was sent to kill him. But maybe he already knows."

"The bitch!" the child said with a precious, toothless smile. "But she has such wild stories. On the whole, I don't miss them."

"What he cannot know is that she's been distantly controlled by Silas. He'll find out later and it'll be better. I don't like the idea of them facing off again. It's serves no purpose for me. Especially when Alberg comes back from where I'm sending him. Because it has nothing to do with him being a hunter that Silas wants to kill him. I've known that for a long time."

"I really don't care much," the child said, "about Alberg. I don't trust him. I'll see later if he can be of any use."

He started hopping. "What say we skedaddle?" He went to the door and came back saying, "I hear the elevator."

Del Padre took a candle out of his robe, which he lit with a 200-year old lighter. Then he opened the wall again. They both went into the dark tunnel. The wall shut behind them.

They walked underground for a while before Del Padre stopped. He felt around for a minute, then pushed a precise place on the wall. Little Paul shivered from the cold, not from fear. Another opening and part of the underground branched off. They closed the wall and started walking.

"You know," Del Padre began, "we have to prepare an action together. If we go separately into battle, we'll be picked off one by one."

"Yes," the child replied. "It's easy to say, but it's already impossible to make the children march in line with each other… and yet, I've got my troops under control. So then, make everyone march together."

"I could say the same thing about the natural men and Silas could repeat it about the mutants. For the brains who have stayed on their native planets, maybe it's more serious. But there are the foreign worlds."

"That's not my business," Little Paul declared. "On the foreign worlds, they don't like anything that exists in the solar system…"

They kept talking while hurrying away. The darkness of the underground soon engulfed their candlelight along with their oversized shadows.

CHAPTER XII

When she arrived on Venus, Iona took a room in a hotel near the astroport. She started by letting her mind wander and she thought nostalgically about her big apartment with a terrace in Euroafrica. But this was just one superficial and random distraction. Deep down, she was not very proud of her behavior with Alberg. Not having the courage to kill him was one thing; having the gall to denounce him so he'd get hunted and killed was something else. Because she knew him well enough to know that he wasn't going to turn himself into the police to ask them what they wanted with him and to submit to a chromosomic test to prove he's not a mutant. He was simply going to open fire. And they would end up taking him down. Plus, it was possible that on Mars denouncing someone led to summary execution without an arrest or any kind of verification, which meant it would be a massacre, but they'd get him.

Silas hadn't left Venus because he called her on video soon after her arrival. He had obviously found her like he'd found Alberg at the start of this whole, wretched affair.

"I'll be over in ten minutes," the immaterial figure spoke on the 3D platform.

And he cut off. Iona was ready and waiting. After all, she had fulfilled her mission, in some way or other…

"Congratulations," he said when he came into the room.

He looked distant but determined. She told him what she had done before leaving Mars.

"You denounced him?" he was startled. "You couldn't kill him yourself, a big stud like that! So, you subcontracted. You're slipping, believe me. And don't imagine that I'm happy with this solution. Alberg is a poisonous snake. He could easily escape them."

He started pacing the floor.

"Don't go anywhere. I'll found out."

He left without saying another word. Iona did the only thing she could do—she lay down and stared at the ceiling where colored shapes floated by. She didn't sleep and it felt like a long time. But Silas came back. He'd been gone for six hours.

"Lucky that sales are sacrosanct," he said, "and that the police are in an equipment-shortage because the public is constantly buying everything up. You didn't check if there are hidden microphones…"

"And you," Iona responded, "how did you get your info?"

"Oh, the same thing. Videotaps by the Spaceless must be pretty rare. Especially in public offices."

Coldly, objectively, as if he had nothing to blame her for, he informed her of the results of his research. He didn't blame her for falling into the arms Alberg either, or for not killing him.

"I managed to contact Aphros through a natural man who told me that Del Padre was on Mars. And I reached him in Arespolis, not without difficulty."

"And?"

"And Alberg sold out to the mutants on Mars. After that he escaped with the help of Little Paul."

"The child! So, it was him I saw on the Spaceless at Arespolis!"

She failed to tell him that her heart leapt with joy at the thought of Alberg being alive.

"And Del Padre sent him to Earth."

"What an idea!"

"I'm just saying what he told me. So, if you want, you can rush over to the Spaceless again but this time to Villagea. And you can finish your mission there."

"What?! Kill him when he's come over to our side? It frightens me to think that I denounced him after he'd teamed up with us."

"Well, get over it and keep the fright for your next show. If I want Alberg killed, it's for reasons you don't know about.

I told you he represents a great danger and none of his turn-coating is going to change my decision."

"I refuse."

"You should've refused sooner. You sabotaged the mission. Now it's up to you and no one else to clean up your mess."

Iona said nothing. She had to admit that Silas was right. But how could she kill Alberg now when she didn't have the heart to do it the first time, when she'd been thrilled that he'd escaped the police, when she was glad to see him on their side? No matter, she'd wait and see. So many things could happen... Silas could get himself killed in the meantime and since she was only beholden to him... A little voice was telling her that these thoughts were as reprehensible as her denunciation of Alberg. But she shut it up. She'd see and that was that.

"Yes," she said. "You're right, in the end. When should I leave for Villagea?"

"Right now."

She got up, looking meek.

Silas looked skeptical. "And this time I'm having you watched."

They left the hotel, one after the other.

CHAPTER XIII

Alberg was walking through the underground, keeping the candelabra raised in front of him. A light, icy breeze made the flames flicker and he was constantly afraid of seeing them blown out. So far, however, he couldn't get lost because the tunnel went straight under the surface of Mars without branching off at all.

While walking he kept glancing at the walls. The tunnel must've been bored a long time ago. Centuries, no doubt. Probably at the time when the brains had gone into battle for the leadership of the people. And it was Alberg using it now as if it'd been dug out specially for him. He thought vaguely of that era which they hardly speak of in the marketed history books. They simply said that the brains were against colonial expansion and they'd been relegated to their former duties in the end. They'd left at their jobs only a few psychologists, sociologists, demographers and statisticians. And they were always pared down by competitors.

The tunnel ended abruptly in a dead-end after rising steeply up a slope. Alberg examined the end wall. There were two small circles of shiny metal at eye level. He guessed it was a mechanism, so he put down the candelabra and pressed the circles.

The wall pivoted without a sound. He went through and it swung closed behind him. He looked around.

He was in a tight space, poorly lit by a luminescent ceiling. In one corner was a toilet. Across from him was a door behind which he could hear muffled voices. He stepped forward, opened the door and stood there frozen to the spot.

He saw a big room full of people. All the walls were hidden behind rows of bunks. Many of them occupied. Only the wall in the back was half free of bunks, the rest beong taken up by the thick bars of a grill behind which uniformed soldiers were passing by.

Alberg stepped back, closed the door and went back to the tunnel. Del Padre had tricked him. He'd knowingly sent him to get caught in a trap. The road to freedom led to a prison toilet. He searched for the opening mechanism but there was nothing on this side to move the wall. It was a one-way trip. Shaking with fury Alberg pounded the wall with his fists and the butt of his radiant, but in vain. It was no use shooting—the radiant only effected living matter.

The door behind him opened. A man stepped in.

"Are you coming out of here?" he asked.

Alberg turned around. He wanted to kill they guy on the spot but instead he said, "It's okay, keep your lid on, I'm coming."

He squeezed by the guy.

The man said, "You weren't with us during the raid."

Alberg turned around, "Oh no, I just came in through the toilet."

The guy shrugged his shoulders and closed the door. Alberg entered the big cell. Three fourths of the occupants were 15- or 16-year-old kids and half of them were girls. The others were indefinable characters that looked menacing. He went to a bunk and sat down. His brain was spinning.

He was obviously the only one who had money and a weapon. He thought for a moment of bribing the guards through the bars, but they would just take him out, grab everything he had and throw him back in. That was obvious. As for the radiant, he could probably use it to threaten them to open the cage, but outside, he didn't have a ghost of a chance.

No, it'd be better to wait and see how the situation developed. He certainly had to keep his things to use them when opportunity arose. He lay down on the bunk. Above him, a couple were hugging and having a whispered but heated discussion. He had only just noticed them. They must have been thirty years old between the two of them.

But what was Del Padre thinking? What kind of rescue sends you into a cell? It was absurd. Indeed, Del Padre did seem pretty crazy.

He heard creaking and turned his head. The grill was opening. A column of soldiers was coming into the cell, pointing weapons at the prisoners. No radiants but those electric pistols that gave you horrible jolts and made your muscles cramp up.

"Let's go!" an officer shouted. "Everyone front and center and no fighting! Don't forget the stunners can stop your breathing for a few seconds."

Alberg jumped up and followed the others who were gathering together in the middle of the cell. They were surrounded by soldiers, who then pushed them outside like dogs herding sheep.

Then they lined up and filed past a photoelectric screen. When they were all through, the officer shouted again.

"There's one too many. But it doesn't matter. I don't want to know who it is or how he got in. If there's one missing, I'll deal with it!"

A few servile snickers among the soldiers. Still surrounded, the prisoners entered a courtyard where bright spotlights lacerated the dark night. Some white buildings recognizable as a Spaceless. But it wasn't the one where Alberg had landed a few hours earlier. A few hours! It was amazing for him to think that only 15 hours or so had passed since he'd killed that mutant in the raincoat inside the Clothes Counter in Aphros. And now they were forcing him into another Spaceless tunnel bound for an unknown destination...

He went in with the others. Shooting at the soldiers at this moment would be suicide.

The young couple were next to him. The boy spoke eagerly, "We're going to fight the rebels, us others. Her too. I hope you didn't choose the work zone."

"Obviously," Alberg grumbled, not understanding a word of what was said.

What rebels did he mean? Rebels against whom? Or what? Mutants revolting? And this work zone, what kind of work? Inventory or accounting?

The red light flashed on. The doors closed. Alberg figured that no matter where the convoy was headed, he could always get away. One simple opportunity was all he needed. He mulled it over. He would take the Spaceless to Venus and get his second payment of 50,000 sollars. If the money kept rolling in like this, he'd buy an asteroid some day and stick all these morons on it. Yes, but for now he was in a trap.

CHAPTER XIV

During the trip, the strange passengers didn't act like the ones on the Venus-Mars Spaceless. They kept talking among themselves, but in completely separate groups. The marginal people, like night-prowlers, traffickers of women or drug dealers looked grim and talked with no one. The others were children. Among the children there were groups that didn't mix. Some talked kind of passionately but were guarded against prying eyes and ears. Others gesticulated freely and spoke without worrying about who could hear them— bragging and boasting and defiant threats and hotheaded challenges. Alberg didn't try to make sense of anything he heard or saw. He was too busy making plans for his escape.

And then, all of a sudden, he understood that he had already guessed where they were sending him, but he'd unconsciously refused to believe it. Little Paul's words: "The Senate who sends us out into foreign worlds at 15 years old." And all these 15-year children around him. Then the words of Iona: "The people exist but not here." And what he'd just heard the child say: "I hope you didn't choose the work zone." That's why some of them, although it looked like they were incarcerated, didn't act like prisoners but like emigrants while others were more like deportees.

Del Padre had purposely sent Alberg to foreign worlds. Was it to get rid of him without having to kill him or were his plans even more devious? That visionary giant could be up to anything!

Alberg constructed a rough chronology of the events he'd lived through, events that, with minor variations, must have happened here over and over again.

They started with raids in the slums and anyone who couldn't prove they had steady, legal work was sent to the annex cell of the Spaceless. As for the children, that must be a little different: those who had fallen for the war propaganda came running to the authorities on the day of their 15th birthday. They went looking for the rest. Some must have managed to hide for a few months, but on the whole, there were few resistors. Farel had clearly explained that this state of things was a direct result of his idea of discipline.

Obviously, such methods were rather surprising to a Venusian. On Venus the going-away of children was regular, official and spectacular. They had parties where the children were spoiled, praised, put on a pedestal, so to speak... Only the hard cases were tracked down in areas that were locked down and they didn't go quietly. These children were always armed. They fired without a second thought at the police and soldiers, which made things complicated because they couldn't kill the children who were going to be sent to foreign worlds. No one talked about this except for a few adults, dumb parents who felt those animal emotions for their children, incompatible with logical planning and the efficient use of the products of producers.

On the whole, Alberg thought, it all came down to the same thing. And the procedures of Terrians might differ from both the Martians and Venusians, but they would inevitably lead to the same results.

Of course, there were those had passed the business test and stayed on their home planet. Barely one out of ten. They were the most eager to turn in the resisters.

But organized gangs lived outside the cities in the vast spaces abandoned to wild nature. These outlaws survived by attacking the suburbs after the few, native, hydroponic crops had been replaced by the total import of goods. These gangs of reprobates had been gradually depleted by capture or death, but new members kept joining and over the years they had increased. At least it was like this on Venus. Mars, in fact, seemed to have fewer problems.

Something was striking on Mars: the importance of the army. Venus had one, but the soldiers were constantly on secret missions. Maybe that was the difference between the two

207

planets as far as the children were concerned: the Martian army, for the most part, stayed put.

Still, Venus hunted the mutants hard, but the chief of the Department of Extermination had told Alberg that the Senate directives were easing up... at least to the extent that they didn't advise killing mutants on sight. Plus, on Venus natural men were free to circulate even though everyone knew that they formed alliances with the resistant children. Whereas on Mars it was not a good idea to walk around amidst all those uniforms if you were sporting long hair and a white robe. Alberg had no information about the fate of natural men on Mars, but he doubted it was much different from what lay in store for mutants. That was no doubt why he saw no natural men on the Spaceless...

The red light turned orange, then green. The doors opened. Alberg, who happened to be right next to them, got hit with the dazzling light, the heat and the noise all at once. He was among the first to go out into the thundering hell where, on an esplanade beaten by the blazing rays of two bluish white suns, men in white clothes were running around, yelling orders, running in and out of white buildings that were falling into ruin. The sky glistened like a silver mirror, studded with constant bursts of bright red, while the deafening explosions rattled their limbs and guts and lungs.

Alberg staggered towards a shaded area. His clothes were already so soaked in sweat that he could wring them out. It was in the shade that they were herding the new cattle with a lot of yelling and screaming. Alberg thought his head was about to explode when a man in a white helmet and black stripes on his shoulder shouted in his ear:

"All those for the work zone go to the right. Fighters off to the left."

Naturally, anyone who had the right to choose had already done so before leaving. Work was not appealing to him. It was harder to refuse work than to desert—hard labor sites weren't as easy to escape as the chaos of a battlefield. And Alberg had not wasted his time at Gun and Murder.

He went to the left. There they asked him nothing. They tossed a bundle of clothes, a radiation rifle, a pack of provisions and they pushed him into a stuffy room where others were getting dressed. He did the same, but was careful not to attract their attention when he slipped his radiant pistol and his money into the pockets of his white uniform.

He walked out and lined up. The shouting continued. They made them march in step towards a foul-smelling mess hall.

CHAPTER XV

The mess was full of soldiers in white uniforms, uniforms that Alberg could already appreciate for their insulation, and they carried white helmets at their sides. There was a general air of hysteria.

Almost all of them were younger than 16. They laughed and shouted at one another, all keyed up, like it was the end of a party they'd all been invited to. But judging by the explosions and the trembling ground, this was no party. Alberg, who knew how to fight, watched them and shook his head. Whatever kind of battle was raging, they wouldn't last long.

He swallowed a mouthful of the gruel in which small, green webbed feet were swimming—lizard soup. They also gave out packets containing a tablet and two lozenges. He bit into them. They were tasteless but made a kind of paste in his mouth that was almost impossible to swallow.

"So," he said to the guy sitting next time, "we're going to go."

"Yes," the answered. "The rebels had better watch out!"

"No kidding," Alberg uttered. "We have to protect the work zone."

The other looked at him. He was a child. "Yes and no. Those bastards come in and kill our soldiers instead of working. The best would be to send them back to the power plants and the crop-livestock units. But they'd rather die. So, we're going to help them."

"They'll end up getting what's coming and the planet will be rid of them."

"The planet! There's an entire system in revolt. The double star C.122 in sector K.X.3844 of the galaxy. I remember the prep course really well, eh? This is our bridgehead here."

Alberg understood. There'd been a psychological preparation before the departure. For the children at least. In order to channel their militant instincts. The adults whom they nabbed in the raids were too much to worry about.

"Obviously," the child continued, "you know nothing about it. You didn't take the course. No one in the solar system knows about it. State secret!" he finished up looking proud of himself.

So, that was the reason for the troop movements on Venus. The army was sending reinforcements to the planets of C.122. The war, therefore, had lasted for years. The natural men used to talk about massacres in space, but people just thought they were crazy. And basically, no one even cared where the foreign worlds were located in the galaxy.

Although Venusian, Alberg, by chance, was part of a Martian contingent. Considering the importance and the apparent immobility of the Martian army, Arespolis participated less than the other capitals in the expeditionary corps. Like this it was keeping itself ready for an eventual attack against Venus. But it certainly suffered some retaliation for this because the mediocre standing of the planet was not a result of the ascetism of its inhabitants; it was definitely linked to the reluctance of its Senate. It was obviously the Earth who supplied the greatest force. The Earth who must have been equipped with a Spaceless that landed on another C.122 planet.

"The Spaceless don't go everywhere," he said.

The child was chewing his tablet.

"Why do you say that?"

"Let me explain."

He didn't think of the child as a youth anymore. He treated him as an equal.

"There are Spaceless for short trips: Earth-Mars-Venus. And for the foreign worlds, the tunnels Mars-C.122, C.123 and C.124. the same for the Earth and Venus where you can go to any of the three systems. Obviously, to reach another sector there are just ships that go the same speed as the cargoes. But why go elsewhere?"

"Well, to keep on settling there, to meet other intelligent races…"

"Those are brain ideas. I don't think you should talk like that in public. You know who's heading the revolt on C.122?"

"No."

"A group of mutant brains. Yes, mutants! That's why we're having such a hard time. But we'll get them. The Earth alone, if it mobilized all the economic potential of C.124, which it owns, could crush them."

"Why don't they do it?"

"Venus is against it. It wouldn't hear of it. But it won't hear anything when Mars has reduced it to ashes. Wait for C.122 to fall to its knees and you'll see!"

"And what if the two other systems revolt next?"

The child said nothing at first. Then, "That's not possible. C.122 revolted because…" He lowered his voice, "What I'm going to tell you isn't in the prep course. The system revolted because it belongs to Mars and Mars didn't maintain enough forces here."

"It was keeping them for Venus?"

"Exactly. But that's the flip side of the coin."

A sharp whistle tore through the mess. Everyone stood up and froze. A tall, slim man had just entered. On his white uniform, which floated on his body, you could see two red stripes. His voice sounded like a barking dog:

"I'm Colonel Merelborn and you're going to get to know me, you bunch of filthy mutants! Outside, in four lines, double time. Go!"

When they were all outside in the ghastly rays of the double suns—a big and a small that were distant from each other—he talked to them again:

"Operation Jungle. Objective: clear out the nuclear stockpiles. Don't worry about the radioactive zones, the half-cycle is less than a minute. The rebels use their own missiles."

He guffawed.

"They don't want to make the planet uninhabitable… and since they don't have radiant weapons…"

He made a grand gesture without any apparent significance.

"You bunch of filthy mutants, try not to die. I'll still need more neutron fodder."

Some wingers came down vertically and landed in the courtyard. They'd been hastily built. Their magnetic thrusters jolted them along. Nothing at all like the elegant private vehicles that circulated in the skies of Venus. These here were like soapboxes.

More soldiers came rushing out of other buildings and climbed into the wingers, shouting and swearing, so rapidly that their prior training was obvious. The company that Alberg belonged to filled an entire vehicle. There were 250 of them. The winger took off jerkily, throwing them against one another.

Alberg wondered how he was going to slip away from this hornet's nest—the rebels' missiles might be clean, but they were missiles. Even though atomic weapons had been given up a long time ago, Alberg knew that one of those missiles could wipe out all the soldiers sent on the mission. He was going to have to hide. None of this mess was anything like hunting mutants. Not to mention the difficulties of deserting under such conditions. He could go over to the enemy since there was an enemy, but that would just be more of the same. None of this was of any interest to him. It was gratuitous.

The winger was wrapped in a red halo.

Someone spoke over the rumbling engines, "The shield."

"What shield?" Alberg asked.

"We've just crossed the energy shield protecting the base. From now on, watch your asses!"

Through a window Alberg saw a streak of fire flash by 300 feet from the winger. One of the ancient missiles.

"Those things probably date back to Hitler," he said. "We've just got to get hit by one…"

"No worries. We've got a shield, too."

213

The winger reeled abruptly, fell 300 feet in freefall and then went spinning back up. The hull was burning hot. The air outside flickered with thousands of glowing spots that tortured the eye.

"What did I tell you?" the soldier said, half-strangled by his seatbelt. "It's not going to really heat up til later. There are no individual shields for the soldiers."

Through the window Alberg watched the ground bitterly. A gray expanse, almost flat, leveled by the nuclear explosions, all the way to the horizon towards which the winger was rushing with every piece of it vibrating. The rebels didn't have radiant weapons as Colonel Merelborn had said, but for Alberg, radioactive weapons were enough. That Merelborn! What a bonehead!

While he was eyeing the ground, the landscape gradually changed. Clumps of half-burned vegetation appeared. Then they became thicker. Soon they were flying over a dense jungle in which a clearing had been hollowed out by explosions.

He flailed about trying to find something to hang onto: the winger was dropping like a stone. It steadied itself a few feet off the ground and landed softly in the clearing. Every soldier was out in less than a minute, spreading out under cover. The winger shot up and disappeared.

The child whom Alberg had spoken to during the flight was not far away.

"They've just got to drop one of their damned missiles," Alberg grumbled, "and Operation Jungle is finished."

"No," the child said. "We're too spread out. They know it. A surface-to-surface wouldn't do much good."

"A surface-to-surface?"

"That's what they call them. A very old expression."

"So, they're going to leave us alone?"

"No. They've got rifles with tritium bullets."

"What's that?"

"Nuclear bullets. One of those can wipe out everything within almost 100 feet."

"Super. And what are we supposed to do?"

"Destroy the launch sites of the surface-to-surface mis-siles."

An order was shouted from a clump of yellow leaves. The child started running, bent double. Alberg followed him, around 100 feet behind. The leaves slashed his face. He could taste the blood running down his cheeks into his mouth.

"But what the hell am I doing here?" he thought to himself. "Running like a lunatic on a planet with one sun too many!"

Explosions could be heard in the distance and wailing along with them. To his right, a tree with a ten-foot wide, black trunk sprang into the air and came crashing down with a horrendous din. Around him the bushes vanished in bright flames. Alberg kept running. He stumbled over a man on the ground rolling in the spiky leaves. A red insect, as big as a hand, jumped on his face. He slapped it off and the insect let out a weird shriek, like a weak neighing. Alberg got up but the man signaled him to stay down. As he was lying down by his side something whistled through the air. 300 feet behind them a grove of trees disappeared in a flash of flames.

"I've had enough," Alberg said.

"It's only the beginning," the man replied.

This guy was not a child. He had gray hair peeking out from under his helmet and deep wrinkles lined his face.

"How can we get through this?" Alberg asked.

"Can't. If we tried to get through straight ahead, they'll drop on us before we make it."

"We could go off into the brush where they're not shoot-ing. And then we'll find a way."

"What, are you scared?"

"Of course," Alberg grimaced. "This isn't fighting man-to-man. They're massacring at random without seeing any-thing. Me, I don't give a damn about any of this. I have work to do elsewhere."

He suddenly realized that it wasn't true. From now on he was out of work. He was a person of independent means like those old men who stole a lot during their lives. Or rather just

215

retired like Merelborn would be someday or Corlis after a lot of killing. They managed to make him inactive; there were others who were made silent. But he wasn't banned from doing something else. Anything was better than this absurd scuttling around under a hail of nuclear missiles.

"Why didn't you choose the work zone?"

"Because I was hoping to get through this more easily."

"Well, now you understand."

"Why not run off to the side?" Alberg repeated.

"Because it's the jungle with creatures you can't imagine that have nothing to put in their mouths."

The word "jungle" didn't mean much to him. They talked about in the old books and he'd seen magnetoscope reels in really bad shape that showed pictures. But they were flat pictures, barely decipherable.

"Okay," Alberg said, "the beasties are going to gobble me up. Farewell."

"What?! You're crazy," the guy said. "Stop!"

But Alberg was already crawling at a right angle to the line of fire. He turned on his side to wave goodbye to the grizzled man. He saw the helmet was crooked. He crawled on for two or three minutes.

A whistling detonation exploded. Alberg closed his eyes to the flash. Then he looked back again. Where he had just been was completely barren, not a tree or a bush remained. Instead was a circle of glowing gray about 40 yards in diameter. The man in the white uniform had vanished. He would never straighten his helmet to regulation position.

"That was clever," Alberg thought, "to choose white for the uniforms. What a target!"

And then he told himself that his worst enemy was the double sun. Certainly, they hadn't found anything better. No enemy was visible. But maybe they were also wearing white uniforms. He looked up. The huge trees formed a canopy of leaves that was thick enough to block most of the bluish light. But what filtered through was enough to justify the almost opaque visor of the helmet. He kept crawling through the bushes and thickets of spiky plants.

More red insects, stirred up by his movements, were climbing onto his back. One of them went at his sleeve and put a hole in it in under a second, even though Alberg could see that the fabric had metallic fibers. He shook the insect off of him and crushed it with the butt of his radiant rifle. The creature writhed on the ground with its weird whining noises. Others came in three columns. Then even more columns converged on Alberg. The tiny cries harmonized with the rhythm of their feet like a military march. Alberg got to his feet and, bent over, started running. A few insects were hanging onto his boots, climbing up his legs. He scraped them off with his rifle and then went back to crawling.

A bullet whizzed by his head and exploded less than 300 feet from him, destroying a parcel of the forest. It was not a good idea to show himself. He was still in the target zone. What if all of Merelborn's troops had been surrounded since their landing?

Alberg kept going. The whinnying noises faded and the explosions were now very far behind him. He slung his rifle over his back to be freer to move. And he hurried on. He was picturing with some relief the moment when he would be out of the combat zone entirely.

He was running, still hunched over, but then he suddenly stopped. Out of the thicket a few feet in front of him a black mouth sprang forth as big as a door. The mouth was connected to an equally big, cylindrical body with countless feet. Alberg thought of grabbing his rifle but he knew the black monster could tear him to pieces before the weapon was in his hands. His old reflexes came rushing back. The radiant was in his hand. He fired without aiming.

The beast rose up, the body standing like a column, the head 30 feet in the air. Alberg backpedaled, reached for his rifle and fired again. A dim ray shot out and hit the monster's head. The beast fell backward, crushing trees and didn't move.

217

It was 50 feet long. In the gaping maw he saw a forest of black teeth as sharp as needles.

"Here's one of the creatures my former comrade in arms was talking about," he thought.

As he got closer, he heard a high-pitched whine, so he dropped to the ground. Before him, the corpse of the animal disappeared in a blinding flash. The explosion came right afterward.

But when Alberg opened his eyes, he could still see nothing. He managed to roll onto his side. He felt like he was caught in the middle of an endless vibration. As if his body was one big tuning fork. At the same time, he vaguely heard voices approaching, but he couldn't make out what they were saying.

Then he sank into a dark void.

CHAPTER XVI

The huge city of Villagea erected its peaks and commercial buildings into the sky, surging up out of myriads of low houses where the inhabitants lived. It was 8 pm and the sun, already set, was casting its last rays on the golden summits of the buildings.

Getting off the Spaceless, Iona walked through the astrostation. The glowing hull of a giant cargo ship was floating down into the landing zone like a balloon. One came every day after years of voyaging from foreign worlds. One light year away from the solar system, the crew had started to prepare the unloading of fabricated goods and staple foods.

They had stopped production of this model of cargo ship almost a century ago for two reasons: first, because the Lorentz-Fitzgerald temporal contraction brings them back to Earth after 75 years while the foreign worlds were at least 15 light years from the solar system: then because the cost of manufacturing these ships was still not recuperated when they decided to invest great sums in the Spaceless. As for the crew, it lived a separate existence, isolated from the problems of the three planets as well as the foreign worlds. Its members along with their families aged five times slower than the population of the home ports. They were nomads outside of all jurisdictions. For them, the loading and unloading of freight—the purpose of their strange way of life—were unimportant. They avoided all contact with the people on the ground at both ends of the line, naturally strangers, and they paid no heed to any changes that occurred during their absence. A separate civilization was born in the belly of the cargo ships with its own traditions and its own technology.

Iona stopped to watch the cargo ship landing. She'd always been fascinated by these ships and the mysterious little communities they were home to. There must have been a lot of mutants. Maybe they hunted those who were not... What would happen if someone decided one day that their voyages were no more use? Did their brains have the means to force the planets to maintain the status quo? No one knew anything and anyone who wondered had never said anything about it.

She had left Venus in the middle of the commercial carnival and although there was no celebration to enliven the gloomy atmosphere of Mars, she was now back in a festive city. The sounds of revelry reached all the way to the terminals of the astrostation.

It was part of Iona's professional responsibilities to know that this festivity was going on, but she'd forgotten. It was Children's Week.

There was hardly any other artistic creation on the three planets aside from what the children did. Rare were the adults who dedicated themselves to unprofitable nonsense that demanded the effort of production instead of the joy of trade. Thus, luminous painting, liquid sculpture, noise music or subjective cinema, everything was the work of children. Tonight, Villagea was an endless gala of opening nights and sneak previews. Some children had even written books—that obsolete custom—and had organized signings.

Iona went to the main bar in the astrostation. It was full of children drinking alcohol. A lot of them were loud and restless, their naturally expressive personalities magnified by drunkenness. Only during this week did they have the right to drink like adults.

Most of them recognized Iona. They gave her an ovation. She wound her way through the tables, smiling and waving. One of them who couldn't have been much younger than fifteen gave her a wink. He was decked out in spectacular extravagance. Iona looked at him curiously.

"Are you participating in the Week?" she asked.

He stood up, "Have a drink with me, if you want me to answer."

Iona sat on the edge of an armchair and ordered a raspberry beer. "Well, my dear viewer?" she said amusingly.

He leaned over and kissed her on the lips. Then, coldly, he spoke. "I'm showing stabilized steam forms. A senator this afternoon bought a Narcissus and Prometheus for his private home. And I'll no doubt get an order from the State."

"Are they expensive?"

"40,000 sollars."

Iona raised her eyebrows and thought of Alberg. Considering the exchange rate, this child was earning, with a single work, one and half times what the hunter got for murder.

"What's your name?"

"Wilfrid."

This was the second shock. The first lieutenant of Little Paul was called Wilfrid.

"What do you do with your money?"

"I invest."

"In what?"

"That's nobody's business." He raised his glass and whispered, "But for you, I'll make an exception."

He snapped his fingers. Quickly and quietly a group of children gathered around, isolating him. And they turned their backs.

"I supply the resistance with food and weapons. There are hundreds of thousands around the Villagea. They're spread out in small groups of hundred."

"That's what they say," Iona said. "Why are you telling me this?"

"For two reasons. First, I don't think you're capable of betraying us. And secondly, you must know that if you do, you won't be living for long."

Iona felt uneasy. The exact same feeling she tried to create in her shows. Little Paul, Wilfrid and the others were the subject of rumors and accusations. But they'd never stopped them. Or never dared try. These children formed a vast web. They knew about everything. Maybe this was the moment to get a lead?

"Have you heard of a mutant hunter called Alberg?"

He looked at her suspiciously, "Why?"

"I'm looking for him."

Wilfrid waved it off carelessly, "That's your business. An unpleasant fellow. Someday, he'll be the hunted. But for now, I have no information."

"He isn't in Villagea?"

"If he is, I think I'd know."

Iona sat there pondering. Wilfrid was telling the truth. Who had lied? Silas or Del Padre? But she couldn't rely on the word of one informer.

"Thanks, Wilfrid," she said. "You know I'm on your side."

"We'll see about that," he replied. "We judge people by their actions."

He kissed her again. She left, troubled, and headed for the bar where she had noticed a natural man—barefoot, draped in a white robe and wearing a headband. He was drinking a glass of water and munching on corn.

Iona ordered another raspberry beer and turned to him, "How goes your campaign to resume hydroponic farming?"

The natural man took a swig of water and shrugged, "Badly. Half of us don't even believe in it. And you, what do you think of it?"

"It's good," she said enthusiastically, "really good. You'll have to do some experimental farming yourselves."

The man's face lit up, "Oh yeah? And do you think the authorities would approve of that?"

"No, of course not, but if you always had to ask that question before doing anything…"

"Right…" the man crunched another piece of corn. "I see…"

She said nothing for a moment and then, "You could get the mutants to work. They'd become independent, useful and safe."

"That's not a bad idea," the man agreed and emptied his glass.

"By the way, do you know a mutant hunter called Alberg?"

"Yes. And you?"

"I know him and I'm looking for him."

"Why?"

"Gotta stop what he's doing."

The natural man straightened up and slapped the counter. Ten people dressed in gray came out of the crowd and surrounded Iona like the children had done earlier. But this not for the same reason. The natural man had just taken off his wig.

"I'm arresting you," he said. "Alberg is a mutant."

Iona stepped back and said flatly, "I know. I'm the one who denounced him in Arespolis. Word gets around fast."

The policeman snickered. "If you denounced him, that means you knew what he was. You had relations with a mutant and in full knowledge of the facts. They saw you with him in Aphros."

"But, come on, since I denounced him!"

"That doesn't change a thing. Besides, you said seditious things about the authorities to me. And you just had a suspicious conversation with the children. You're going to explain all of that. Let's go."

Iona put her back against the bar. "I'm not leaving. You have nothing against me. Absurd fallacies. Objections to meaningless chatter. Baseless assertions."

One of the men came up and slapped her hard in the face. She tasted blood in her mouth. It took four of them to pull her off the bar she was clutching onto. But when the officers turned around, all the children stood up. The huge room suddenly fell silent. It was a sea of ice-cold eyes.

The men in gray had taken out their guns. They moved forward determinedly, but their faces reflected their anxiety. This crowd made them think twice.

Most of the children present, boys and girls, were around 13 years old. They wore leather pants, pink or green or blue or orange, and white shirts decorated with black skulls or photograms of cadaverous colors. A lot of them were sporting necklaces of human bones stolen on the way to the incinerators. All of them had knives or iron bars that they had flamboyantly drew from their metal belts. How many of them had radiants? No doubt a great many. If the police fired, they'd be disowned by their superiors, but posthumously because they most likely would be massacred right there.

Wilfrid gave a brief order. 20 or so of the biggest children stepped up. They were bare-chested and had tattoos of genitals and weapons. Their hair, fashionably burned by matches, fell to their shoulders out of the oversized antiradiation helmets they had swiped from some army supply store. They parted the others, creating a passage that opened up before the policemen, who went down it, dragging their prisoner hastily toward the exit.

On the street that went downtown, the magnetocars of the police had been surrounded by other shock groups dressed like savages. The cops pushed away a few drunken kids who staggered up to them yelling insults and threats.

"None of this bodes well," one of the cops said as he got into his vehicle.

The magnetocars started quickly amidst the boos and jeers. Less than a minute later Wilfrid mustered his troops.

"Operation A nd B. No radiants. A show of force. Call up the Bullies to keep things in line. Primary objective: free the woman they just arrested."

Ten children piled into the magnetocars and sped off in different directions. Others started talking into the mini walkie-talkies on their bracelets. The astrostation terminal was emptied out in the blink of an eye.

After half an hour the festive atmosphere all over Villagea had mutated into an ambiance of revolt. The entire city hummed and buzzed. Police brigades took up their positions at the main intersections to cordon off the 3D buildings, to guard the Spaceless, to occupy the esplanade of the Senate, to build blockades around the weapons shops. The men wore gray uniforms, antiradiation helmets and carried paralyzers. Each of them had a light metal shield hung around his neck.

But all the avenues, streets and neighboring squares were teeming with children between the ages of 8 and 15. The youngest of them were holding strange weapons—strong springs mounted on tubes that could be wound up by means of a crank. From out of the tube the steel arrow could hit its target at 200 yards and go right through a human body. Others were carrying long blowguns whose sharp darts had been soaked in polluted water.

The children were always prepared for war and could be called up at any time. Thus, some had big slingshots that could launch balls full of acid or had bundles of fireworks containing yperite, otherwise known as mustard gas, slung over their shoulders. It didn't all look like the work of children alone, but stuff bought or stolen from labs and monasteries.

Great waves of them singing and shouting in high-pitched voices, but it wasn't chaos. Divided into fairly equal groups, they were framed by the Bullies. Bare-chested, helmeted, the Bullies had radiants and even rifles. Above the city, the surveillance chiefs were soaring around in hundreds of wings, side by side with their police units.

Two armies faced off without engaging. The rumor spread that Wilfrid was at the Senate where he was talking with the opposition senators, the others having refused to see him. Another rumor spread then—Wilfrid would be arrested.

Right away missiles went flying. The smell of mustard from the yperite wafted through the city, which was swept clean by a strong, artificial wind. But the steel arrows pierced the shields and the balls of corrosive acid burned through the clothes and skin. On the other side, hundreds of children, temporarily paralyzed, were carried away, suffocating. Explosions sounded off pretty much everywhere—the children had old firearms and were shooting bullets.

They handed out radiant rifles to the police who already had dozens of casualties from arrows and bullets and hundreds of wounded.

In the midst of this spectacle, the Bullies were overrun. In a tidal wave of shrieking, the painted children rushed at the

225

enemy, dodging the rays and attacking with knives and axes. The men in gray could only use the weapons they'd been given.

CHAPTER XVII

The Senate Palace was built on one of the hills that over-
looked the city. On another hill stood a bizarre building with
multicolored walls, surmounted by turrets and spires covered
with bells that chimed in the wind. This kind of baroque castle
looked like it was built of caramel and had always been the
butt of jokes among the people.

In fact, it was not caramel, but titanium reinforced concrete. Its basements contained a power plant that allowed it to
be surrounded by an anti-radiation shield and its walls were
pierced with holes that harbored the long, black tubes of long-
range radiant arms.

The Candy House, as it was often called, held within it
many secrets that the Senate police had tried for a long time to
penetrate to no avail. The investigations couldn't be made
official and every inspector caught was disavowed by the Senate. This state of things was a direct result of the Constitution.

Moreover, according the designs used to build it and
renovate it, the Candy House had an underground airport and
astrostation with a private tunnel to the Spaceless.

A network of corridors snaked under the city of Villagea,
accessed from the surface by huge, rapid elevators. Hundreds
of magnetic vehicles could circulate in these underground passages, ten times faster than on the surface without the traffic.
Of course, the Senate knew about this anthill but it had no real
idea of its importance. It also knew that some adults were part
of the Special Guard, the "shadow" police able to mobilize at
any moment when called upon. For the most part, they were
parents attached to the old-fashioned ideas that had once ruled
over family relations. In public, these ideas were so openly
ridiculed that it was hard to imagine there were more than a
few hundred members of the Special Guard.

When Iona was arrested, a middle-aged man was standing in the high chamber of the Candy House. He was dressed

in pink velvet and was playing a complex game of pool in which the balls were soap bubbles that never popped. Nearby, files were piled up on a desk; a book lay open among them: Humorous Treatise on Legislation.

An image appeared on the 3D platform next to the desk. A man dressed in green satin. The pool player straightened up.

"Lewis," the image said sternly, "you're sure you've got nothing better to do?"

"Oh, Binker," Lewis replied, "all my routine business has been attended to."

"Me too," Binker said. "But it's not finished for you. The host of the scary stories show has just been arrested. While Little Paul's gone, Wilfrid is taking charge of the children. It looks like it's going to get really messy."

Lewis dropped his frivolous attitude. "So, we have to act immediately. Would you take care of the legal formalities and all that? I'll deal with getting her out."

"Very well," Binker sounded a little anxious. "The big guns, then?"

"My friend, "Lewis said, "this arrest is only a technicality that the Senate can certainly fall back on without seriously harming its prestige. On the other hand, if the children don't stay calm, they could start a chain reaction with unforeseeable consequences. You know the Senate and its pig-headed policies. It'll be ready to do anything to maintain order, meaning it'll stir up more disorder instead of settling a trivial grievance…"

"I think you're right," Binker admitted. "I'll deal with the broadcasts and the surveillance of the army chiefs. Meet in one hour in the audience hall."

"Right."

Binker's image clicked off. Lewis left the room by a small elevator and went to the central command office where he pressed a red button and sent out a series of messages. Then he put on a red helmet; which clashed with his outfit. He grimaced at himself in the mirror and left with a sigh.

In the next hour, while the streets of the city were flooded with children and police, another feverish activity was going on in every apartment building. Called on their individual micro-receivers, the reservists of the Special Guard left their families and ran down to their basements. There they entered passages known only to them and followed the corridors that led to shops and small arsenals. They put on their red helmets, armed themselves and got into the magnetocars that were equipped with big paralyzing blasters. These magnetocars were bright red. Some of them sped off into the underground to line up on the ramps that led to the surface. Others went towards the airports in the suburbs and stopped on an underground esplanade where hundreds of red wingers were waiting. Over each of these was a slab that slid open, allowing for simultaneous vertical takeoffs.

When the clashes started becoming serious in the city, the red magnetocars came out everywhere and their drivers tried to cordon off the fighters. Long lines of red helmets formed a vast net while their paralyzing weapons went to work.

Above Villagea, the red wingers soared in like a cloud at sunset because they reflected a blood-red light. Not knowing what was going on, the police and the children started spinning around. Some of them fell to the ground.

And in all the receivers a sharp voice came through. The same voice thundered out at every intersection. It said:

"We, Lewis and Binker, the Ludocrats of Earth, declare a state of emergency. Starting right now, the Senate is under our control. Whoever obeys its orders will be subject to the harshest punishments. In every city on the globe, the Special Guard is on alert. The police chiefs and the generals are under our surveillance. The senators shall be confined to the assembly. It will immediately grant the demands of the children. The state of emergency will last 24 hours after which the Senate will be restored to its full powers. We will remain on alert, however, and not give up our vigilance. We are ordering all senatorial forces to go back to their quarters so that the traditional festivities of the Children's Week can continue in normal fashion. We, Lewis and Binker, the Ludocrats of Earth, have intervened in the interest of everyone. Let's hope everyone is aware of this and we won't have to prolong this period of temporary dictatorship provided for in the Constitution."

In the Palace surrounded by red helmets, the senators were confused and dismayed. All of them had deluded themselves about the Ludocrats and the Special Guard.

CHAPTER XVIII

He was floating in a milky void. He didn't know where he was or who he was. A foamy void like beaten egg whites. The beaten eggs he used to eat when he was a little boy. Eggs preserved for 75 years before coming to the family table. The family? A woman with a worried voice, memories of bewildering words: "Stop analofyzing in front the children. Watch yourself. Think a little more slowly. You're very often wrong. You know the neighbors are listening at the doors?" And the hazy face of a man with black hair, a man shrugging his shoulders. And again a child holding a knife, coming in at an angle, saying, "You know, just because you're bigger than me doesn't mean you can do whatever you want. See how sharp this is? And look at the point…"

The images melted like a candle. A candle? Like stearin, better. What is stearin? And a candle, what's it used for? The images reformed into the outline of a man running. He was running but not escaping. He turned his head. A head with yellow eyes. And he fell slowly, tumbling down. He, too, melted in a lake of light out of which cries were rising like some drowning victim calling out from the depths of the water.

Now it was a man they were beating. Someone screaming for mercy but the torturers were whipping him with steel cables. And he who was still drifting in his cottony void interrupted them: "Leave him to me. You don't know how to handle this. They'll pay me more than you for the job."

"Everything's okay," someone said as if in answer. Alberg opened his eyes. The white void was the ceiling. He felt like he was just lifting his eyelids but his eyes had already been open for a long time. Except he didn't know he was seeing. The image was really there, on his retina, but the brain was still not registering it. The colored nothingness finally became something. And the voice that had said, "Everything's

231

okay," belonged to a young woman who was leaning over the air bed on which Alberg was lying.

"What happened," he asked.

"You were completely irradiated," she said. "They bled you dry and properly cleaned out your guts. Now you've got brand new blood and you don't make the Geiger counter go crazy."

"Oh," Alberg said weakly.

None of this mattered to him. He was sleepy. And indeed, he slept.

In his dream he felt ready and he struggled up clumsily. Walls of air kept him from falling to the floor. "Yeah, I'm not as strong as I thought."

Now he remembered. A tritium bullet had exploded in front of him, close range. But he hadn't been disintegrated, just irradiated. In the past it meant certain death. Today they had more effective radiation, longer frequencies, which blocked the intracardial nerve conduction. The same ones they used for radiants and rifles. And for the big guns.

He wondered, "Where did I come up with all this?" Did he learn it all at Gun and Murder? His mind went in a different direction.

Where was he now? Was he in an infirmary of the Merelborn column or had he fallen into the hands of the rebels who were going to torture him for information? Information about what? He didn't know anything about this war except for what the child had told him: C.122 and the rest.

Something told him he wasn't a prisoner of the rebels. He didn't see what could make him so sure. He didn't believe in intuition and yet he knew nothing about his situation. Observing details, more or less consciously, and automatically processing them in his brain? Here again he was surprised by this kind of thinking. He wasn't used to analyzing everything, to speculating like this. He knew what he had to do to track his prey, to escape a counter-attack, to get his pay under the most trying of circumstances… thoughts directly linked to action.

But then he realized that these new thoughts were also linked to action. The more information he had, the more foresight he'd have. And more foresight made him more effective. Strike better and dodge better.

The nurse came back. "So, up and at 'em?"

That was a fitting phrase. He wanted to smile, but a man dressed in white was walking by in a hallway at the edge of his vision. The man had looked over at him, briefly. Alberg started talking without realizing it.

"When you've blackmailed him, you'll still have to figure out if you'll need to carry it out or not. Given the fragmentary observations I've got, you'll be made to do it so that he'll take you seriously. Right now, your future together will be the result of new factors that I can only estimate in such a broad range. The problem with the future is that it's like a body of water: we see better what's near the surface than what's hiding deep down."

He stopped, flabbergasted.

The nurse was staring at him, wide-eyed. She muttered, "Wh... what are you talking about? How could you know that?"

A red light flashed on in Alberg's mind. Something terrible had happened to him. Something he'd do better to keep hidden.

"I think I'm not completely back to normal," he spoke weakly again. "I must be hallucinating."

The nurse watched him for a moment. Her face turned stony. "You're not hallucinating at all. Everything you just told me is intimately related to my private life, and I'm wondering how you know about it."

Alberg thought, "Here we go, I've put myself in a fix. Now they're going to try to find out what happened and they'll find out something I won't want to know."

He bitterly missed the time when he spoke curtly and brutally, when he calculated only two or three steps in advance, just for immediate action. But that was in the past. It was the radiation that had transformed him. On second

233

thought, he had to admit that there was something to it. The radiation couldn't radically metamorphosize a man's clairvoyance by suddenly honing his observation and augmenting his mental acuteness. The radiation acted as a developer of predisposed terrain. He thought of his memories on first awakening when he was still in the field. A memory of his mother's words, maybe from when he was two or three years old. "Stop analyzing in front of the children..." It was about his father. His father with conclusions that were too quick, too valuable not to arouse attention. His father with a mind too brilliant not to be suspicious. His father the mutant.

His father whose nose he had broken when he was ten years old, maybe to avenge the unconscious certainty of being the son of a mutant, meaning something scandalous and repugnant. A father who desired the death of his son so as to put an end to the transmitted traits he possessed and that the public opinion considered a defect rather than a gift because the public opinion was created by inferior people who were bitter and afraid. Still, the public opinion took precedence and put pressure on minds, even those that understood its absurd hostility.

"You know," he said, "I have no knowledge of your private life. I'm coming out of a coma. But maybe you brought up the subject around me with a colleague, for example, and my sleeping brain registered what you said..."

He stopped talking. He was starting to go too far.

"I didn't bring up anything of the kind with anybody," the nurse said. "I believe we'll have to proceed with some chromosomic exams."

"Listen," he confessed, "I'm a mutant hunter. How would you like it if I turned out to be a mutant myself?"

She looked confused. "Maybe you don't know about it."

"Right," he agreed. "Now, whether I'm a mutant or not, don't you think I can be useful if we talk a little about your personal problems? It's better for me to avoid an unpleasant exam with all of that... let's say notoriety."

For the first time a little smile appeared on the nurse's face. But he'd already known for a few seconds that he'd won.

It was necessary since he knew he was going to leave the hospital soon through the door to the left of the main entrance because with the location of his room…

They had a conversation after the curiosity, impatience and anxiety of the nurse made her open up. She acted like someone in centuries past meeting a clairvoyant psychic. But Alberg did better than said psychic. At the end of their talk, the nurse had whittled herself away for him and even more in the next hour during which her menacing breakup with the chief physician turned into a new romance.

Afterward, nothing much happened for 24 hours. Alberg got his uniform back, which had partly protected him, as well as his helmet. His weapons, they told him, remained in the hands of the military police who were keeping them for him until his medical leave was over.

However, the formalities and execution of the urgent orders had kept them from searching his uniform. Thus, he still had his radiant and his money, though he had lost the cumbersome rifle.

When he left the hospital, the chief physician shook his hand with a grin, "So, are you satisfied with the care you received? What did you think of your nurse?"

The red light flashed in Alberg's head. "Very satisfied. My nurse was very dedicated."

"Isn't she nice? And well, your advice was of great use to her…"

"Hmm, hmm," Alberg nodded.

"You know, when it's sound advice. Especially when sounded by something not altogether human…"

"Yes… I don't follow you…"

"Come on, come on," the doctor said, "you're way ahead of me." He patted him on the shoulder and added, "Pay a visit to the Cedille. You'll see some surprising things there."

"Cedille?"

"The suburbs of C-town. But be careful, the rebels have infiltrated there, too. Who knows into what camp your poor feet will guide you…"

He bid farewell to Alberg with an ambiguous gleam in his eye. On the sidewalk the convalescent looked back three times at the secondary exit he'd come out of, the one to the left of the main entrance…

Night was falling. A night that was going to last two hours because the setting sun would soon be replaced by another, which would be rising in nearly the same place. And it was still a good season. The planet had a dozen. During most of them, there was no night. The longest one ensued under a merciless sun that went around in a little circle at the zenith and whatever shade it left was roasted by the second sun revolving at a 45 ° angle around the first.

Alberg started off into the stuffy night. The streets were full of soldiers like on Mars. Nine tenths of them, moreover, wore Martian uniforms. But there were also some civilians. Alberg was quickly struck by something unusual: because of the heat the civilians wore different clothes from the Venusians protected by an infrared shield; different also from the Martians on the cold planet—but they all looked elegant and luxurious. All except for a few who became more and more numerous as Alberg got closer to the periphery. These were covered in rags. One of them held out his hand to Alberg, so he shook it. The man tore away from the careless grasp, shook a fist at him and ran off, skirting along the walls. Alberg stood there speechless as some soldiers broke out laughing. The look he gave the closest one froze the laughter in his throat.

The soldier finally just shrugged and said, "No need to get sore. We were all new here once."

"Who are these misers who wear rags on their backs instead of buying new clothes?" Alberg asked grumpily.

The other laughed again. "They're not misers. They're poor."

"Poor? That hasn't existed for 300 years."

"Back home, no, but here, they're everywhere. That guy didn't want to shake your hand. He wanted money."

"Money? For me to give him some? He's crazy! He just has to do like me, like everyone—earn it!"

236

"You don't get it," the soldier said. "Either he can't earn it or he's only paid one or two sollars a day."

"One or two… a day!"

He was about to scream. Then he shut his mouth. He suddenly understood everything. At the same time, he realized that for a moment he'd turned back into the old Alberg. His gift could go dim.

"Let me explain," the soldier said patiently. But another touched his arm and gave him a knowing look. The soldier resumed, "Yeah, if you want an explanation, go find out for yourself. I don't want to get locked up. Later, pal."

They all left, arm in arm, singing loudly.

Alberg watched them go away with an uneasy feeling. First of all, he didn't recognize himself. He was different from one minute to the next. Different in abilities, personality and attitude. He tried to get hold of himself but he slipped away as if he were both the donkey and the carrot.

Secondly, what happened on C.122 troubled him. For a moment he wondered with terror if he'd been offended by the condition of the poor, if he was sinking into the depths of a ridiculous morality that was going to bind him hand and foot. But he sighed with relief—what really bothered him was the newness and complexity of the situation and thus the difficulty he would have to exploit it. All right, there was the positive Alberg who knew what was important and wasn't upset by bleary-eyed whining.

Obviously, it was not a well-oiled machine. The three planets of the solar system lived in opulence and their people were circulating fortunes that passed from one to another like a peace pipe according to the rules of the complicated game they called business. But all of this was possible only by the presence on foreign worlds of other peoples, probably more numerous, who produced the consumer products and manufactured goods for a measly wage. These objects were used as pawns in the game of business, which would sink without them. And whether they ate the objects or used them, they had to be continually renewed. Maybe this wasn't so nice for the foreign worlds—just look at the C.122 revolt made possible by the prehistoric ideas of supremacy that Mars fostered. But, on the whole, they had to like it. The armies of the three solar planets were there to make sure of it.

The trickiest part of the issue, Alberg was thinking, was in the process of selection that kept around the table only the players who were most skilled in this kind of game. The others were left to fill the ranks of producers—who reproduced themselves without any further intervention—or else maintained the military might destined to discourage any ill will.

"Clever system," he thought as he entered a zone reeking of filth. "A system running smoothly but it has cracks: mutants, natural men, children. And then this rotten war on C.122. And also, those narrow-minded Spartans on Mars who lose sight of what's important by wanting to play the conqueror like in the age of cavemen. It's thanks to them, ultimately, that everything's on the point of collapsing. It is, therefore, thanks to them that I'm going to get something out of this. Because I have no intention of leaving the profits of this operation to all those weaklings who dream of taking the reins. A good revolution pays for anyone who controls it. It pays in money and power. I don't care about power, but the money... and since the two go together..."

He kicked a bowl and whispered to himself, "Although power, after all..." But he shook his head. Power was another need of the weak. When you were strong, you had no need to prove it to others. It was only for people lacking self-confidence, seeking validation of their personality in the servility of others. A false validation, obviously, since its search came out of idleness and insecurity. He, Alberg, would never let himself fall into that trap.

The street had become squalid. Adults and children in rags stood in front of adjacent alleys, gazing at the sculpted magnetocars raised on golden rods to drive over the trash. Inside the vehicles they glimpsed officers with their women decked out in jewels, only one of which could have bought an asteroid and furnished it with an atmosphere.

238

Alberg smiled. Didn't this lack planning? The poor shouldn't be idle in the streets but working, no matter what the wage. As for the officers, they didn't need anything more than their pay. Of course, they did all kinds of work to keep those whores, but it only resulted in an outflow of money. Money should go back into the government coffers. No doubt it got back there somehow and some way. Alberg suspected that the Senate on every planet was getting fat off this circus. But why such devious ways? When you had the power, you didn't need to sneak around to steal. Or else they didn't really have the power. He felt nothing but contempt for these amateurs.

But him, hadn't he spoken absurdly in the mess hall during his last meal before the attack? To go elsewhere, to keep on settling there, to meet other intelligent races... And to the child that was all brain talk. He didn't have the knowledge of a brain but he had the weaknesses. Luckily, and to make up for it, he had the strength of a mutant. He knew how to be wary of himself. When you were a little thick, the worst enemy was inside. The others you could shoot the moment they were felt down to the bone.

Incidentally, he'd forgotten about another fault in the system. The brains were indispensable but fleeting elements. They would be the hardest to make use of in the course of affairs. But the brains were living in their instruments and their calculations. They didn't have a political spirit. He'd get the better of them.

For the present, he was thinking of what the doctor had said: "who knows into what camp your poor feet will guide you..." As he was passing by an empty lot, hidden from the street behind a half-burned, green plastic fence, he almost ran into a man. He stepped back, his hand already reaching for his radiant. But the guy coming out of the shadows looked puny and withered with blinking eyes. Rags hung off his body like parasitic plants on the walls of a ruin.

"Soldier," the wreck said, "you want to know what real love is"?

239

Alberg looked him up and down. The rags had once been a tailored suit and behind the perpetually moving eyelids his eyes were darting.

Alberg smiled, "And you know? Judging by the state you're in…"

The bent over and folded his hands together, "Don't mock. War, too, can ruin you. And a lot more than the night I can offer you."

Alberg looked up at the sky where wispy white clouds stood out against the darkness. He knew that the night would last two hours.

"Your merchandise must be well-seasoned," he said, "since its perishable."

"You'll see. It'll cost you two sollars."

Two sollars! Indeed, the price they pay on C.122 had nothing in common with what Alberg was used to.

"Sold for two sollars!" Alberg said. "I'll follow you."

The wreck limped ahead of him. How could these people suffer a disability instead of healing it? Alberg remembered that for them there was no way to find the necessary sums.

His guide turned down a dead-end street at the end of which stood or rather leaned a dilapidated house. It looked like it was built of some kind of clay instead of rot-proof, synthetic material.

Alberg had been to many seedy places, but not this bad. The low-ceilinged front room he entered was full of drunks and half-nude girls with shaggy hair. Some of the drinkers were wearing fragments of uniforms. Others, partly undressed, were spilling wine on themselves. Murderers, dealers and pimps—Alberg had rubbed shoulders with this scum on Venus. But the money that flowed over there bestowed on them an appearance that was hardly distinguishable from the rest of the population. Basically, it was pretty much the same here where poverty and filth reigned on every level except in the expeditionary forces. But you couldn't tell them apart from the others here either. A few tough guys whose fortune must've amounted to 200 or 300 sollars, sported some untorn clothing.

They could wash down small pieces of black-market meat with drinkable wine.

"You owe me two sollars," the guide said.

Alberg pulled out a five-sollar bill. He had no change. He ripped the bill in two and gave half to the guy demanding his due.

"Here," he said, "I'm giving you half a sollar more."

The other burst out moaning, which only made Alberg laugh. In the end, the other half of the bill changed hands. The moaning turned into outbursts of gratitude. Alberg was pleased with his joke. But he was a little upset at himself for giving in to the impulse of generosity.

The guide left to carry on his hustling. The boss of the foul place must also have given him a few coins. Indeed, handouts only end up deforming everything. You have to adapt to where you are and not get tender-hearted.

Alberg sat down. Straightaway, a grimy girl came up to him but he cut her off before she could open her mouth.

"I'm not here for you," he said. "Can you find me some civilian clothes?"

The girl shook her disheveled hair, "Deserter? It'll cost."

"How much?"

She got a cunning look that was mingled with greed, worry and scheming. She tossed out a number that she figured was extravagant. "1,000 sollars!"

"That's too much. By far. I'll pay 200."

"500."

"Sold for 500," Alberg sighed as if she had ruined him.

He leaned closer.

"Can one join the rebels?"

She narrowed her eyes, "That's even more expensive."

The barter they had just made led her to believe that she was dealing with a rich client but who didn't throw his money down the drain.

"1,000 sollars for you," she offered. "Not one sollar less."

"When?"

She glanced around. "Now. You'll get the info and the clothes at the same time. Give me 1,500 sollars but under the table. If they see you, I'll be gutted within the next ten minutes."

"Let's do it differently," Alberg said. "Take me where I have to go and I'll give you the money with nobody to see."

She looked at him and kept a lid on her impatience. "Follow me."

In the alley, Alberg tried to use his supranormal insight to plan the attitude he should adopt. But for the moment he was just a man like the others. "Ach," he told himself, "I got by just fine for years with my little slice of common sense. When I'm back to a mutant with a big head, that'll be great, but in the meantime, I just have to act normal."

They went down the street that Alberg had already taken, then took a series of noxious alleyways lit by nothing but the reflection from the clouds in the black sky. They walked without speaking.

As they neared a house in ruins, Alberg heard a rustling noise and jumped back. The iron bar struck the woman on the forehead. Swift and silent, the man wielding the weapon lunged at Alberg. He didn't have time to take even one step before he collapsed. Alberg had fired from the hip.

The woman was lying on the rubble.

Alberg leaned over her, "Where is it?"

She groaned. Her face was bathed in tears. "The money..."

"I'll give it to you. Where is it?"

"The second house on the left... next to the big warehouse... Give me the money."

"No," Alberg declared. "You don't need it anymore."

He left her there alone in the dark.

While hastening to the designated house, he thought that the people he was going to see would naturally know the woman. At one time or another they would find out about how he'd treated her, which could play against him. He turned around and went back.

The wounded girl was still conscious. She reached out for him in gratitude.

"I was just kidding," Alberg said as he stepped over the mugger's corpse.

He put 1,500 Martian sollars into her hand. Since she couldn't hold onto to them, he stuffed them into her shirt and hefted her over his shoulder. Then he started off again toward the house.

He saw the warehouse first, which looked like it was about to cave in. Closer up, the light from the clouds showed that it was not in such bad condition as it appeared and that its door was firmly closed. Nearby, the dark house. Alberg knocked on the door.

"Don't move," a deep voice came from the corner of the warehouse.

Alberg froze.

"Good," the voice continued, "Put the woman down and your hands in the air."

Alberg obeyed. A shadow detached from the warehouse—a man who was aiming a radiant rifle at him. Covered by the gun, Alberg was quickly searched and lightened of his radiant.

"Bring her inside. The door's not locked."

He entered and stood still in the dark with the woman on his shoulder. She was starting to get heavy. The man came in behind him. The click of a magnetic lock. A dim light turned on, revealing a table, a few chairs and a simple couch dating back two centuries.

"Lay her down."

When the woman was lying and groaning on the couch, the man stepped up. A well-built guy wearing the uniform of a Martian officer.

"But it's Dora!" he said. Then he turned to Alberg and asked, "What happened?"

"We were attacked 50 yards from here," Alberg explained briefly. "I took the guy down and carried the girl who was guiding me. She's in bad shape."

"I know."

The man had already gone to a chest and taken out a lightweight, electrochemical apparatus that he set up around Dora's head. Alberg was familiar with these ultra-fast, hemostatic, antiseptic, healing devices. They were capable of decompression in case of head wounds. For a little while they were even thought to completely regenerate damaged nerves.

"She'll pull through," the experimenter said. "So, who are you, where do you come from and what do you want?"

"I'm Alberg, I come from Venus by way of Mars where I was stuck on this expedition to C.122. I want to desert, meet the rebels and, if possible, see what's happening on C.123 and C.124."

"Is that all?" the man said. "And what's to tell me you're not a spy?"

"Nothing. You can just keep an eye on me. Does the name Little Paul mean anything to you? Or Del Padre?"

The man was startled. "You have news from them?"

"I saw them in Arespolis. They saved me from the hands of the police only to stick me in those of the army. I still don't understand."

The other nodded. "They must have their reasons. Especially Del Padre. His plans are never simple."

"In any case," Alberg grumbled, "it almost got me killed."

"But it didn't. I think I'll ask Weldoor what we should do with you."

"Who's Weldoor?"

"You'll see. Me, I'm Lespart."

Alberg gave me a little sign of greeting. "Give me back my radiant?"

"No. Don't take me for a simpleton. Even if you want to join us, you'll still have to prove it."

"Okay. What do we do?"

"I'm going to leave Dora here. She'll be on her feet soon enough. You and me are going."

He grabbed his rifle.

"I didn't think you had radiant weapons?" Alberg asked.

Lespart looked at him, "It's true. We have very few. But we're not so badly armed despite everything."

"I've seen that," Alberg said. "You almost got me. You shoot bullets that destroy half the forest."

"That's the least of them," Lespart replied. "But soon we'll have better."

"Radiant cannons?"

"Even better. Come on, let's go."

He held his rifle under his arm. Alberg followed him.

When they were inside the warehouse, it was easy to see that it was far from crumbling to the ground. And a good thing because there was a big winger in it, obviously built for space travel.

"Get in," Lespart said.

Alberg climbed into the forward cabin. Lespart sat in front of the controls.

CHAPTER XIX

On learning of the uprising of the children of Villagea, Del Padre and Little Paul had taken the Spaceless to Earth separately. For Little Paul there was no problem. He often traveled under his real name, which avoided questions. His name was Binker and no administration on the three planets would risk hassling the son of a Ludocrat.

As for Del Padre, the situation was different. He was persona non grata everywhere, but on Mars he was risking his life. However, he hadn't yet figured into the plans of Senator General Farel to cause bloody riots on Earth. That was what would happen if they'd tried to imprison Del Padre and even more so if they tried to execute him. The natural men on Earth would have brought the whole trade economy to a standstill and Venus would have followed suit. Causing trouble and instability on the neighboring planets, however, did figure into Farel's plans, but not yet. Acting too soon would have created an anti-Martian movement that would have cemented the shifting relations of Venus and Earth. A more powerful army than Mars was needed to confront such a coalition.

Thus, Del Padre had only suffered through a little harassment and could leave Mars untroubled. In the Spaceless he wondered whether he had done rightly on the videophone with Silas to steer the mutants onto a wild goose chase. What he had in mind was really the destruction of the senatorial system and his tacit alliance with Silas risked being undermined by this subterfuge. For it to pay off, it was necessary, first of all, that Alberg live up to the idea Del Padre had of him, meaning that on seeing foreign worlds he'd start wanting to join the still latent battle. Then it was necessary that Silas be right, Silas who had confided in him long ago that Alberg was, in his opinion, a mutant and not a minor one. Finally, it was necessary that Alberg not get killed. These were a lot of conditions to meet.

But for Del padre, it was well worth the effort. He was trying to fight the Senate to make the philosophy of the natural men triumph and not to put the power into the hands of the mutants. Silas was an ally who would turn dangerous as soon as the seat of power was vacant. Whereas Alberg was part of no social group. He was just a greedy, unscrupulous rogue whose eventual disappearance wouldn't cause the slightest outcry.

Del Padre didn't understand the worry Alberg caused in Silas' mind, a worry that had made Silas condemn Alberg to death. Del Padre had to guess this, of course, because Silas hadn't told him anything. He would protect Alberg when Silas decided to act, which might already be happening. He was planning to use him and, if necessary, eliminate him. But he needed him because he himself was just a theoretician, a preacher, a master. Not a man of action capable of anything. He was fully aware of the fact that he would recoil in the face of certain actions, but he would not hesitate to get them done by someone else to accomplish his goals.

As for the children, they weren't dangerous to him or to Alberg. Even less to Silas. Anybody could use them by following the necessary rules. They would be the first beneficiaries of a power shift since they wouldn't have to go off to foreign worlds anymore. Of course, their new destiny wouldn't be their responsibility... you couldn't trust a savage like Little Paul whose credo was violence considered as one of the fine arts.

When the Spaceless was arriving at its destination, Del Padre drew up the first sketch of the role that the children would have to play in the natural society. On the new breeding farm, all the children would be shepherds. They'd drop their crazy artistic whims and pick up the shepherd's pipe.

The giant with long hair stepped into the astrostation amidst snickering and respectful looks. He headed immediately for a house where he knew they were expecting him. There he talked with a normally dressed person who was, however, a genuine natural man. He gave him a mission to contact the clandestine cells on foreign worlds in order to give Alberg a warm welcome. It was not an easy mission to accomplish because the foreign worlds showed little sympathy for the people of the solar system no matter what side they were on. They held them responsible for the slavery on C.122 and in all other systems without exception. However, Del Padre was hoping that the uprising of the children would be considered of utmost interest by them. He didn't forget to advise his messenger to remind the leaders that a real revolt in the solar system would lock down part of the army and this would give the rest of the galaxy greater freedom to maneuver.

Then he went to meet the most diligent and determined of the natural men on Earth in order to assess the situation and estimate their current forces.

Meanwhile, Little Paul met with Wilfrid and gave him a thrashing for starting a riot prematurely. Wilfrid could've killed him with a single blow, but Little Paul would've seen it coming and slayed him without remorse. Afterward, Little Paul admitted that the experience provided a good lesson for them. In short, they could mobilize the children in an hour. The lesson wouldn't be forgotten.

CHAPTER XX

Other planets besides the one with the war raging were revolving around the double sun of C.122. It was towards one of these that Lespart piloted his winger. During the few hours that the trip lasted Alberg tried to get some information about where they were headed, but it was a lost cause. Lespart didn't say a word. Alberg ended up shutting his mouth. At one time he wanted to kill him and take over the controls, but where would he go? There was no way he could get back to Venus on a mid-haul winger. Although he knew how to fly, he was no expert. He would get lost and the winger would become his tomb.

"Besides," he thought to himself, "there's nothing like being introduced to the right people instead of dropping into the middle of a group who all want a piece of you."

The fifth planet, where they landed, was just a block of ice. They had to put on heavy spacesuits to leave the craft.

They went down a tunnel that took them under the surface. At the end of it was a small cave where a permanent base was set up. An airlock, a few men, a branch of the Spaceless.

"Where are we going?" Alberg asked again after Lespart had introduced him as a defector.

This time Lespart deigned to answer, "C.124. That's where we'll meet Weldoor."

He went over to a cabinet mounted on the wall, opened it and took out two green suits. He threw one at Alberg.

"Change into this. It's a technician's uniform. We'd be free to move around with the tech students but we're a little too old for that."

"Oh," Alberg was surprised. "They study on foreign worlds?"

"Children arrive here at 15 years old," Lespart explained. "Do you think they're ready to produce anything at all? They're only given a general education from 6 to 12 and business classes from 12 to 15. So, here there are a lot of tech monasteries where they spend at least five years. Some of them who hadn't shown any particular promise on their home planet can even enter the science monasteries and become brains."

While speaking, he took off his officer's uniform and put on the technician's. Alberg did the same. When they were ready to go, they entered the Spaceless. The same light warning lights but no speaker. They took off.

Because there were only two of them, the ambiance of the huge cabin was a little irreal. They stood apart from each other, completely silent. Lespart had already proven that he was no chatterbox. Alberg was trying to put together a plan of concerted action to propose to the mysterious Weldoor. But even if Lespart seemed impressed by Alberg's acquaintance with Del Padre and Little Paul, Weldoor might be more indifferent. And when Alberg couldn't use his recent gifts of analysis and foresight, he felt more defenseless than ever.

They stayed like that during the time it took to get through non-space, always a constant time although always imperceptible. The stillness of two beings preoccupied with their own thoughts, floating in a luminous void, like fish in midwater.

The light gradually changed hues. The walls of the cabin reappeared. The doors slid open. Lespart went out first, followed by Alberg. They were in another underground where men in green suits accompanied them without saying a word.

When they came out on the surface, Alberg shrank back from the appalling, blinding red light that engulfed everything. He forced himself to keep going with the others while trying to see around him.

He was under a gigantic transparent roof that must have been miles long and whose plastic dome was fitted with black beams at least 1,500 feet above the ground. In the red light stood metal buildings that supported huge, slanted gutters pouring out water unceasingly. These gutters overlapped all the way to the distant dome and the water streamed from one to another down to the ground into giant reservoirs.

Alberg was mesmerized. He gazed at the countless elevators accessing the gutters—fast little rockets full of men in black. The closest tanks and the lowest ones were overflowing with black leaves. Thinking about it, he figured the leaves must've been green, just like the men's suits, just like his, but were turned black in the red light.

"Hydroponic farming," Lespart answered his unasked question. "There are hundreds of greenhouses like this one over the surface of the planet. All the fruits and vegetables you eat in the solar system come from here. It feels weird, doesn't it, to see that men are working to make them grow?"

"Yes," Alberg responded. "But I hope things will change. There are enough hands on the three planets to free them from this parasitic existence and let them live on their own."

He noticed the approval in Lespart and smirked privately. The fate of foreign worlds didn't matter to him. He watched the armed guards crawling among the scaffolding and thought that the producers deserved their fate. The day when they would revolt, they would massacre their masters who, in turn, would have it coming to them. To Alberg, it was all just power relations—the moral value of an act was judged by its success.

"We have to get out of here," Lespart said. "If we're stopped for a check, you're a specialist in synthetic fertilizers and you're coordinating between the hydroponics and the chemical manufacturing plants."

"How can the Spaceless remain secret?" Alberg whispered.

"Some controllers got suspicious and tried to do some individual investigating. They were taken down, against their will, into the Spaceless station they'd suspected, but somewhere along the way they got lost. Heaven only knows where they are now."

251

Alberg frowned. What happened to you when you were thrown out beyond space?

"Let's go," Lespart said.

They followed a long procession of circular wagons that had just stopped near them. The wagons were full of workers and technicians among whom they forced their way. The procession shot off again on cushions of air, passing through magnetic hoops every 100 yards that first pulled them in and then push them forward. That was how they left the huge greenhouse and went straight across the rocky landscape flooded with blood-red light. The wagons rode sometimes on top of long viaducts, sometimes inside tunnels from which they came out whistling.

At one point they sped along the shore of an ocean whose waves washed the reefs with a pink foam like spittle from the mortally wounded. The waves themselves looked like blood splatter. The ocean was a great big hemorrhage. Then the wagons entered a region studded with enormous, pitch-black buildings and huge panels tilted 45 degrees that blinded with the reflection of the red sun.

"Those are the nuclear power plants and the solar batteries," Lespart commented, keeping his voice down. "The factories are not far."

And indeed, they soon rose up on the horizon. After seeing the monstrous hydroponic greenhouses, Alberg was not expecting buildings even more colossal yet. But the closer they got, his mind balked at what his eyes were showing him. Some buildings must have been 6,500 feet tall. A tiny insect at their base, the wagons took several minutes to pass by them despite the accelerated speed. They entered one of these nightmarish constructions like a dart piercing a shield.

When Alberg climbed out of the wagon, he was assaulted by a cocktail of foul smells and irritant gases. He stepped onto a platform cluttered with boxes and pieces of machinery surrounded by a crowd of black suits screaming, swearing, scolding and insulting. Lespart led him into the crowd where the technicians they traveled with disappeared. The two of them climbed into a chute that shot up so fast Alberg felt dizzy and sick. In under a minute, they were at a railing overlooking a vast empty space. They had stopped not at the top of the building but on a narrow ledge that ran around it halfway up, meaning more than 3,200 feet. There was an open door on the face of the building, apparently guarded by two armed soldiers. But Lespart paid no attention to them. He went through the door, followed by Alberg.

"They're in a daze," Lespart said. "Semi-depersonalization just enough to keep standing. That's how Weldoor guarantees the involuntary cooperation of the sentinels whose mission is to cut him off from the outside world."

They walked down a corridor with luminescent walls.

"And how does he do it?" Alberg asked.

"You're too curious. But I already hinted at it before leaving C.122 when I mentioned the development of our new weapon. The two things are not unrelated."

A man emerged at the end of the corridor. "C.124," he said and fell silent, waiting for the response.

"1, 2, 4, 8, 16, 32…" Lespart said.

"Okay, you can pass." The man disappeared.

Lespart came to a closed door and looked at Alberg.

"This is where I leave you. My work's done. I hope you get along with Weldoor. I'll warn you that it won't be easy."

He shook his hand, gave him back his radiant and went back the way they'd come.

"Oh," he said over his shoulder, "if you're a spy, I'll toss some flowers in the sea for you. That's usually where they finish their mission."

He left. Alberg saw his figure shrinking, then vanishing through the door to the ledge. He turned around to face the double doors. They were open. Albert walked into a big room furnished with an iron U-shaped table. From behind the table ten people were looking him over with no kindness in their faces.

Alberg noted their white clothes, their penetrating eyes, their well-tended hands. He was dealing with a group of brains. The one in the middle had a wide forehead and shaven head.

"Come closer," he said. "We were informed of your arrival in the hydroponics, but don't make any sudden or suspicious movements. You were placed in a forcefield that will blow you up."

Alberg stepped up. He was on alert. Luckily—or maybe it was because of the situation—he felt in control of his gifts of perception. He knew that he was in front of Weldoor, which was easy to guess, but he also knew that Weldoor had heard of him and had been expecting him even before Alberg had met Dora. Since this was the case, the information must have come from Del Padre. A communication by Spaceless video? No, a messenger. They'd advised Weldoor to be welcoming.

"Greetings, Weldoor," he said calmly. "I believe you can trust Del Padre's messenger."

The one next to Weldoor cracked a little smile.

"Not bad," he said. "He just surmised that only by looking at us. And right now he's thinking I'm a mutant like him. Isn't that right Alberg? How does it feel to find out you're a mutant after being a hunter for so many years?"

Alberg smiled back. "I knew hunters like me. It might help save my hide someday. In the meantime, I don't claim to know what Little Paul is up to by teaming up with Del Padre, but I can tell you that he's in full agreement with Del Padre and myself. He's proven to be a man of action by his daring sabotages. Now, however, he needs someone determined. The opposite of a theoretician. He thinks I fit the bill."

"And how do you get along with the mutants?" Weldoor asked.

"Not as badly as you think. I already made a pact with the ones on Mars when I was still a hunter."

"We know," Weldoor affirmed. "But I don't think you made up with Silas."

"That will come," Alberg assured him. "The circumstances won't let us stay enemies anymore."

Silence.

"What can you do?" Weldoor asked curtly.

"Replace Del Padre," Alberg shot back. "He's got plenty of troops, but he believes too strongly in his idea of a natural life, which erodes the trust of mutants and children. With me, it'll be nothing like that. And I'll see to controlling the children. As for the mutants, they can manage on their own. I'll only ask them to attack at the same time as the others."

Silence again. One of the brains who was sitting at the far end of the table spoke up.

"I don't think we need this individual. The most important thing right now is to fight against the technocratic ideology of the clandestine fighters on C.123."

"I don't agree," another said. "We can deal with those issues after taking the power."

"I see what you're thinking," a cold voice from the other end of the table said. "You're hoping the mutants will grab all the power after eliminating the others!"

"I will no longer tolerate racist accusations in this assembly," Weldoor declared. "I also won't tolerate activities that aim to break up the unity of the three systems."

"And you no doubt want to preserve the unity with the malcontents in the solar system?" another piped up. "We need not worry. If they're unhappy, let them do as we do. I know, I know, you're all hoping for the settlement of the solar armies over there. But the rebels are just a handful. Everyone else on the three planets is satisfied with the state things that crush and disgust us."

"No," Alberg said. "They aren't just a handful."

From some of their looks and tones of voice, he was sure that something serious had happened in the solar system.

"What's just happened," he said to prove it, "Del Padre's messenger described to you in enough detail for you not to underestimate the power of the children, for example."

He didn't know exactly what he was talking about, but he saw the effect it had. Without a doubt the messenger had given information that was, of course, to be kept confidential by the solar authorities and their army of surveillance and was not to be given to the clandestine army.

"The troubles didn't spread far," Weldoor said slowly. "What makes you think that you, Alberg, can rekindle it?"

Alberg looked at all of them for a moment, then, "Based on the cause of the troubles, an incidental and unsubstantial cause along with the persistence of a latent revolt."

"But the storyteller woman has been released and everything's back to normal."

This was something Alberg had not divined and he almost let them see his surprise... his surprise and a little worry. "Especially since they didn't treat her too badly," he hazarded a wary guess.

"No doubt. What do you envision to do as a replacement?"

"Attack a senator. Dorf or Garon, even though Garon is an opponent of Dorf."

"But you're aware that all attacks fail all the time."

"They weren't carried out by professional hunters. The failed attacks make the people laugh. A successful attack will weaken the Senate and solidify resentment against it."

Weldoor thought about it. "Maybe, maybe... I'm going to speak bluntly: I don't trust you and I wouldn't listen to Del Padre, who's an old fool, if the force of rebellion wasn't as strong as it is on C.124. But, in the present situation, I feel we must use all the means at our disposal to get rid of some of the army."

He looked around the table.

"I put to the vote the following proposition: Alberg goes back immediately to Earth and launches an offensive in 24 hours. We wait 48 hours to act in turn."

A few disapproving voices were raised but the vote took place. Weldoor's proposition was accepted by a majority of three. Alberg sat on the edge of the table.

"One other circumstance will favor our projects," he said. "I'm saying this to calm the minds of those who voted 'no'. You all know that Mars is nursing plans of expansion and dominion. You are fully aware that it's thanks to these dreams of power that the revolt on C.122 could break out. I myself have heard Farel calling for war in a grandiose speech. If a large-scale uprising takes place on Earth, it'll have repercussions on Venus, but difficulties on Mars. Since the terrian armies will be stuck at home, Mars will intervene on Venus with the excuse of bringing back order. By seizing the opportunity, Farel will free us of both the Martian and Venusian armies. It's an important point to remember if I can incapacitate half the terrian forces."

A long silence. And then:

"How can you make sure it gets to that point?" Weldoor asked. "Events might unfold like that, but they might turn out differently, too."

"You'll see," Alberg said simply. "Don't you worry, you'll be more than satisfied."

Weldoor shrugged his shoulders, "It is, indeed, possible. But I don't rely on inspiring speculations. So, take care of your part of the plan and leave the rest to us. I might have information that could be useful. You might like to know that Garon uses the Senate's priority shipping to get a device tested on C.123 at regular intervals. He has to maintain this device in good working order, which our specialists have managed to examine, at least superficially. It's a projector that can materialize an image at long distance. I say 'materialize' because it's not just matter of a simple 3D projector but of a solid form. So solid that it even casts a shadow. It seems that this shadow delineates a special area, a kind of hub of radiation. You can draw the conclusions yourself."

"They've already been drawn," Alberg said.

He wasn't lying. And on his response the meeting was over. They took him back past the sentinels and an agent of Weldoor followed him all the way to the Spaceless station where he introduced the two of them as technicians responsible for surveillance.

This Spaceless entrance was near an astroport where they were loading a piece of cargo over half a mile long. Alberg almost bumped into one of the men on the cargo crew. He was wearing shiny body armor. He smiled at Alberg like he was smiling at a dog.

Puzzled, Alberg entered the Spaceless with his guardian angel.

CHAPTER XXI

It was at the entrance to the Spaceless that Alberg and Weldoor's agent had taken risks: for the latter of being discovered and as for Alberg of being searched while he was carrying a radiant. On arrival it was different because the technicians coming from foreign worlds were hustled into special buildings so that they'd be seen as little as possible. So, it was as usual, which allowed Weldoor's agent to get civilian clothes with a little help from the area called "technician reception". They left secretly with the construction workers, the builders of building machines who were the only ones in the solar system really needed.

Alberg wasn't familiar with Villagea but he got a pretty precise picture of it starting with the location of the astroport, the layout of some streets, the distribution of companies on these streets. He told his guardian angel directly that he had to contact Del Padre in a hotel in the southern suburbs. He pretended not to know the exact location but he remembered the neighborhood. Like that he was free to stop the magnetocar they'd taken where and when he wanted. He made sure to do it in front of a secluded property surrounded by overgrown grounds. The nighttime was a help to him. Without warning the agent was killed and his body hidden in the bushes like Alberg had done before in Arespolis.

Alberg had good reasons for acting like this or at least reasons that he thought were important: he had no intention of starting anything whatsoever before three days time and certainly not in 24 hours. Thus, the action he planned would have greater freedom. In fact, with the revolt breaking out on foreign worlds before Earth they would send reinforcements out there, which would weaken the enemy back here. Alberg had already calculated that through the Spaceless stations of the ten main cities the Senate could send more than 300,000 men in 24 hours, since the war materials were already on C.124 and could not go through the Spaceless anyway.

There was one weak spot in his reasoning: Weldoor would certainly be informed of both the disappearance of his agent and of the delay in launching operations. Alberg figured that it was a risk worth running. Weldoor had himself revealed that the tension was mounting on C.124 so high that he feared being overwhelmed. Under these conditions, maybe he'd give the order to revolt after sending emissaries directly to Del Padre, Little Paul and Silas.

Alberg, therefore, had to guarantee the coordination between the three subversive factions on the one hand and on the other hand to get them to agree to act only after Weldoor. He would convince them that the benefits of the earth revolt were not on foreign worlds and that Weldoor would get a taste of his own medicine since he wanted to launch his own action only after Earth, which would bear the full weight of the senatorial counter-attack.

In the course of the night, Alberg avoided showing himself in public. He thought the authorities on Mars had given his description to those on Earth, accusing him of colluding with the mutants. Moreover, the disappearance of two technicians from the welcome center would be connected to the murder of one of them as soon as the corpse was found. So, it was with great caution that he approached a natural man who took him to Del Padre. Before this he had gathered some information on what had recently happened in Villagea. Everything, apparently, had gone back to normal except for the curfew. In order to appease the situation Garon was trying to get reforms passed by the Senate.

The meeting Alberg had with Del Padre did not take place in a friendly, relaxed atmosphere. Alberg was still a little resentful of the way Del Padre had planned his escape from Arespolis. He admitted that it was thanks to Del Padre's quick measures that he had awakened his dormant abilities, but he didn't whisper a word about it. As for Del Padre, he avoided mentioning Iona's denouncement, leaving Alberg to his misunderstandings. However, on the practical level, they reached an agreement: they would start to stir things up again while Alberg tackled the terrorist attack. They targeted Dorf, the garish, stubborn puppet. Del Padre approved of Alberg's projected delay.

Through Del Padre Alberg next met easily with Little Paul. Contrary to their previous conversation, which had taken place alone and in a secluded house, this second conference occurred in a picturesque ambiance. It was in the back of a dive bar where all the exits were guarded by war-painted Bullies armed to the teeth. It was harder to manage. Little Paul and Wilfrid together built up a mountain of mistrust and skepticism that Alberg could get through only by calling upon his faculties of observation and analysis. He did manage, in the end, to get the support of a Bully commando team to attack Dorf.

It was Little Paul who then arranged a meeting for him with his father, the Ludocrat Binker. For this Alberg went through the underground network of Villagea and was received in the Candy Shop where Binker didn't have to be begged to promise the support of the Special Guard. Binker considered Alberg insignificant but the 24 hours of dictatorship had gone to his head. He'd decided that the children's tribunal was no longer enough for him and the Senate's authority was becoming too burdensome. He had also convinced himself that Lewis was useless in this new vision… So, he looked upon Alberg as a pawn that might be interesting to maneuver. With this in mind he graciously accepted to put Alberg in touch with Iona, whom he could summon whenever he wanted.

Alberg had two reasons for wanting to see Iona: first of all, he missed her a little, even though he was loathe to admit it. Secondly, it was through her that he figured on getting Silas to accept being an ally. This idea lacked neither arrogance nor audacity, but that wouldn't stop him. Still, he asked Binker to fail to mention the name of the person Iona would be meeting. A few microscopic elements in the attitude of both Binker and

Del Padre had led him to take this precaution. Since Iona was being closely watched after they'd let her go, he'd decided that she should go at a particular time to a particular ruined monument where they could easily keep an eye on the surroundings.

The meeting took place the day after Alberg's arrival. Coming from the north he had to cross a transparent bridge under which flowed a permanently lit river and then enter a semi-abandoned zone where the chosen monument stood.

Compared to the big buildings on the north bank, the ruins were nothing colossal. But among them a visitor felt both devastated by and imprisoned in an ancient dream.

It was a rusty metal structure shaped like a pylon standing on four feet. The top was over 600 feet high and the old documents proved that it was missing a third of it. Alberg found a metal staircase partly restored, which he started up. After three minutes of climbing he was out of breath and stopped to contemplate the landscape. He had not gone very high but he still felt dizzy from the height, a lot more than from behind the window of a modern and much taller building. With the wind whistling through the struts and beams, he got back to scaling the stairs, which lasted another ten minutes. Then he stopped again, panting, lungs on fire. He leaned over the railing after making sure that there was something solid under all the rust and looked around. Everywhere was the same nightmare of gnarled iron, the same madness of useless structures. His knowledge didn't include many references to visionary architects, but there was no need for references to get smacked with the genius of naïve design who had proposed building such a marvel and had actually done it. This was the summit of grotesque wantonness.

Alberg gathered his strength and once again hit the little winding staircase. He kept going for another ten minutes, telling himself that the choice of such a place should have perked up his ears. It was certainly a singular observation point, but also an excellent trap. A shadow passed over the beams stained golden by the setting sun. He looked up. A winger was soaring by silently, turning around the rusted giant pylon, then going a little farther off. It was a tiny machine with an open cabin. Alberg caught a glimpse of an arm waving in his direction. He figured Binker was having him watched and at the least sign of danger the winger would come hover at the edge of the tangled metal mess so he could hop on. Only him? No. On looking up he had also noticed a human form standing motionless in the iron web maybe 60 feet above him.

Iona was holding on tightly to a beam in the gusts of wind getting stronger as the sun got lower, a sun disappearing far behind the sea of tiny buildings that were crumbling at the foot of the decapitated giant. Frozen among the spiky and twisted tresses of iron, she was watching the dark figure ascend and recognizing it. The rays of the setting sun turned scarlet and stained Alberg's face blood-red when it peeked through the tangle.

CHAPTER XXII

Iona, too, felt caught in a trap. She retreated, put her back against the very edge of the railing, then stayed there in the hissing wind. She was gathering her forces to defend herself. Alberg was quick on the draw. She should have killed him in the middle of his movement. But at the same time, she was wondering why Binker had thrown her into an ambush.

"Did you lose them?" Alberg asked after catching his breath.

She kept silent and then, "Not easily. You know about it?"

Alberg had gauged his attitude in one second. He smiled. "Know about what? About your imprisonment or what you did?"

Barely started and the meeting was racing to its brutal finale. She got ready. But Alberg just shrugged his shoulders.

"No, but you can tell me. Let's reshuffle the cards and start over." By chance, or almost, he added, "You couldn't kill me, so you betrayed me. I'll let it slide this time, but only this time."

Iona took this for a bluff. She kept her eyes on him. But the attack annoyed her. Knowing Alberg's reactions she pushed it.

"Yes," she said defiantly, "I got them believing you were a mutant. I guess they all went after you and I'm not sorry for it. Now you understand how it feels to be hunted and shot at on sight."

But these last words were lost in Alberg's explosion of laughter. She was speechless. He didn't usually react like this.

"But you didn't lie!" he finally said. "Maybe it wasn't a truth to be spreading around and I should probably throw you off this metal wreck… but, then again, it's true I'm a mutant. I spent all these years killing my brothers."

He looked like he found it all very amusing. She felt the disgust and outrage he aroused in her all over again. Clearly, he wasn't lying. He certainly had good reasons for telling her all this. However, disgust and outrage once again caused her hair to spark and her teeth to glow. Alberg saw it.

"You're full of principles," he said, "but you like cynical brutes. I think we'll get along. Because with me, I like females who aren't strong enough to strike out in the open."

He approached her. Once again Iona felt helpless. She glanced at the distant ground. The twilight had turned gray. The wind was howling now through the beams. He took her in his arms with a completely new gentleness that abruptly transformed. Around the gigantic metal carcass, the surveillance winger was circling in the growing darkness. The two bodies lying on the catwalk formed one. The pilot figured they had no more need of him and flew off so as not to attract the attention of any would-be observers to the ruins.

It was totally dark when Alberg and Iona spoke to each other again. The climate control fabric of their clothes protected them from the colder and colder air, but their hands and face were frozen. The darkness spread under and around them. Towards the north, it was fended off by the lights of the business district. In the east, less than a mile away, stood the huge façade of the monastery of sciences, studded with its 10,000 windows. Strangely, Alberg wanted to cling to this moment like clinging to a buoy at sea. He felt as if he was starting to live more intensely than by fortune and hunting. He had an unnatural knot in his throat that he would have extracted with pliers if he could. In the dark, he arranged his face to chase away such a hateful state of mind.

"How did you find out you were a mutant?" Iona asked him.

He told her. And like that he lost the only secret shield he could use to fight against her if she decided to kill him. He could no longer count on only his quick draw and agility. He knew it, but for him it was like yielding to forces long held in check. With the valve opened he felt again the cold and calculating Alberg that he had always been glad to be. The fire part. He went so far as to realize that if the fire part was too strong, it would burn everything up...

"I have to see Silas," he blurted out.

She recoiled. He explained to her what he had planned. Like her at the start he challenged her a little by explaining that it was only to serve his own interests and not to change the status quo that he had benefited so shamelessly from so far. It would be much more useful now that he was the one who changed. Although he was being hunted, his hunters would see that they were on the wrong turf. But he wouldn't even give them time to get back on track. Even though Iona had gotten close to Silas again with Alberg out of the picture, she was persuaded. She gave him the necessary information.

"Be careful," she told him. "You'll be risking your life because Silas thinks of nothing but murdering you."

In the darkness Alberg noted the intonations of her voice. "Is he the one who sent you to kill me at Aphros?"

She didn't answer.

He didn't press her but he added, "He knew before I did that I was a mutant. He saw me as a rival. Very well, I'll be careful. And I've got an ace up my sleeve."

He paused, pricked up his ears. He put a hand on the railing. It was vibrating gently.

"They're here," he said coldly. "How are our troops going to get by without us?"

But Iona had already noticed the men slowly climbing the iron staircase. She pulled out an object that Alberg couldn't see and she fingered it deftly. A tiny transmitter. Less than 30 seconds later the surveillance winger was hovering three feet away from them. They took a dangerous leap off the railing and both landed safely inside. The winger soared up and shot off to the south. On the horizon, other wingers were arriving, flashing their red lights.

The pilot took them down to the top of the trees that had replaced the houses. Iona gave him orders. He headed west, skimming the leaves until a huge clearing made a breach in the wild vegetation. He set them down there.

The police wingers were getting closer. Coming out of the forest, sliding on invisible rails, the dark mass of a radiant cannon appeared. The first winger crashed into the trees with a purple haze that lit up everything around. The others beat a quick retreat.

CHAPTER XXIII

The arrival of the police had made Iona's explanations pointless. Alberg was where she had wanted to send him.

This part of the forested suburb was held by a large and powerfully armed group. The winger pilot, on Binker's orders, had a mission to protect and guarantee the escape of Iona and Alberg, but he couldn't allow the Ludocrat to be get caught up with the armed resistance. So, he got back in the air as soon as the Senate's machines had gone. Iona preferred to stay with him. The disturbances were still near enough to stop them again. The Senators must have known that this kind of initiative would end in more trouble, probably by another reaction from the Ludocracy, meaning between the army and the Special Guard. Now, the Guard was recruited from a civilian population of adults who were all part of the established order. It was dangerous to give them reasons to question it.

Numbering in the hundreds, the group was made up of resistant fighters aged 15 to 25. It was supervised and advised by a few dozen mutants who were over 30. Alberg was taken before two twins close to 60 whose eyes shimmered in the dark like a cat's. In the camouflaged metal hut that served as their HQ, he saw their abnormally big foreheads and their faintly orange hair. He realized that they struggled to speak in a way that could be understood—their natural flow must have been over four sentences per second. Alberg accepted their hospitality while waiting for Silas to return. He calculated that the following day would be "D" day. What could Weldoor be doing?

The night was calm. Alberg slept deeply under both the protection and the surveillance of the resistance. He was awakened the next morning by Silas himself. Alberg got up painfully. His limbs and back were aching from the primitive mattress of leaves.

Silas regarded him with surprise mixed with disgust. He looked grim when he said, "You've gone mad to throw yourself into my hands."

Alberg had half a smile. "You've known forever that I was a mutant like you. Probably the only one who could someday stand in your way. A being more dangerous than a hunter who missed you. But you're wrong. I've known I'm a mutant for too short a time to care about those who are like me."

While he was talking, he kept an eye on Silas' reactions. Seeing what was going to happen, he added:

"No, don't try to kill me, I'll see you coming and get the jump on you. Instead, just listen to me. You can decide for yourself whether or not it's in your interest to have me as an ally. A temporary ally, of course. If you want war afterwards, you'll have it."

They were alone. The door of the hut was guarded by four resistance fighters.

Silas made a negligent gesture and said, "Speak. I'm listening."

Alberg described his position with the children, natural men and Ludocrats. He told him about the conversation he'd had with Weldoor. He confirmed that he was ready to act this very day and he had troops on alert. Nothing showed on Silas' face but certain involuntary movements, invisible to an ordinary observer, revealed to Alberg the depth of his reactions. And Alberg took it into consideration when choosing his words and the extent of his proposition.

"You should've died a long time ago," Silas answered fervently. "Maybe we'll wait a little longer for you to show us your abilities as a coordinator."

He had apparently answered before taking time to think. But he had thought plenty during Alberg's speech.

What was heard in their conversation was just the tip of the iceberg. The rest of what remained silent was much more important.

"Let's do a Yalta," Alberg said.

An old conference lost in the mists of time, but whose name passed into common usage.

He continued, "I'll launch an offensive and you back me up with mutants and resistance fighters. I have no authority over them. I'll take care of my own troops, who are very important for you."

This time Silas paused.

"Naturally," Alberg explained, "this can't be a fool's bargain. Neither of us can act like Weldoor and I both acted. We're not 15 light years away from each other…"

Silas still kept silent. Then he said slowly, "The Spaceless has been entirely confiscated. Soldiers have been flooding into it by the thousands all night long."

It was Alberg's turn to be speechless. Two fundamental points stood out from this information: firstly, Silas was leaning towards an alliance, otherwise he would have said nothing; then for some reason Weldoor must have launched his own attack on schedule.

"You see," Alberg finally declared, "now's the time to act."

Silas shook his head doubtfully, "It seems to confirm what you said, but are you sure you can get the children, natural men and the Special Guard to mobilize together at the same time?"

"Yes, if the mobilization is in concert with the mutants and resistance."

"And the trigger?"

"My attack on Dorf, as I told you."

Silas looked at him, "Are you aware that a reform was passed last night in the Senate despite him?"

"No. What reform?"

"Garon managed to get a law voted through to send off children starting at 16 years old."

Alberg smirked, "Nice reform! I don't think the children are going to be happy about that. But Dorf's position isn't exactly something that'll appease them."

"Another thing. The Palace of the Consortium is guarded by troops. They've put up an anti-radiation shield around it."

"The Palace of the Consortium?"

"Yes. Haven't you heard of the Sale-Purchase Consortium with millions of small shareholders and a few big ones?"

"Vaguely."

"It controls the commerce of the three planets, but they don't talk about it much. If its headquarters are guarded like that, it's because the Senate is expecting something serious. Has anything about your projects maybe leaked out?"

"Come on, Silas, don't lose you head. You know what I do best. And so do I. The revolt on the foreign worlds is explanation enough for their precautions. The senators weren't born yesterday. They know that if half the army leaves, some people are going to try to take advantage of that. But they must be thinking of the children or the natural men or someone else. Not everyone at the same time."

Silas looked convinced. Alberg changed the subject.

"I've always wondered," he said, "why they make such a big stink about all the attacks on Garon and so little is heard about the ones Dorf scraped through."

"It's the opposition that shouts all over the place about them, not the majority."

"Funny opposition," Alberg mumbled. "Are there any children, natural men or mutants among them?"

"There are brains."

"Right, above all the specialists in projected economic figures."

"I know. I think about it a lot. But we're talking about a Senate that is the manifestation of an adult population adapted to the economic structure. Do you really think that even in the opposition it would have anything that might deny this structure?"

"Of course…" Alberg pondered this. "Still, it's food for thought."

Nothing more was said. Alberg figured there would be something else to discuss when the victorious revolt turned him and Silas back into enemies. Whose side would Iona be on? He repressed this premature issue. Instead of being victorious, the revolt might be quashed. In bloodshed. And Iona might not want to choose between two corpses.

CHAPTER XXIV

When Alberg got back to Villagea, he was unrecognizable. Used to camouflage, the mutants had changed the shape of his face and the color of his skin. A psychogram would have revealed his identity, but they'd first have to think of stopping him to put him through it.

It was raining. Alberg remembered the storm rains on Venus. Here it was different. A freezing drizzle from the gray sky. He supposed that the Senate had mobilized the meteorology specialist: a cold and monotonous rain discourages potential rioters. But the Senate did not gauge the full extent of the tension. It believed that the revolt on foreign worlds was just an extension of the latest troubles on Earth. If it had information about a coordinated strategy, it would not have stopped at making the rain fall...

Silas had sent Alberg to the children's general staff, which was meeting in a huge, underground chamber belonging to the communications network of the Ludocrats. Access was through the basement of a building and Alberg vaguely recalled what he had heard in his general education classes: the network dated back centuries and had primitive trains moved by electricity. The archives held the original maps but the whole thing had changed so much that the maps were useless. Anyway, Alberg didn't care anymore after he'd been to the Candy Shop.

When Alberg was among the children's general staff, he assessed the strength of Binker and Little Paul. The Ludocrat had laid a trap for Dorf by asking for a meeting to agree on a common course of action. He knew that he'd be meeting a twin, but his agents in the Senate had given him the real Dorf's schedule so they could get to him. Three commando units of children armed with radiants were already ready to strike. The first would get Binker out of harm's way, the second would attack the Dorf stand-in and the third would back up Alberg in his attack on the real senator.

Alberg had to wait until later in the afternoon and the inaction was agonizing. However, he was in full possession of his wits when he headed downtown near the Palace of the Senate. Binker had asked for the meeting not to take place in an official building but rather in the rooms of the Senate Club located more than half a mile from the Palace. They knew, moreover, that Dorf was leaving the Palace at the same time but for a different destination. It was on the way to his magnetocar that Alberg was going to lie in wait while the commando team mixed with the crowd.

Everything went off as planned: Binker's car was attacked by children who grabbed the Ludocrat in the traffic jam. This action was performed spectacularly and much more easily by Binker's refusal to have an escort. The children dragged him into the underground and broadcast a threatening statement to the people, demanding Lewis to act with the Senate so that the recent, ridiculous reform be extensively amended. Binker was their hostage. All this was so believable that no one except Lewis suspected it was all staged.

But at the same time, another commando team was shooting in the streets and from the windows, keeping the fake Dorf and his hefty police escort under fire. The double was killed along with some of the police. In the rapidly closed off quarter, they went chasing the attackers, but in vain. They, too, had taken refuge in the underground. The police who dared enter were exterminated.

Almost simultaneously, Alberg spotted the anonymous vehicle that was carrying the real senator. He jumped off the sidewalk, forcing the magnetocar to slow down, and fired through the windshield, killing the driver and the two other men inside. In the same movement, he dropped to the ground. He barely avoided the crossfire from the two anonymous vehicles in front and back. Aided by the total confusion all over the street, he slipped into the crowd. The armed men ran after him, straight into an ambush by the children, which only caused more chaos. Like in the other attacks, the assailants escaped into the underground.

After the first pirate broadcasts that showed Binker as a hostage and that gave the Senate an ultimatum, others followed that revealed the strategy of Dorf while announcing his death. Being head of the opposition, Garon, during the next hour, made a hard and fast announcement that declared a state of siege:

"The Senate won't be intimidated by a handful of agitators whom it has been proven are working for the brains rebelling on foreign worlds when they're not the paid thugs of senator general Farel whom we all know supports Martian nationalism."

Garon remembered the recent reaction of the Special Guard, so he took care not to accuse the children despite their inflammatory broadcasts. In his view, this was not the time either to call up the usual scapegoat—the mutants. Turning the outrage of the peaceful citizens on them would have been a wrong move. As for the natural men, their influence was too complicated to identify and they still commanded a certain respect. For the assassination of Dorf, Garon had decided to adapt. The children's broadcasts could've been scrambled rather quickly. He didn't try to claim that Dorf was still alive, but he promised that the terrorists would be mercilessly punished.

On the other hand, the electronic equipment in the attacked vehicles had done their job: within half an hour the walls and the store windows were plastered with the 3D photo of the changed Alberg alongside one of his true face. But in the underground, other mutants were busy giving him a third one.

After all this, Villagea was the scene of a fiendish search. Although they hadn't called attention to the children, they made them pay the price and thousands of them were stuffed into prisons. Many resisted individually and were summarily killed on the spot. The resistance in the southern districts turned violent enough to bring in battalions of the regular ar-

275

my. In a blaze, the monastery of sciences became a furnace in which disciples fought side by side with children. The battle lasted until nightfall. The death toll was heavy.

In the morning, Alberg conferred with Binker. Two issues worried them: first, they knew that Garon, though head of the opposition, was going to ally with the Senate, but such a violent repression hadn't been expected. It might discourage the rebel forces. Second and in some way this made up for it, only a small faction of the children had been mobilized. By focusing on the savage reaction of the Senate, it might become easier to recruit the ones who hadn't taken part in the fighting.

"We need to follow up this very morning," Alberg said, "otherwise, everything's going to fade into terror. The plan of attack can't be interrupted: action, reaction, extension of action. And it's only in the third phase that we can count on Silas and Del Padre who will begin the final disorganization of the enemy forces."

Binker agreed, "True, but a general uprising of the children of Villagea can only be the result of a kind of chain reaction that won't start from simple disgruntled propaganda, which, by the way, would be really hard to spread under the noses of the senatorial forces swarming the streets. We need a new explosion to light the fuse."

Little Paul entered the underground room where the meeting was being held. He had red hair and was limping.

"Bunch of bastards!" he said. "If you'd seen what happened. But of course, you just sat on your asses while we got ourselves killed."

"I can see you weren't in front of the magnetocar when I killed Dorf," Alberg muttered, insulted.

Little Paul looked at him admiringly, "That's true. You did your job. But my father's a joke. Isn't that right, pops, aren't you a joke?"

"Be quiet," Binker said. "Everyone does what he can depending on his position."

Little Paul snickered, staring at him with his pale eyes.

"Let's get back to what we were saying," Alberg proposed. "The explosion you're talking about could be the death of Garon."

This time Little Paul looked at him with something like sympathy. "You think you can kill him?"

"I got Dorf."

"Not the same thing. Garon has a reputation of being invulnerable."

"And me," Alberg responded, "I have a reputation of being a good hunter... at least I used to."

"I think," Binker stumbled over his words, "that Little Paul is right. And if by some miracle you succeeded, we'd have all the liberal adults on our backs after already offending the conservatives."

It was Alberg's turn to snicker. "We have nothing to hope for from the adults, but there's not much to fear either. Maybe they'll become dangerous when we ask them to start producing instead of just trading products... but not before."

Without transition he turned to Little Paul.

"Is it still raining?"

"Yes," Little Paul answered. "But the rain hasn't washed the streets clean yet. There's too much blood. They didn't use only radiant weapons."

Alberg thought about it. "I need sun," he declared strangely. "Can you send an expedition to blow up the antennas controlling the weather?"

Little Paul grimaced. "Not easy. But doable."

"Do it. You'll see the results."

"Okay, I'll take care of it." He left the room without saying another word.

"The ideal," Alberg said, "would've been to take control of the antennas ourselves to make sure. But it's May. There'll be sun if the artificial rain is cut off."

"How do plan to do it?" Binker asked.

"Well now," Alberg replied, "that's none your business. I know we're on the same side, but I like having free rein."

From certain micro-expressions he knew that Binker had already lost some of his resolve, that he was not far from switching sides and maybe doing a little favor for Garon like saving his life, for example...

CHAPTER XXV

Little Paul had taken less than an hour to choose his half-dozen Bullies and explain his plan. There was Big Joey, Van Horst 18, Cyanure the Young and three other berserks of lesser repute.

In one of the weapon depots built by the children, there were a few small nuclear explosives the size of a pencil, secretly brought back from foreign worlds. Little Paul put one of these in his pocket and climbed into an anonymous winger. His six partners piloted six others equipped with radiant weapons. The seven machines soared off in scattered formation toward the site where they controlled the atmosphere.

The site occupied 20 acres at the east end of Villagea. In the middle of the buildings stood the 2,000-foot tall antennas that made it rain or shine in the city. Army troops ringed all around the installation with a battery of radiants posted every 300 feet.

Big Joey went in first at 5,000 feet altitude. Before he even began his descent in near freefall, the red warning lights flashed on the ground. He dove at one of the batteries while spraying his lethal radiant over the gunners. But the next closest battery got him in its sights. Big Joey's winger was wiped out.

Five others came down like falcons, Cyanure the Young at the lead. The defenses were put out of commission at a distance of 1,500 feet within seconds. But four of the wingers ended up crashing beyond the installation into the nearby trees. The fifth came charging back at high altitude. It was sighted as a target just when Little Paul came racing in near ground level...

Little Paul tossed his micro-bomb out the window. It was set to explode in five seconds, which gave him enough time to get away. But for an instant he was distracted by the fall of the last winger piloted by Van Horst 18. He nicked an antenna and had to steady his winger while dodging the battery fire that was still coming from the other side of the buildings. During these maneuvers that would have been tricky even for a more experienced pilot, he bumped another antenna. Thrown into a spiral, the winger crashed just over a mile away in the suburbs.

One second before impact a blinding light wiped out the installation. The antennas bent and melted like giant candles while the buildings vaporized. A black mushroom cloud slowly took shape 1,500 feet over the city. A muffled din of horror rose out of Villagea.

Little Paul lay among the wreckage of the winger in the middle of the street. His eyes were open and he was still breathing. In his present position he could see an arrogant building façade decorated with a huge insignia—a graph with an upward curve and a motto readable from a distance: "I matured along with my fortune."

Little Paul knew that he was not going to mature. He looked over the roof of the insolent building and saw the black cloud spreading its crown in the sky. A crown that looked almost like it was a cap on the insignia. He felt satisfied with his success, but fear and despair came to cloud his eyes. A big sob was rising in his throat for the first time in years. The armor of the children's chief was cracking and leaving a little boy defenseless and terrified by death.

Before his mind went dark, he clung desperately to the certainty that the children would no longer have to go off to foreign worlds. He departed with a victorious smile on his face, sealed by a trickle of blood.

CHAPTER XXVI

While waiting for the results of Operation Weather, Alberg thought it better not to go out in the streets too much. Also turning down Binker's invitations, as he found his intentions more and more questionable, he tucked himself away in a place that looked abandoned. In reality it was a place used for meetings by natural men. They came by night to discuss their methods of defiance and ended with hate speeches vented at the 3D platform, which they spat at incessantly. As opposed to them, Alberg didn't use it as a target for his tirades. He turned it on and waited for news.

The explosion that made the ground tremble caused only a whiff of burning air. Considering the proximity of the weather control station, it was obviously just a small bomb coupled to a system of implosion that limited damage to targeted area.

Just a few minutes later a speaker appeared on the platform, announcing a statement from Senator Garon, who replaced him immediately. He said only a few words, condemning the acts of the terrorists and calling the people to assemble in the main publicity stadium. The stadium stood in the northern districts, a huge ellipse that could accommodate 700,000 spectators.

Alberg got up and left. He hailed a magnetocab that took him to the stadium. There he found a place in the bleachers as close as possible to the podium, which was 15-20 feet high. Few people had come as quickly as him, but Garon's call must have been heard because the stadium was filling up. Usually used for audio-visual jousts between companies, the arena had been automatically fitted with extra seats. Garon was no doubt thinking, and with good reason, that direct contact with the people would make it easier for him to get things back under control or better to stand fast against the troublemakers.

The news of Little Paul's death was starting to spread. For a moment Alberg felt a little upset, but he dismissed it with the simple thought that from now on there would be no children to get in his way. Although Little Paul had proved useful so far, he would probably have turned into a dangerous enemy later on. For the present, his final feat was bearing fruit: the sky was slowly clearing up, letting the bright sun appear. Alberg looked up and closed his eyes with satisfaction.

Garon arrived when the stadium was full. It was three in the afternoon. The senator climbed up on the podium surrounded by troops. His dark outline stood out against the small, white stage. The shadow at his feet was drawn out. when Garon raised his hands before him and demanded silence with a voice coming through the speakers, Alberg slowly raised his hand, armed with a radiant, and fired. Then, coldly, he shot the spectators in his immediate vicinity and he fell down among the corpses. He had not targeted Garon. He had shot at his shadow.

The senator's form bent over, fell to the side and lay motionless in the sun, curled up like a foetus. The bleachers were already swarming with police who were selectively searching spectators higher up from Alberg. Simple logic from the angle of fire led them to believe that the shooter had shot Garon and the spectators were in his line of fire. As for the dead bodies, both real and not, they carried them to one of the exits where they lined them up on the ground. Alberg quickly crawled around a corner and got lost in the panicking crowd.

The streets around the stadium were full of people whose fear was turning into heartburn. Groups were wildly discussing what happened and a new worry came out: someone had finally succeeded in killing the opposition chief considered to be invulnerable. The fact that even the opposition was denied by the fanatics made the crowd think. The word "fanatic" made Alberg smile when he heard it. If any word did not fit him, it was that one... What he liked most was that his idea worked out so well, asking Little Paul to destroy the weather station. It resulted in the death of the children's chief, the appearance of the sun, the reaction of Garon who was so over-confident that he showed himself in public and being exposed to the sun, was exposed to death as well.

So, Weldoor proved valuable at least once when he talked about how Garon projected a form of himself and the protective zone that the shadow of this material form created. Somewhere in a senate chamber the real Garon was lying on the floor, struck down by radiation that had fried his wave-frequency umbilical cord that linked him to his image.

Alberg kept walking like in a dream. He was thinking of the wads of sollars that he still possessed. He was surprised to realize that he was more and more detached: he likewise felt a kind of exaltation at the idea of the power he was crushing. He had to admit that he would've been really astonished by a pre-diction of this.

But it was done. He was no longer seeking riches nor even the wealth that comes from power. He was interested in nothing but domination. He was going to become something other than a little mutant hunter. Something else entirely…

He was back to his cold logic. Right now he had to get back to the natural men's hideout to await further news. He was anxious to find out how the Senate was reacting and what measures would be taken all over the planet. Anything could happen. Either a violent repression or just a simple nomination of two opposing vice-presidents with surveillance of the cities by the army.

He was about to hail a magnetocab when a vehicle pulled up slowly next to him. Through the sliding door he saw a 12-year old child gesturing to him. He got in and found himself next to another, older child.

"We all feel," the second one said, "that you have de-graded the life of Little Paul. But Wilfrid has decided to sup-port you since you managed to kill Garon."

And then silence. Alberg thought that Wilfrid might not be disappointed by the death of Little Paul. He also thought that Wilfrid would only support him as long as he was judged useful. He considered the power of the children who were always trailing him and who could have easily killed him there on the sidewalk. But everyone was powerful in a way: mutants, natural men, the Senate, the army... Everyone was powerful until the sudden crash.

The magnetocar entered a garage that sloped down. It went into the basements and stopped in front of a space hollowed out of a wall. Everyone got out of the vehicle, Alberg last of all. The hole opened onto a big room where Wilfrid was giving instructions to a group of Bullies. In one corner was an empty, silent 3D platform. Wilfrid looked at Alberg. "Little Paul is dead because of you, but his death bore fruit. Since you got away with it, I'll trust you until further notice."

He gestured to the Bullies to post themselves by the door.

Then he went on, "I have some breaking news, came in just now. There are riots on Venus and the Martian army is on its way, supposedly to help the Venusian government suppress them. In fact, the Senate on Venus has no way to oppose Farel's projects. It's going to end up, practically speaking, in the colonization of Venus by Mars, which is not to our liking. We have to speed things up here."

"None of this surprises me," Alberg responded. "But we'll act a lot more easily in a climate of disorganization."

An image suddenly popped up on the 3D platform, immediately followed by another.

"Dear friends," the speaker said, "I want to introduce you to the Secretary of the Planetary Union of Families. Mister Secretary, you have the floor."

The Secretary pushed out his chin, laced his fingers and declared, "In view of recent events, the Union has called an emergency Counsel by videophone. It falls upon me to inform the public of the decision made unanimously: *because of the role already taken by the Special Guard and faced with the danger of seeing it play an even more subversive role against the legally constituted Senate, the Counsel of the Planetary Union of Families has ordered the dissolution of the Special*

Guard and the delivery of all its equipment to the senatorial authorities."

The Secretary narrowed his eyes and disappeared from the platform.

The speaker then added, "Echoing this decision, we have just learned that Their Excellencies the Ludocrats Lewis and Binker have left Earth for Venus. At the astroport they explained that their place was at the side of the beleaguered Venusian Ludocrats."

Alberg and Wilfrid looked at each other. But their attention was quickly focused back on the platform. The speaker was opening his eyes wide, then fell to the side as if blown over by a string wind. He was replaced by the image of an armed man who started talking in a monotone:

"Pirate broadcast. Don't turn it off. A commando team of mutants belonging to the annex administration of the Senate has just gained entrance to the personal apartment of Garon. They found not only his corpse but a large quantity of documents that are now being examined. We are already certain that Garon was, in reality, the secret president of the Sale-Purchase Consortium. In consequence, the Senate is nothing but an extension and a slave. Be aware that..."

"That's why the opposition didn't worry so much about the majority," Alberg commented with a laugh.

But nobody else could laugh because the image fell, too, doubled over. It was replaced in turn by three men in uniforms. The most colorful of them took the floor.

"In the absence of the Their Excellencies the Ludocrats Lewis and Binker, the senior officers of the general staff declare the dissolution of the Senate, obviously unable to maintain order and guarantee the security of the Consortium, which is necessary for the survival of the planet. The senior officers of the general staff take responsibility for the temporary replacement of the Senate by a triumvirate formed of a general and two colonels. Peace must be preserved here while the army does its duty on foreign worlds. The triumvirate calls upon the level-headed adults to help it in its task because the operations carried out on foreign worlds require the massive deployment of reinforcements. We're counting on everyone's sense of civic duty."

The platform went gray again, empty and silent.

Alberg shrugged his shoulders. "Basically, two things to notice: one, a lot of people must have known about Garon's secret activities, beginning with anyone holding any position of authority in the Consortium. That's why his death could cause such panic resulting in the suppression of the Special Guard. The Union of Families is, in truth, an organization of stockholders. Moreover, it's obvious that the Consortium, after manipulating the Senate, wants to ensure their basic survival by maneuvering the army."

"Undoubtedly," Wilfrid said, "but from what I've heard, I have the impression that the army isn't counting much on the Consortium. Under these conditions, the Consortium can't count on it either. I think the general staff doesn't want to control such an unstable planet and is no longer up to pursuing military operations on foreign worlds."

Alberg thought about that for a moment. "I think you're right. But there's another reason. The situation in the solar system is going downhill fast. Maintaining authority here demands peace elsewhere and immediately. Well, after Mars has swallowed up Venus, it'll turn on Earth. And the combined forces of Mars and Venus is likely to crush the army of Earth, even imagining the expeditionary forces on foreign worlds and with total calm here. Therefore, right now, the power of the army can't take hold except under the influence of a suicidal dinosaur. It's not the case for those who have more weight in the general staff, but the case works in the long term too because if a military dictatorship sets up, it won't last longer than 30 years, at the end of which the cargo ships will stop delivering since the rebellions on foreign worlds will have triumphed in the meantime... unless the captains of the cargo ships put the pressure on, which I don't believe will happen."

All of a sudden, he realized that he was talking to a child. He looked at Wilfrid's face that showed no expression and he understood that any adult would have understood him better.

"Do you think," Wilfrid said, "that the military dogs want to secure the future of their descendants? I myself believe that they're only interested in their own future. And a future less than ten years is plenty for them."

Alberg retreated. "The short-term suits them just fine. I'm just pushing the argument."

He was thinking: "This ambitious little bastard has already given up all romanticism. I wonder if I've gotten this far…" Ultimately, the one who was pretending to establish a dynasty or at least set up a system was starting to free himself from his personal desires. This was not the case, obviously, with the newborn Triumvirate. This was not Wilfrid's case either. Alberg was a little bitter about it. But not all the children were like their new leader. They still believed in many things, good and bad. It was because the leaders believed in nothing that they became leaders and because the troops identified their leaders with their own personal aspirations. Alberg believed in nothing, of course, but he was counting on leading troops down the right path. And he was starting to get an idea of what the right path was…

With a faint crackle the 3D receiver awoke again with a new image. It was a fat man wearing an armband.

"Units have just been formed to uphold lawful order. They are made up of volunteers who used to be in the old Special Guard whose equipment has been given by the Triumvirate to these units. We are calling all conscientious adults to sign up. The recruitment office is in the old Palace of Ludocrats."

He vanished.

"These people are reacting as fast as their puppets are falling," Alberg remarked. "But their haste testifies to their fear."

A Bully who had come in from outside went straight to Wilfrid. "All the Spaceless are guarded by large contingents, but they're being whittled away by the hour because they're actually getting in the Spaceless."

"That's good news," Wilfrid looked at Alberg. "Legality is no longer a symbol justifying the Triumvirate, so the claimants are going to have to support themselves."

"Yes," Alberg added, "but the people who've stood up to defend their children might not be so forceful when their children attack them."

Wilfrid had half a smile, "I see what you're saying. Me, I don't trust it. It's true that a surprising number of parents were moved and answered the call of the Ludocrats, but at the moment their wealth and their tranquility was not really in danger. Right now, it's totally different. And I'm afraid they'll get used to shooting us sooner than giving up their lifestyle."

"Possibly," Alberg said, "but they'll have to count on the mutants and natural men."

Wilfrid kept silent. After a few moments he turned to a Bully:

"Get in contact with Silas and Del Padre. I want to meet with them as soon as possible."

The Bully, with his hair floating over his shoulders, hastened off to the sound of swishing leather.

CHAPTER XXVII

The next morning Alberg set himself up in the reception office of the Senate Palace, a kind of madly luxurious audience hall. Without a shot being fired he had become Archicrat of Earth. He was the one who chose the title because he still had a little honor left.

The night had not been too chaotic. The support units of the Triumvirate quickly put down their weapons, declaring that they were not being helped by what remained of the army. It had started with the invasion of natural men who, by their resistance, had slowed down all movement and sown disorder. Then a million children had poured into Villagea and hordes had done the same in most other cities. The final blow was delivered by the mutants at the head of rebels organized into powerful phalanxes. There'd been very few victims.

Everything had gone off without a hitch during the meeting held without Alberg. He had been proposed for the power by Wilfrid and Del Padre against the advice of Silas who had stayed faithful to his distrust. But Alberg was a good fit for the children and natural men because he didn't represent any particular group of people and even though a mutant himself, he could stand up to Silas. Alberg was invested with a pompous title and to all appearances held all the power. But Wilfrid and Del Padre considered him a puppet in their hands.

This was not exactly his idea. Temporarily alone in the audience hall, he thought of how fast a large body could fall apart, especially when circumstances got out of hand and made it rotten. Who could have predicted that the Senate with its formidable army was going to collapse or scatter to the winds? Who would have believed that the Sale-Purchase Consortium was also going to lose its traditional support of the general staff so quickly? And how negligently had Ludocrats kept the secret mercenary troops? To answer these questions you just had to look at the children's apathy, building up for a long time; you just had to remember the fury of the foreign worlds; and the persecution of mutants was a losing battle just like the children refusing to become adults; in fact, the entire human race was being called upon to change and the behavior of men was like an army of caterpillars hunting butterflies.

As for the natural men, they'd been underestimated. Alberg had decided not to make the same mistake. He knew that all his allies considered him a straw man under the illusory authority they were preparing to pit each other against.

But after a long period of greed, followed by a short moment of being drunk on power, Alberg was reaching another level: he needed to legitimize the actions that had brought him here and legitimize them not with respect to himself but before all of humanity. With this diversion alone he could look at himself in the mirror and not see confusion or inconsistency. He was gradually being imbued with the sincerity of his mission and the justice of his views. For the first time, he was feeling responsible for others and considered that the elevation to this responsibility proved the quality of his revelation, his illumination.

It was in this serenity of mind, faintly tinged with a teasing smile, that he took the plunge and started signing decrees. The first reestablished the Senate police, provided with the funds of the Special Guard and completely under his personal authority. The second ordered the arrest of Del Padre, Wilfrid and Silas. Among the rest he wrote, in a few short and concise sentences, a declaration of independence of the foreign worlds, a repeal of the law to send off children, a project for the implementation of a policy of metropolitan production, the mandatory work service for natural men just like for the commercial agents and a governmental organization in charge of using the abilities of the mutants.

When this preliminary work was done, he remembered that the coup and the rebellions had always led to civil wars or foreign interventions. Things were going pretty smoothly so far, but it was this new system coming in that would see a brutal reaction. He himself, perhaps, represented the first phase of this reaction. The discontent (to say the least) of his old allies would soon come to light. And soon also the attack of Martian and Venusian armies, which would try to reestablish the old order under Martian control.

Before going personally to liberate the police chief who'd been in prison since dawn, he had one last doubt. He looked over the decrees he'd signed and found them both humane and rational. But he had two questions: Would he always act like this if he remained in power? And if yes, were there other ways to proceed than imposing progress by the voice of a single man? Pondering these two questions, he was convinced that they could cripple his project. Thus it was that he ignored them.

In fact, he had been led to this attitude in part by skimming through some revolutionary philosophers of the 19th and 20th century, long ago banned from all libraries but still present in Garon's. To prove his sincerity, he had them reprinted and distributed widely among the children...

CHAPTER XXVIII

In the following days, Alberg's police, despite their power and strength, didn't manage to catch any of the ones he had ordered to bring in. It was the first serious failure but he started an intense propaganda campaign among the children, based on the decree he'd signed in their favor. He quickly realized that the children were the group he could count on the most and he took great pains to maximize his popularity with them, going so far as to grant Wilfrid amnesty.

The events had shown that the common attitudes of the old rebel groups only worked together against the Senate if they were united under an outside authority, even an artificial one. Once it turned into a real one, they didn't unite against it if they hadn't joined together against the former one. Alberg's power fed on this division just like on the strength of the police and on his popularity with the children.

He was working now 14 or 15 hours a day, aided by economists and sociologists as well as by the ex-triumvirs in order to reorganize the discombobulated society gripped by fear and also to rebuild an army that could stand up to the inevitable threats from Mars, which they'd heard little news about.

But a silent opposition was becoming more and more overt around him: the mutants refused to become the trained animals in the pocket of the State. And the natural men didn't see the new society in the same way as Alberg. As for the adults accustomed to business, they kept trading, arrogantly, and formed armed groups to protect free enterprise. Alberg worked on the systematic destruction of these groups, but it seemed only to extend instead of diminishing their importance.

And then something even more serious happened: the children began to slip away from him. They had devoured the books exhumed from Garon's library, works that the methods of electronic reproduction were able to print millions of copies of in a few days. Their organization transformed; their demands were no longer the same. They stopped showing respect for the natural men and some of them started publishing pamphlets and studies to include the mutants in the theories of their new favorite authors. Among the mutants themselves, these theories grew like wheat in the sun. Some brains, who had stayed in the solar system to lead a silent opposition against the Senate, took the initiative of holding wide-ranging conferences in which Alberg's reforms were analyzed under 400-year old critiques.

Alberg knew he had to act urgently. First of all by immersing himself in the works he had so recklessly made available; then by adopting, as conspicuously as possible, the theories they talked about. But something told him that things had gone beyond his control and he was starting to be considered useless.

Then came the deserters in rags, stepping out of the Spaceless. There were more and more of them, spreading news of the total destruction of the armies on the foreign worlds. The brains on C.124, they told, were using psychic weapons against which the equipment of the terrian forces proved as effective as ancient catapults. They added that Weldoor had been assassinated, that the three systems were entering an ideological war and that they were talking over there of blowing up the Spaceless with nuclear bombs so as to cut off direct communication with the solar system.

Alberg reacted to this situation on two levels. He recruited and armed all the deserters, thereby increasing the regular troops able to assist his police. As soon as these forces were big enough, he outlawed all organizations that had formed because of his own recklessness and imprisoned their leaders. Then he took certain precautions for the security of the cities—people were unaware of the repercussions that were possible on Earth from the destruction of the Spaceless on foreign worlds.

293

It was during the evacuation of Villagea that he was ambushed by his enemies.

He was in a magnetocar at the time, flanked on all sides by vehicles full of armed men and he was wondering how his mutant aptitudes of observation and analysis could have left him so unaware. How could he not have foreseen the explosive power of the studies and manifestoes he'd made public? All he'd seen in them was a surprising analogy with the current problem and he didn't imagine anything coming out of them but the quaintness of old works that might give some texture to his reforms by legitimizing them historically.

But instead of making it all look nice, these old books ended up sinking him. He was considered a self-taught revolutionary, driven primarily by the need for action, but without theoretical foundations and dangerously convinced of a monopoly on the truth. Around him they talked only of dialectics and self-governance and these terms once buried in the past turned him into an anachronistic tyrant whom the natural men, on the contrary, were accusing of spreading ideas more dangerous than the Senate.

The streets were full of people fleeing the city, which caused huge traffic jams. The evacuation was being obeyed without the need for force.

In the middle of one of these traffic jams, thousands of natural men suddenly jumped out on all sides in their white robes floating in the wind. A group of them rushed Alberg's magnetocar and started smashing it with iron bars. The police made a massacre but were ultimately outnumbered. Alberg was snatched from the car, beaten and carried away unconscious.

When he came to, he was lying on an air bed in a strange room. He turned his head and saw a woman standing next to him. It was Iona.

"Do you feel better?" she asked.

Alberg felt she was acting oddly. She was starting to undress while looking elsewhere.

"I'm all right," he gently tapped his bruised limbs.

She lay down next to him. "Good thing. You're going to need your strength."

He scrutinized her face, trying desperately to use his gifts of observation and deduction. But the blackout had sent them away. He was left to his own natural devices, which could see nothing but an ambiguous attitude in Iona.

"What happened?" he asked.

"The natural men kidnapped you and we got them to give you to us. There's a price on your head."

Alberg chuckled, painfully. "That reminds me of something."

Iona stared at him without saying a word. Finally, she said, "But I won't try to earn the reward."

Alberg smiled as he thought: "Look, she'll always be this weak before me."

"Of course not," he said aloud. "Here's what you're going to do. You're going to show Silas that he'd be better off keeping a close eye on the natural men and siding with me. This time an example must be made."

"No," Iona said. "You don't understand. I'm not going to earn the reward because you've already made me disgusted with such behavior. But I am going to kill you like I should've done the day I first met you."

She hadn't finished talking when Alberg's hand was on the butt of his radiant. But he froze in mid-gesture: Iona's eyes opened wide and turned red while her hair lit up with sparks. Her phosphorescent teeth were blinding.

At the same time, Alberg felt all kinds of pain surging through his body, paralyzing him like a lead weight. He opened his mouth to scream but no sound came out. Aghast, he stared at Iona who had turned into a cavity of two glowing furnaces. It was her eyes that radiated the unbearable waves of heat that was stretching him like a bow. He no longer saw the room. He no longer heard the cries and hubbub of the crowd pouring in through the windows. He felt himself fall forward into the two lava lakes that now filled his vision. In the midst of this universe of red-hot iron, he saw Little Paul's face pass by, a bloody face fused into a permanent, ironic smile. He also saw the face of Dora, the prostitute from foreign worlds. Then it was a kaleidoscope of faces—Del Padre, Carlis, Merelborn, Silas, Weldoor and others whose features melted together in the throes of an infernal pain. And always, in the center of this dance of faces, there was Iona who had become horrifying.

A distant voice was saying: "You couldn't remain alive, Alberg. You tolerate only your own passing fancies, your personal decisions, your ideas and your convictions. You don't accept objections because you think everyone else is wrong and only you are right. You are the stuff tyrants are made up and it would just have gotten worse and worse. I needed all my strength to kill you, but I know that I have done a favor for all of Earth."

And the voice was soft, broken, full of sorrow.

But Iona's words sank into an ocean of fire. Alberg felt himself being consumed from the inside, as if his whole body had become the site of a blaze that left nothing visible outside it. In the end, a thought rose up in his mind: he was dying a martyr because he had served as an instrument like all the others. For him it was the most absurd, the most ridiculous death, dying for a cause destroyed by its results. His last image was of Iona, but a different Iona, the one who had inspired love and for whom he had sometimes felt his hardness melt away. It was, however, the same woman just as he had always been, ultimately, the same man. Now, he was losing his manhood. He was becoming a dead man.

He melted away into a kind of roaring laughter that never passed his lips.

CHAPTER XXIX

On the vast, vitrified expanse, Iona sat motionless in an inflatable armchair that she had brought herself. The sky was serene. A June sky where the breeze carried off the metallic clanging of the robot dockers and the faint voices of the men directing the activity. The cargo ship was over a mile long and 1,500 feet in diameter. The giant automatic cranes moving around it looked like praying mantises around a pumpkin.

Many things had happened since the death of Alberg. First of all, what they'd feared would happen had happened: nuclear bombs placed at the entrances of all the Spaceless to the foreign worlds had exploded on Earth and probably on the other planets of the solar system, obliterating several cities, which had luckily been evacuated on Alberg's orders. In the non-space tunnel, the exit got tangled with the entrance, which explained why the bombs exploding 15 light years away had vaporized this end too. It was why the astrodome in Villagea, along with the suburbs, had been turned into a vitrified esplanade. This, however, didn't stop the cargo ships from landing because the radioactivity of the explosions lasted for just a few hours. But the stars that the Spaceless had made neighbors became inaccessible. No one was boarding the cargo ships.

Elsewhere, the dissensions between Silas, Wilfrid and Del Padre had reawakened stronger than ever, ending up in sporadic battles between the clans. Stuck in their secret hideouts, the leaders of the Consortium had led a clandestine campaign among the adults, still nostalgic for business as usual. Rediscovering Alberg's reasoning, they had relied on the fact that merchandise would still be coming in for years even though the source had dried up for good. There was, therefore, a bright future for at least one generation. In the meantime, they would see to conquering other systems and showing them the benefits of siding with them so that they could replace the foreign worlds with other means of production that the children would be sent to labor in just like in the past.

Very quickly millions of people had protested in the streets of many cities to demand the election of a new Senate. They had clashed with millions of children blinded by rage and by the fear of seeing their liberation revoked. Bloody, deadly battles had taken place. Wilfrid had then launched coded instructions.

The next night, two thirds of the children took advantage of their parents' sleep to murder them. In the morning piles of discarded corpses littered the streets of the city. Flushed out of their lairs, the former members of the Consortium were hanged by a tribunal of children.

Faced with these exterminations, the natural men fled. On the plains and in the forests they created the antiquated microsocieties they had dreamed of. The adult mutants withdrew to the outskirts of the cities, trying to compensate for their inferior numbers with a flawless organization and powerful weapons. As for the brains, the children had taken as many as they could get hold of and given them an ultimatum: provide the Earth with weapons for the children to defend against the inevitable attack by Mars or else be executed. In the blink of an eye the laboratories turned into silent hives where teams of researchers worked night and day.

In the midst of this chaos, Silas was plotting with the mutant children in whom he instilled the idea of their superiority. He had already managed to form active groups that infiltrated everywhere decisions were being made. That same morning, a violent dispute pitted Silas against Iona on this subject. She had threatened Silas with the influence she still had with the children to denounce his strategies and oppose this new form of racism.

But she no longer felt strong enough to throw herself into the battle. Alberg's execution, the necessity of which she still couldn't accept, had cost her too much energy and too much self-sacrifice. Besides, she trusted the children to guard against any backsliding in whatever form it might take. On the other hand, they had found out during the day that although the Senate on Venus had quickly laid down their weapons, the Venusian children, with the help of the mutants and natural men, had formed a secret army that would counter the Martian forces on Venus for years to come.

As the minutes passed, she realized that she didn't have much to do in this society on Earth, that she didn't understand half of what was going on and it just didn't need her.

A crew member from a cargo ship was passing by and gave her a look in which she saw a glimmer of interest. She stood up in the wind, leaving behind her inflatable chair, which flew away.

"Can I come with you?" she asked.

The spaceman smiled, "Come on. We'll have to vote on it, but I think you'll pass. This happens so rarely!"

She walked to the huge ship next to the man with his shining body armor. She didn't remember having pictured this departure before even though she often thought of the mysterious life on the cargo ships. She wondered what kind of organization they had in these mountains that crossed the interstellar gulfs and how she was going to be received. Did they know about the inflammatory philosophers who had caused the downfall of Alberg? If not, was she going to tell them?

"I wonder what the captain's going to say," she said softly.

The spaceman laughed loudly. "There's no captain," he said.

She looked at him. The stories told about these cargo ships were more or less modeled on Solarian reality. They had nothing to do with the truth.

It seemed that the truth was inconceivable for the sedentary homebodies on the planets. As for the philosophers who became the foundation of Earth's new beginning, maybe the people on the cargo ships considered them too conservative.

Iona made her way to the side of the ship, which was like a cliff looming over a sea of crates and boxes, tanks and bags. Printed labels on the packages listed their contents:

"Space Dust. Volume searched: 400,000,000 cubic miles. Volume obtained: 2 cubic microns. Usage: personalization of apartment dust."

Iona wondered who would be interested in this now.

She was thinking of Earth's past. After playing hooky for three centuries, History was back at the crossroads and taking a different path. But from the crossroads you could already see new forks… maybe they were the same? If History never went backwards but if it encountered the same crossroads, then it was still just going round in circles.

But the history of the planets was moving along a plane. The history of the cargo ships was taking off perpendicular to this plane. Like the children born of men, the cargo ships were the children of History. Iona hoped they had invented the straight line.

Stepping into the outside elevator whose cage was stuck to the dizzying height of the ship's flank, she turned to look into the distance where the gray ground cut through the blue sky like a broken window. A huge city was standing there. It was in one of the houses in that city that she had killed Alberg. She had stayed her hand for a long time, but she had done it in the end.

The elevator started. Iona had a knot in her throat as she rose above the landscape blurred by the budding tears in her eyes. Before they reached the top, a sob rose up from her belly and escaped with a cry. She threw her arms around the spaceman's chest and he put his arms gently around her shoulders.

www.ingramcontent.com/pod-product-compliance
Lightning Source LLC
Chambersburg PA
CBHW030346020726
47493CB00003B/707

* 9 7 8 1 6 4 9 3 2 1 9 8 5 *